HEROES OF THE RANGE

Zane Grey's great western novel NEVADA first introduced Jim Lacy, gunman and near-renegade, who changed his way of life to fight on the side of justice. In BEYOND THE MOGOLLON RIM, Nevada Jim takes up his sixgun once again and hits the trail on a lonely manhunt, with a vengeful outlaw gang lying in wait for him.

Al Slingerland, a trapper so wise in the ways of the redmen that he was known as "The White Indian," made his initial appearance in THE U.P. TRAIL. In THE TRACK OF BLOOD, Slingerland tangles with both Indians and whites, as he protects a beautiful young Indian girl from her attackers.

THE LIGHT OF WESTERN STARS was the Zane Grey novel that featured Chris Oliver, the halfbreed in whose veins flowed the blood of mighty Sioux warriors. He answers THE CALL OF THE WAR DRUMS to save a beautiful white girl, at the risk of his own life!

Other volumes in the
ROMER ZANE GREY Series:

Zane Grey's Laramie Nelson:
The Other Side of the Canyon

Zane Grey's Buck Duane:
The Rider of Distant Trails

Zane Grey's Arizona Ames:
Gun Trouble in Tonto Basin

Zane Grey's Buck Duane:
King of the Range

Zane Grey's Yaqui:
Siege at Forlorn River

Zane Grey's Arizona Ames:
King of the Outlaw Horde

ZANE GREY'S NEVADA JIM LACY

BEYOND THE MOGOLLON RIM

Romer Zane Grey

Based on characters created by Zane Grey

LEISURE BOOKS ∞ **NEW YORK CITY**

A LEISURE BOOK

Published by

Dorchester Publishing Co., Inc.
6 East 39th Street
New York, New York 10016

Printed in the United States of America

CONTENTS

BEYOND THE MOGOLLON RIM 7

THE TRACK OF BLOOD................109

THE CALL OF THE WAR DRUMS.......223

BEYOND
THE MOGOLLON RIM

I

Hettie Ide tightened her fingers about those of the lean-faced rider at her side in the shadowy depths of the little church. "Nevada," she murmured, "in just two more weeks we will be standing where they are now, and you'll be fumbling for the ring just as awkwardly."

Jim Lacy — the Ides had never gotten around to calling him by his real name, but had continued to use the one they'd tacked on him back in the hell-for-leather, wild-horse-hunting days in the Forlorn River country — shook his head.

"I'm wishing it was right now," Nevada drawled softly. "Waiting until we get to San Diego don't set well with me."

"I've told you I feel the same way. But Mother—"

"Sure, sure. I know how it is, sweetheart."

The droning voice of the Reverend Mr. Kingsley rose higher as he extended his hands, and held them over the heads of Marvie Blaine and Rose Hatt.

"I now pronounce you man and wife."

Marvie, young brother-in-law of Ben Ide, turned to his bride. She wore no veil, no elaborate wedding gown, only a simple white dress hurriedly whipped together by Ben's wife Ina and his sister Hettie. Taking her awk-

9

wardly by the shoulders, he planted a kiss on her lips, and drew back, smiling, embarrassed.

"My turn now!" Ben Ide said, stepping up and taking Rose in his arms. "I guess a brother-in-law has the right to be first in line."

The other wedding guests surged forward—Hettie, Ina, Mrs. Ide, Judge Franklidge and his daughter, the Tom Days—all offering congratulations and best wishes. Nevada, never fully at ease at such times, held back until their exuberance had subsided before claiming his moment with the flushed, happy girl.

"Good luck to you, Rose," he said. "Marvie's a fine boy."

"I know he is," she replied, a look of understanding passing between them. Rose Hatt, daughter of the notorious Elam Hatt, sister of the now dead outlaw, Cedar Hatt, marrying into the wealthy Blaine family. It was a big step for her. "I don't deserve such happiness," she said. "But I'll be a good wife—and I'll do the best I can."

"I know you will," Nevada said. "Marvie's lucky, too." He turned to the young bridegroom. "She's yours now. It's up to you to take good care of her."

"Don't worry about that, Nevada," Marvie said. "I'll spend the rest of my life—"

"Forget that her folks weren't as law-abiding as they might have been. It's no fault of hers, so don't ever mention it."

"I won't—you can count on it! I aim to make her the—"

"All right, folks," Ben Ide's voice broke in, overriding the excited talking. "Everybody head for Clem Walter's restaurant. The wedding dinner's there."

10

Nevada felt an arm slip under his, and he grinned down into Hettie's calm gray eyes.

"I'm so happy for them," she said. "There's so much ahead for them. I—I regret all those years we were apart—the ones we lost. I feel—well, cheated."

"We'll make them all up," Nevada said, drifting toward the doorway with the others. We've a lifetime together waiting for us."

Outside, Winthrop's single street lay quiet in the warm spring sun. Somewhere a dog was barking, and the sweet smell of lilacs growing along the front wall of the church filled the air. Marvie and Rose stepped out onto the landing, the others close behind them. Ben Ide pushed to the edge of the porch.

"No need for any of you gentlemen to stop off at Haley's Saloon on the way," he said, grinning broadly. "I've ordered champagne sent to the restaurant. Fact is—"

"Jim!" an urgent voice shouted from across the street. "Jim Lacy!"

Nevada, in the act of handing Hettie down the step, paused and swung quickly about. A familiar figure was coming toward him at a hard run from the passageway that lay between the bank and Mason's Feed Store.

Cash Burridge!

The lean rider hadn't seen Cash, an impulsively reckless friend from the old days in Lineville on the California-Nevada border, since that morning he'd warned him to leave the Mogollon Rim country or get caught in the rustler clean-out he'd undertaken—and successfully completed.

"Get out of here, Jim!" Burridge yelled, waving his arms. "They've come to kill you. Cud Richardson—

Ed's brother! He's right behind me."

The shouted words were almost instantly drowned out by a crackling burst of gunfire. Burridge halted in mid-stride and spun half about as bullets thudded into the front of the church.

"Back inside!" Nevada shouted. "Fast, all of you!"

Another burst of gunshot erupted close to the bank. Ben Ide sagged to one knee. Marvie Blaine staggered, clutching at his shoulder as a dull red stain widened about his contracted fingers.

"Get inside!" Nevada yelled again and, seizing Hettie about the waist, hurled her toward the doorway.

Behind him, Franklidge and Tom Day, jolted from their stunned lethargy, began shepherding the women into the chapel. Nevada leapt to Ben's aid. Slipping an arm under the wounded man's shoulder, he lifted him to his feet.

"Come on, pard," he said in a low, unhurried way, "Let's get you inside, where we can fix up that leg."

Ide swore deeply. "Not bad hurt. What in the name of hell is this all about?"

Gunfire rattled a third time. Bullets splintered into the flooring, thudded into the wall, plucked at Lacy's sleeve. But there were fewer shots this time. Down the street voices were shouting—one voice calling for the marshal.

Nevada, grim-faced, laid Ben Ide on the first pew, and wheeled to Tom Day. "Slip out the back way—get the doctor," he urged, his voice strained. "They won't see you."

Hettie clutched at his arm. "Who is it?" she breathed, searching his face with a terrified look in her eyes. "What's it all about?"

Nevada shook his head. "I'm not sure. But it is nothing good. I want you to stay right here, and keep others from following me. They'll listen to you if you stay calm."

Her fingers tightened on his arm. "You're not going out there?" she said in a shocked voice.

"I've got to, Hettie. Cash is in a bad way and needs help."

"No—you can't! You're not even wearing your gun!"

Nevada's hand dropped to his hip. He swore silently. Like all the other men in the wedding party, he had put aside his weapon.

"Reckon I can manage," he said, and stepped quickly to the doorway.

The day had begun with promise.

It was to see the wedding of Marvie Blaine, Ina's nineteen-year-old brother, and Rose Hatt, who had come to live with the Ides after Nevada Jim Lacy and other ranchers had cleared the Mogollon country of a ruthless band of outlaws—the Pine Tree gang.

It would all work out well. Ben and Hettie's mother, in failing health for the past year, had been ordered to San Diego where a milder climate would be of benefit. It was decided that the family would escort her to her new home, leaving the ranch in the care of Marvie and Rose, although—as Ben observed to Nevada as they perched on the top rail of a corral awaiting the family he doubted there'd be any large amount of work done by Marvie.

"A man doesn't get married every day," Lacy had replied.

"You and Hettie going to tie the knot, too?" Ben Ide

asked.

"We decided to wait until we get to San Diego. Your mother wants it that way—though it'd be fine with Hettie and me to get the job done right alongside Marvie and Rose."

Ben Ide nodded. "Obliged to you for humoring Mother. She's always talked about a fancy wedding for her only daughter."

"I know that," Nevada drawled, "but I'm getting a mite anxious. Your sister means more to me than life itself."

"I don't have to tell you how much you mean to her," Ben Ide said. "I'm dead certain she's as disappointed as you."

Nevada stared out across the sage-covered flats toward the frowning Mogollon Rim. "We've come a long way since those wild-horse-trapping days on Forlorn River," he mused. "Don't think Hettie's been out of my mind hardly a minute since the trouble here I was falsely accused of being right in the middle of. Kept me on the run, drifting—just trying to forget. Only I never could."

"Where did you go, Nevada?" Ide asked, looking up. "I always intended to ask. We tried to find you, let you know your name had been cleared, and the killers you flushed from cover exposed for what they were."

"Just kept dogging along. I went back to Lineville where I knew folks who figured me for a friend, and didn't mind if I was a gunslinger named Lacy. Worked around there for a spell. Then my heels got to itching and I struck out for Arizona. I showed up at Tom Day's ranch, and he put me on and asked no questions.

"When it came to my name, I sort of held back, not

wanting to mention the one you'd hung on me—
'Nevada'—for fear you and Hettie might hear of it.
And I sure wasn't going to tell him I was Jim Lacy, the
gunman half of the lawmen west of the Missouri were
after.

"But Tom's a real gentleman. He just sort of grinned
at me, and said: 'Well, I'll call you Texas Jack. The
name sort of fits that drawl of yours.' So Texas Jack I
became. Judge Franklidge called me that, too, when I
later on hired out to him." Nevada paused. "Mighty
fine people, those two. One thing I'll always be thankful
for—the kind of friends the Good Lord lined me up
with."

"I'm the one to be grateful," Ben Ide said quietly.
"If you hadn't stepped in, I'd have been strung up as a
horse thief. You and that fast gun of yours."

"That's over and done with. I'm through with being a
fast gun. We've put the Pine Tree rustling bunch out of
business and we can be grateful the law's no longer
interested in me because I had a hand in doing that."

"A hand in it!" Ben Ide echoed. "It was practically
you alone—"

"I'm sure it was Judge Franklidge who set everything
straight," Nevada said, ignoring Ide's protest. "He
probably made them take a real hard look at the
record—at the kind of men I'd gone up against."

"You never were a killer," Ben Ide said. "A gunman,
maybe—a man who uses his weapon when he has no
choice, but always—"

"Hold on," Nevada interrupted, grinning, "you're
making me sound like some kind of a hero—one of
those knights in shining armor I've heard you reading to
little Blaine about."

"It's the truth, Nevada. If Franklidge hadn't put the law straight, I'd have seen to it. I owe everything to you, Nevada. After my father disowned me—"

"I told you to forget it. It's all in the past, buried six feet under."

"No," Ben Ide said slowly. "I won't ever forget. None of the Ides will."

"You've done as much for me. You gave me the chance for a new life. You made it possible for me to have the woman I love for a wife."

"It was Hettie's love for you that made it possible," Ben Ide said. "All the wild mustangs we ever trapped at Forlorn River plus California Red couldn't prevent my sister from marrying you! I'd hate to be the one who tried to stop it!"

Jim Lacy's face was sober. "Just the same," he murmured. "I'm grateful to the Ides."

A thousand lonely thoughts lay behind the words—ten thousand haunting memories of empty days and nights, endless trails, dusty, hostile towns, and always the deep yearning in his heart for the girl he'd felt necessary to give up—and forget.

But all that was over with now. Never again would they be apart for long. Today was the marrying time of Marvie and Rose; tomorrow the rest of the family would head for San Diego. Once there, with Mrs. Ide comfortably settled, Hettie and he would be married, and then he could really believe that what he had hardly dared to take seriously during all of the lonely years—a happiness that would remain steadfast until he ceased to draw breath.

"We're ready, Ben!"

It was Ina's voice, coming from the house. Ben and

Nevada descended from the corral rail.

"It didn't take them as long as I figured," Ida said, smiling. "Proves a woman can fancy up in a hurry, if she has a mind to."

Nevada moved toward the two-seated carriage, knowing that Ben Ide would drive the surrey. "Do we swing by Tom Day's for them?" he asked.

Ben Ide shook his head. "Nope. They'll meet us at the church. So will the Franklidges."

Nevada nodded in understanding and swung the matched sorrel team up to the porch where the family had gathered. Ben Ide curved in behind him.

Stepping down, Nevada assisted Hettie into the front seat. Marvie handed Rose onto the rear cushion. Mrs. Ide would ride with Ben and Ina, taking over the back of the surrey with her small grandson.

Circling his team, Jim Lacy glanced at Ide. "All set to go?"

"All set," Ben answered, "You'd better keep those sorrels plenty far ahead of us, or my blacks'll climb right over you!"

"Now, Ben," Mrs. Ide said. "I hope you're not going to do any of that foolish racing, are you?"

"No, Mother," Ide replied, "no racing. I just don't want you to breathe in a lot of dust." He winked broadly at Lacy, and raised the reins.

Nevada, placed his foot on the iron step pad, swung up, and seated himself beside Hettie. She was frowning.

"Something wrong?"

Hettie pointed to the gun on Nevada's hip. "I know you have to carry a gun while you're working the ranch. But to the wedding?"

Nevada grinned sheepishly. "I guess I forgot," he

17

said. "When we get to the church, I'll leave it in the buggy."

II

Halting just inside the doorway, Nevada cast a quick glance up and down the street. It was deserted now, except for the sprawled figure of Cash Burridge stirring weakly in the dust. Those along the way who had emerged into the open at the first crackling burst of gunfire, had apparently experienced second thoughts as to the danger of exposing themselves, and had wasted no time in vanishing from the scene.

He was sure that the outlaws were somewhere in the shadowy, weed-filled passageways between the buildings on the opposite side of the street. He was equally sure that without a weapon he could do nothing. Even if he had been armed, an attempt to shoot from where he was standing would have been answered by a hail of bullets that would have endangered the others inside the church.

His gaze passed to the buggy parked next to the surrey which Ben Ide had driven. It was a couple of dozen long strides away, but it was a bit nearer than the stricken man, and the gun he'd have on his hip.

Again he felt the touch of Hettie's hand on his arm. She knew him, knew the direct way his mind worked.

"Wait, please," she murmured. "Let the marshal—"

"He can't be in town," Nevada replied, "or he'd have shown up by now. I can't expect another man to do my fighting for me." He paused, frowning. "How about Ben and Marvie? They hurt bad?"

"Marvie's only scratched. A bullet went through

18

Ben's leg, but I don't think it's serious."

"A bullet meant for me," Nevada said bitterly. "I'm bad luck for anybody who's my friend, it seems."

"That's foolish talk!" Hettie replied, almost angrily.

He shook his head, looked down at her. In the dim interior of the church her face was a pale, intent oval, her eyes soft with a glimmer of tears.

"You're going out there, aren't you?"

"I've no choice," Nevada said, and bending swiftly, kissed her on the lips. Then he swung about and plunged through the doorway.

Instantly guns opened up on him. As he raced for the buggy he felt a bullet rip through his sleeve. Others spurted dust around his feet, or buried themselves in the wall of the church behind him. The outlaws were hiding in the passageways, just as he'd thought.

He reached the buggy, and, breathing harshly, halted behind its thin bulk. He'd have little protection there, he knew. Outlaw lead would quickly enough search him out. But he had no intention of remaining so precariously shielded longer than it took him to seize his gun belt, and the heavy .45 hanging from it.

Keeping the high seat of the vehicle in front of him, he reached into the bed and probed about blindly for the weapon. His fingers touched the worn leather of the belt. Quickly he picked it up, drew it to him. Still crouching, coolness moving through him now, he strapped the belt about his waist and lifted the well-oiled weapon from its holster. He was their equal now. He could meet them on even terms.

"Jim—"

The instant Burridge's voice reached him he crouched still lower, peering under the vehicle, and gripping a

19

wheel spoke to steady himself. Cash was moving, struggling to drag himself out of the street.

"Stay put!" Nevada called, taking care to keep his voice from rising to a shout. "I'm coming."

Gathering his legs under him, he spurted suddenly from behind the buggy. The gun flaming in his hand, he headed on the run for the wall of the buildings opposite. The unexpectedness of the move caught the outlaws by surprise, for there was no immediate crackle of answering gunfire.

Without halting he rushed on to the first passageway. Just short of it, he slowed, and at a crouch moved in carefully, reloading his weapon as he did so. Puffs of smoke coming from the weedy corridor earlier had warned him that one or more of the killers was hiding there. Gun ready, he drew a long breath, rose, and lunged into the narrow area. A man was hurrying toward its far end.

"Pull up!" Nevada shouted.

The outlaw wheeled, his gun coming up fast. Lacy fired. The man staggered, flung out his arms and crashed to the ground in a headlong sprawl.

Immediately Nevada moved on to the next passageway, one considerably larger. Behind him he could hear men coming into the street now, ready to back him. He grinned wryly. Someone else always had to take the first step, fire the first bullet. But it was hard to blame them. Most were family men, with dependents—and it really wasn't their fight.

He pulled up. From the rear of the buildings he heard the quick, hard pound of horses moving out. Throwing caution aside, he ducked into the passageway, and legged it for the alley behind the structures. Three riders, bent low over the saddle, were just disappearing into the grove of trees east of the settlement.

Jim Lacy swore softly, and started to turn back for the street. Then abruptly, he halted. A fourth rider, wearing a fringed buckskin jacket and riding a black horse, broke from the far end of the row of buildings, and raced to overtake his friends. One of the gang had been a little slow in getting away.

Nevada brought up his gun, then lowered his arm again. The distance was too great. He stood for a time watching the outlaw fade into the trees, before continuing on to the street.

Now that all danger was gone, a small crowd had gathered around Burridge. Nevada pushed through them, nodding to those he knew, and dropped to his knees beside the wounded man. Slipping an arm under his friend's shoulders, he raised him slightly. There were two broad stains on the man's back. A single, quick glance convinced Nevada that he didn't have much time left.

"Glad—you—made it, Jim," Cash Burridge said slowly.

"Not soon enough," Nevada answered, with an edge of suppressed anger in his voice. "Somebody get the doctor in the church."

"I—I mean—they didn't get you. It's what they're—out to do. Was anybody—in your party hurt?"

"Ben Ide. Marvie Blaine."

"Sorry for them. Glad they didn't hurt you—or your wife."

"We're not married yet, Cash. It was Marvie and Rose Hatt—"

"Little Rose Hatt? Not good for her—if Marvin is hurt bad. Thought it was you—and Hettie."

"We're getting married later, in San Diego. Cash, if you hadn't warned me in time—"

"Owed you—a favor. You gave me a break. Had to—pay back."

"Wasn't necessary. Cash, what's behind this, what's it all about? I didn't quite get what you said before they cut you down."

"It's Cud Richardson. Ed's brother—fro over New Mexico way. Swears he's going to—to get even with you. For killing Ed."

"The old Pine Tree trouble! And I told Ben it was over and done with, a buried part of the past. Cash, it was a fair fight—just between the two of us."

"I know that. But Cud's the kind—who never forgives or forgets. It was his brother you killed and—even coyotes have kinship feelings."

Nevada's thoughts swung briefly to a long-ago moment of violence near the corrals of the Ide ranch. It had been late in the day, near meal time. Several punchers had been there, along with Ed Richardson—known as Clan Dillon then, foreman for Ben Ide, and, unknown to Ben, the secret leader of the vicious Pine Tree rustlers. Face to face they'd shot it out, and Richardson had died, victim of Nevada's deadly bskill.

The dying man's words started coming in a rush, with no pauses between words, as if a sudden realization that the end was near had made Burridge determined, by exerting himself to the utmost, to tell Nevada everything he felt the lean rider should know.

"Cud aims to start up the Pine Tree outfit again. He figures he first has to get rid of you."

Nevada nodded. "Looks like he'll try again then. But thanks to you, it won't be so easy for him now. How did you get mixed up in it?"

"Ran into him an' the bunch riding with him in Mesilla. I knew Cud from Texas. He told me what he was aiming to do. We'd done a few jobs together—in the old days. Reckon he never thought I'd lean toward you.

"He—he wanted me to handle the selling of the beef they'd be rustling. Him and his bunch would drive the herds to Palos Verdes. It would be my job to have a buyer—be the business end of the set-up."

Burridge's voice faded, choked off. He began to cough deeply. Lacy glanced to one of the men standing close by. "Where's that doc?"

"I'm doing fine," Cash mumbled. "Wasn't that much interested—in lining up with Cud. He ain't the kind of man you can turn your back to. Figured I'd—best go along with the deal. Then I learned what he had in mind—bushwhacking you."

"So you rode in here with them."

Burridge nodded. He started to say something, but fell into another violet spasm of coughing. He brushed wearily at his lips.

"You reckon I could have a drink?"

"Somebody get over to Haley's, and bring a bottle," Lacy snapped.

"No need," a man said, stepping forward. "Happens I got a pint here in my pocket."

Nevada held the liquor to the dying man's mouth, and let him drink his fill. Burridge managed an appreciative smile.

"That helps—the pain's getting real bad. We seen

23

you drive in. Cud hid the bunch along the street. Aimed to nail you when—you come out. Said it'd be a joke on you if you never got the chance—to be a bridegroom.''

Burridge's words had begun to come haltingly again. His voice was weaker. He reached for the bottle of whiskey and took another long swallow. At that moment Doc Able shouldered his way through the thickening crowd. Kneeling, the doc made a hurried examination, and shook his head.

"Wanted to warn you—earlier," Burridge said. "Couldn't get away—from Cud."

"Warning me cost you your life," Nevada said quietly. "I owe you plenty, Cash."

"You owe me nothing. Was just a favor—I had to pay back."

"You've done that, and more. Is there anything you want me to do, like getting word to somebody who's important to you?"

"Ain't nobody. Just look out for yourself. Cud won't quit—until he's cut you down. He won't—"

Nevada waited for Burridge to finish. The words had come slow, with effort, and were almost inaudible. He bent own in order to hear.

"No use," Doc Able said. "The man's dead."

III

Nevada Jim Lacy rose slowly, badly shaken and unable to tear his gaze from Cash Burridge's slack features. Cash had changed. Things had evidently not been going well for him. His clothing was worn, faded and the golden mustache he had once taken such vain pride in was unkempt. Only his eyes had remained the same—a

24

bright, intense blue that seemed to pierce a man.

But the eyes of Cash Burridge would never look out upon the world again, and the flashing grin and engaging manner that had so easily won over new acquaintances, often enlisting them in some far-from-honest scheme, was gone forever.

Cash had known that his loyalty would probably cost him his life. He had been fully aware that the moment he yelled his warning, Cud Richardson and his ruthless companions would turn their guns upon him. It hadn't held him back. With all his shortcomings Cash Burridge was a man—one who had not stopped to add up the costs when there was a debt of friendship to be repaid.

"What'll I do with him, Mr. Lacy?"

Nevada, jarred from his reverie, turned to a tall, darkly bearded onlooker who had elbowed his way through the crowd. It was Rufe Daniels, who did undertaking chores in Winthrop, along with his regular profession of barbering.

"He's to get the best funeral you can arrange," Lacy said. "I'll foot the bill."

"Yes, sir. How about the other one?"

Nevada frowned, his gaze passing to the outlaw he had downed. "I'll pay for him, too," he said. "Every man, even a vicious killer, is entitled to a decent burial."

"Yes, sir. I'll do the job up right. When do you want the services held?"

Lacy stared off toward the Mogollon Rim. "Tomorrow, or the next day, whenever you're ready. I doubt if I'll be around."

He turned then, found Hettie standing directly behind him. She was looking up at him, pride showing in her

25

gray eyes. Beyond her, Marvie Blaine and Rose were looking on from the porch of the church. Marvie was standing at their side with a white bandage on the upper part of his arm, but the others were still inside.

Ben's absence sent a tremor of anxiety through Nevada, but he managed to keep his voice level when he asked: "Is Ben hurt worse than you thought, Hettie?"

"He's fine," Hettie replied. "It was just a flesh wound, and won't take long to heal. It's mother. She's terribly upset."

Daniels and three men moved in, lifted the body of Cash Burridge, and placed it on an improvised board stretcher. As they straightened his lax form, his gun fell to the ground. Daniels recovered it hastily and offered it to Nevada.

"Expect you'll want this, Mr. Lacy. He won't be needing it now."

"Bury it with him," Nevada said. "A man's gun belongs with him, no matter what."

Daniels nodded, and with the three others aiding him, headed for his shop. The crowd began to break up, some of the men pausing to compliment Lacy, and slap him on the back.

"You sure potted that owlhoot hiding in the alley," an angular man with mud on his boots and a quid of tobacco in his cheek said. "Bullet took him dead center of the brisket. Real shooting, I call it."

Nevada moved his head woodenly. Men who stayed on the far side of the street when guns opened up could never know how it felt to be dealing out death—the sickness, the hollow, empty feeling it brought, the dead stop to the heart. No matter if he victim deserved to die, the taking of life was a terrible thing not easily erased from memory.

"I wish I'd had my gun, and been out there with you!" Young Marvie Blaine's voice claimed Nevada's attention. "I'll bet the two of us could—"

"Just be damned glad you weren't!" Nevada cut in savagely. "And start praying every day of your life that you're never called on to kill a man."

Marvie's jaw sagged. "But I thought—"

"I know. You're thinking it's a great thing to handle a sixgun—outdraw another man, cut him down! You think there's some kind of glory in it. Well, think again!"

"Nevada," Hettie broke in gently. "Marvie didn't mean—"

"Neither did all those galoots who came by, and thumped me on the back. If you're smart, Marvie, you'll forget you even own a gun."

Young Blaine's features were frozen. He glanced at Rose and then at Hettie. "What did I say wrong?" he asked, perplexed.

Nevada stared at the boy for a moment, then reached out and gripped him by the shoulder, his fingers tightening in a friendly squeeze. "Don't mind me," he said. "It will make sense to you in a few years." Taking Hettie's hand, he moved off toward the buggy.

"Hettie, you know what all this means," he said, as soon as they were beyond earshot of the others.

The girl nodded soberly.

"There'll be no peace, no safety for anyone around here unless I got after Richardson. He won't quit until he gets me—or I get him."

"I know, Nevada."

"What's worse, he's the kind who'll take it out on you and everyone else who's close to me—if he gets the chance."

27

"I understand I hate it—hate it worse than I can say. But with a posse, it won't take long."

"No posse," he said flatly. "It's a job for me alone. If I head out of here with a bunch of men Richardson will lead us on a chase that could last weeks—maybe months. If I got by myself he'll stop, make a stand."

Fear crept into Hettie's eyes, and as quickly vanished. "Of course I'll worry. There's no sense in my pretending I won't. But I know you can take care of yourself."

"Something I learned how to do mighty young," Nevada drawled.

"I know—but I keep thinking there were four of them. And now it will be three to one."

"Five to start with. Four rode away."

"Four to one, then. Couldn't you take at least one man with you? That would make the odds better—and it wouldn't be like a posse."

Nevada shook his head. "It would be asking too much, even if there was somebody around whom I could trust, and depend on—like Ben. It would be no problem getting a posse together. But to ask one man to side me against four killers—well, it just wouldn't be right."

"Ben would go instantly."

"I know that, but he's in no shape for a hard ride."

Nevada glanced toward the porch. Mrs. Ide, assisted by Tom Day, had come out, and Judge Franklidge had lent his arm to Ben. The others had gathered around them, and were looking expectantly toward the surrey and the carriage.

"Appears they're about ready to head for home," Nevada said. "I want to get this straight with you, Hettie."

28

"It's settled," she replied. "We'll go back to the ranch, and postpone the trip to San Diego until you return."

"No, that's what I want you to understand. You're to go on just as planned. I don't think it's a good idea to keep your mother here any longer than is absolutely necessary."

Hettie faced him. "Tell me the truth, Nevada. Are you afraid Richardson might raid the ranch while you're out searching for him?"

"Possibly. But by going after him, I'll be giving him little reason not to make me his target. It's just that I'd feel better, knowing you were in San Diego. Besides, the doctor told you to take your mother to the coast as soon as you could."

"I know, Nevada, but leaving without you—it doesn't seem right."

"It's right. Just trust me. I'll come to San Diego just as soon as I've handled this chore. Then we'll go right on with the plans we made. One thing I've been sort of holding back from you. I thought we'd go down into Mexico for a honeymoon. It's nice down there, this time of year."

Hettie smiled, and her eyes brightened. "I'd love that. I've never been in Mexico."

"Something else. Figured we could do a little business while we're there. Rancher I've heard of near Mexico City raises a fine breed of horses. Tan color with white man and tail. Thought maybe we could make a deal for a stud and a couple of mares, and get the strain started up here."

"It would be wonderful," Hettie murmured.

"Then we're all squared away. As soon as Ben can

ride comfortably, you will head for San Diego. I'll join you the instant I've made sure Richardson can't sink his fangs in anyone else. Cash died from a rattlesnake bite as surely as if he'd stood in the path of an uncoiling diamond-back. It mustn't happen again.''

Hettie Ide shuttered. "I—I don't know. I'm still not sure.''

He stared at her. "Not sure of what? Is there something wrong?''

Hettie shook her head. "I don't know what's the matter with me. I had the strangest feeling, as if everything was ending right here, that we'd never see each other again. Oh, Nevada—''

He caught her in his arms, and held her close.

"Now, now, you're letting all this excitement get the best of you. We'll meet again—a lot sooner than you expect. Nothing bad is going to happen to me.''

"I wish I could be sure of that.''

"You can. My luck's always been good when guns open up unexpectedly. Take today. In all that shooting I wasn't even nicked. Poor Ben and Marvie caught the lead intended for me. It always has been that way. Good thing for me, but a mite hard on my friends.''

Hettie laughed in spite of her fears. "All right,'' she said, "We'll do it your way. And I'll try not to worry.''

"Fine,'' Nevada said, heaving a vast, inward sigh. He'd dreaded telling her of what had to be done. But she had seen his side of it, accepted it as he had felt she would. Taking her by the arm, he helped her into the two-seater.

"We'll explain it to the others when we get to the ranch,'' he said. "I aim to get an early start in the morning.''

IV

The next day dawned cool and pleasant. Nevada Jim had chosen a tough-bodied little buckskin for a mount, preferring it to the tall, much faster bay gelding that Ben Ide had suggested. Cud Richardson had headed east out of Winthrop into rough, rugged country and Nevada knew it would take a horse with plenty of bottom to stand a grueling chase, in which speed would not be a major factor.

He rode due south in preference to wasting the hours that would have been required if he went first to the settlement and picked up the trail from there. By angling, he could eventually intersect the road a dozen miles or so above the town. Knowing Richardson as he did, he was quite sure that a man of the outlaw's stripe, being certain of pursuit, would be very unlikely to head back for the settlement.

Cud Richardson would want to have all the cards stacked in his favor. He would strive to meet a pursuer on his own ground, and pick his own time for a confrontation. And Nevada was determined to have something to say about the location of the final showdown.

One factor was not good. Richardson and his companions were strangers to him. He would not be able to recognize the outlaw leader if they came face to face, unless of course, Cud bore a strong resemblance to his brother. The only definite identification upon which he could depend was that one of the renegades he'd seen had worn a fringed leather jacket, and a somewhat narrow-brimmed hat.

But he'd find Richardson—or perhaps Richardson would find him. That particular problem did not worry him.

As the sun rose higher, his sense of his grim mission dropped away from him somewhat. This part of his trail led through deep forest, and the shafts of light striking through the tall pine and spruce contrasted vividly with the deep green of the trees. The forest was bathed in an atmosphere at once cool and bright golden, and wild turkey and pheasant flashed as the sun caught them in movement.

The peace that the wilderness always brought to Nevada came upon him as he rode the familiar forest track. He entered a grassy glade, and a startled deer bounded away, an increasingly distant crashing of the undergrowth marking its passage.

The forest gave way to open country then, and his heart lifted as the illimitable space spread out before him—the purple of the sage, the red and yellow of the rocks stretching like a stormy sea lit by a lurid sunset, to the distant mountains. A flight of prairie warblers darted from the trees behind him and shone like whirling dust-motes for an instant in the bright blue air.

Near mid-morning he reached the road out of Winthrop that curved on in twin ruts toward the Mogollon Rim. He halted at once, dropped from the saddle and moved a foot until he found a stretch where the earth was soft. He nodded in grim satisfaction. He had been right. Clearly imprinted in the roadway were the hoof marks of three horses traveling abreast. Only three.

This brought a frown of puzzlement to Nevada's face. He began to search about more closely, and eventually discovered the tracks of the fourth outlaw's mount. The man in the fringed buckskin jacket had apparently not overtaken Richardson and the others—at least, not at that point. It seemed strange, unless the outlaw was deliberately maintaining a distance behind his four companions, the better to keep a lookout on their back trail for pursuers.

Nevada decided that almost had to be the answer. Accordingly, he went back to the saddle, cut off the trail at right angles for a full quarter mile, and then resumed his northward course but on a line paralleling the twin ruts. Anyone looking back now would have seen no one in the roadway.

The sun grew warmer. Nevada loosened his jacket, removed it, and tied it down in its usual place behind the cantle. He had donned the checkered silk scarf he'd worn in years past, associating it vaguely in his mind with good luck. The handmade, scalloped-topped boots and yellow vest had long since worn out, and been replaced with footgear of similar design, and a vest of soft tan broadcloth, heavily corded and frogged to the point of resembling a Mexican *charro* jacket.

Nevada felt confident and in reasonably high spirits. Yet a quiet resentment lay upon him. He'd gone through such time often enough in the past, when he was on the trail of a man he would probably be forced to kill, or who, in turn, would try to kill him. But this was different, somehow.

Responsibility, he guessed it was—responsibility to Hettie on the one hand, and a similar obligation, but not quite the same, to the ranchers, the people of Winthrop, and all those who lived in the area on the other. Everyone was relying upon him to stop Cud

33

Richardson and the new Pine Tree rustling gang he was assembling before the land was again ravaged by lawlessness.

That covered Ben Ide, Day, Judge Franklidge, and the entire law-abiding community. But it was difficult to place Hettie in quite the same category. True, she must be protected—at the cost of his life, if fate took a cruel turn. But there was more than that involved. Hettie was waiting for him—waiting to become his wife, and help him build a ranch of their own, so that they could make a fine life together.

He'd known she was the woman for him the moment of their first meeting, seven years ago, when he'd teamed with her brother, Ben.

Nevada sighed, and stared out across the long flat—the low hills that built gradually until they became massive mounds of frowning mountains. There was no point in dwelling upon what might have been. Find Cud Richardson, settle with him, and return to Hettie. Then their new life could begin.

Staring out over the purple sagebrush landscape, he considered that. Was it possible for him to settle down, and become a rancher—even with Hettie? Or would the recollections of the past, the years during which he'd drifted aimlessly, never halting for long, prove a barrier too strong to overcome?

A restless spirit is a difficult taskmaster, hard to conquer. There had been times when he'd succeeded in convincing himself that he'd like nothing better than owning a ranch, and becoming a steady family man. But there had been dark moments as well, when a voice deep within him had warned against too great a confidence, had whispered that it could never work, that he'd only break Hettie Ide's heart.

Invariably he had resisted that thought. It could be—it had to be. He was entitled to settle down just as other men did, and enjoy life to the full. He could overcome the recalcitrant trail rider within himself, and make the good dreams come true.

So deep in reverie had Nevada been that the outward signs of the ragged gash were upon him almost before he realized it. Pulling in the buckskin, he raised himself in the stirrups, and looked down into the broken land dotted with round clumps of snakeweed, sand peaked piles of greasewood and patches of saltbush.

Here was the true Arid Zone that had given the Territory its name when the Spanish Conquistadors came. Harsh, unyielding, yet possessing a color and grandeur that more hospitable lands knew not. Far off, the purple hills rimmed the scene, rising up in a frowning, jagged line, dark at that distance even in the bright sun.

Closer to hand, the air shimmered over the sunbaked rocks and sand flats, making the image of all he saw dance and glimmer as if seen through a trembling veil of clearest water. The road curved eastward here, Nevada recalled, and followed the canyon to a point where a crossing could be made, one could press on toward the larger Chevelon Canyon.

On a hunch he swung left, slanted across a long slope and returned to the road. They were stil ahead of him—the fourth rider still trailing his three friends. Just how far behind the man in the fringed jacket might be it was impossible to determine, but Nevada made it a point to use more care now, and watch sharply. Once in the canyon, he knew, they could cut off the trail, and angle back for Mogollon Mesa. There were two or three settlements to be found in that area.

Nevada rode on, once again removing himself from the roadway in order to take a side course. He went down into Wild Cat Canyon with the sun pushing hard at him now, and bringing the first flecks of sweat to the buckskin's hide.

A short while later he reached the flat on the opposite rim. Halting once more, he dismounted. It had been a rough, hot crossing and the gelding needed a few minutes' rest. Leaving the horse to graze on the sparse grass, he climbed to a low knoll and looked ahead.

The next break in the land would be Chevelon Canyon, a deep, wild section where a man, if he so desired, could hide with ease. He doubted that Cud Richardson would do so, however. Most likely he would keep moving until he reached one of the settlements. There he would have matters his own way—might possibly have more members of his gang waiting.

And there was that strain of pride men such as Cud Richardson always possessed. He'd want everyone to see and know that he was the one who had brought down the famous Jim Lacy. To Cud it would be a mark of distinction, an invisible medal to be flaunted proudly in all the towns where he walked.

"Reckon I'll have something to say about that," Nevada murmured. "If he nails my hide to the wall, he'll have earned the right to do it."

Raising his glance to the towering mass in the distance, known as Chevelon Butte, he watched the effortless soaring of a golden eagle silhouetted against the empty blue-steel sky for a few moments. Then he returned to where the buckskin waited, mounted and pressed on. Little more than an hour later he reached the larger canyon. There was but one trail leading down into the broad gouge, and he was compelled to take it. The hoofprints of the outlaws' horses were still visible, but on the yonder side he encountered his first change.

The outlaws had swung from the trail, followed a northwesterly course. Nevada grinned wryly. Richardson was running true to form; he was heading for one of the settlements just as he had anticipated. Men like Cud were all alike, they possessed single-tracked minds, and it was never hard to fathom their intentions.

Some time later Nevada halted at a small stream, to rest the sturdy little buckskin, but also to ease his own muscles. He'd grown soft, he realized, rubbing at his thighs and flexing his shoulders. There had been many days in the past when endless hours in the saddle had been scarcely noticeable. But of late he had been doing most of his traveling in a buckboard or a buggy; come nightfall, he guessed ruefully, he'd be paying for all that easy living.

He spent an hour at the creek, taking the opportunity to brew up a lard tin of coffee which he drank hot and black. He wasn't hungry, however, and ate only a little of the lunch Hettie had prepared, and ignored completely the food supplies he'd stowed in his saddle-bags, in case the chase ran into several days.

The sun was well past midafternoon when he mounted and moved on. Gradually, with the passing miles, the heat dwindled and a coolness began to spread over the land. Freeing his jacket, he drew it on, finding it comfortable. Shortly before darkness he pulled to a stop on a low ridge. Miles ahead, in a pocket formed by two towering upthrusts of granite, lights twinkled. A calmness came upon him, took possession of his nerves, and mind.

Richardson would be waiting for him there. There was no doubt in his mind about that.

V

Nevada Jim Lacy knew that the road would be watched. Cud Richardson would not permit him to arrive unannounced. Slumped on the saddle, he studied the general lay of the land. he town, whatever its name might be, appeared from the distance to consist of no more than three or four buildings clustered tightly together in a small area as if for mutual support in the hollow of the hills.

A mining settlement, he guessed, although he could think of no ore deposits in that general area. But men sought gold and silver at random, often basing their hopes and expending their labor on a hunch, an ancient legend, or a purportedly authentic map passed down through generations.

Regardless of the town's reason for existence, it was where he would find Richardson, and that was why he had ridden to the ball in the first place. Find and stop him before he could plunge Arizona's Mogollon country into another bloody war between a gang of vicious outlaws and the law-respecting townspeople.

Moving on, Nevada cut wide of the little-used road that led to the glimmering lights. The last of the sun's flare in the west had gone, and a weak quarter-moon, affording little light, made it slow going for the buckskin as he picked his way over the loose rock. For a time they moved downward, coming finally to a broad, sand-floored arroyo. It originated somewhere above the settlement, Nevada surmised, and since it offered better footing for the gelding, he turned into its brushy expanse.

The buckskin plodded on tirelessly, while the wash steadily deepened until finally Nevada saw that he was hemmed in on both sides by ten-foot-high banks. He began to watch for a break that would permit him to climb out, since he was drawing close to the town and had no intention of entering it without first looking it over thoroughly.

A side gully, steep and brush-locked, coming in from his left offered the sought-for opportunity. Dismounting, Nevada took firm hold of the buckskin's saddle and led the way, breaking and kicking aside the brittle undergrowth to make it easier for the horse. He had gotten into the big pine country, he realized, noting the pointed tips that were etched blackly against the dark sky farther on.

Finally he broke out onto a small mesa that ran on to where it fused with the choppy foothills of the mountains to the west. To the right of its termination he again caught the flicker of lights.

Nevada grunted with satisfaction as he stepped back onto the saddle. By following the mesa, he could enter the town from its rear side, and it seemed unlikely that Richardson would expect him to do that. In all probability his sentry would be keeping an eye on the road.

The settlement was about what he'd expect it to be like—five small structures and one large two-story building that probably, in some previous decade, had been someone's fine home. Now it bore a crudely lettered sign with the solitary word SALOON. Two of the second-floor windows showed light. All the rest—at least the ones visible to him—were dark.

The ground floor was a different matter. Light blazed in all of the glassed openings and the feeble moon was sufficiently strong to enable him to make out the shadowy forms of a dozen or more horses at the hitch-rack. All of the other buildings were in blackness. There should be houses, too, he thought, homes for those who worked in the stores. Probably they were set farther back, below the slight ridge that lay just beyond the town.

He worked his way in closer, taking care to keep well back in the shadows along the base of the towering mountain. Faint music reached his ears—piano chords rendered fast and loud, and with little regard for accuracy.

The reason for the town's existence came to him then. It stood at one of the crossroads that led to Arizona's former capital city, Prescott, miles to the west. It was not a mining camp or supply point for ranchers or homesteaders. It was simply one of those towns that sprang up to offer rest and relaxation to travelers, and break their tiring journeys, to and from widely separated destinations.

He wondered what the name of the place might be; it was even possible he once had been there, coming into it and passing on by a different road.

He swung the buckskin right, moved slowly away from the mountain until he found himself on the lip of a bluff. Below he could see the meandering course of the arroyo which he had followed earlier. On beyond it he located the trail, barely visible in the pale silver of the night.

Tracking it with his eyes, he saw that it entered the settlement at its south-east corner. That was good. If Richardson's man was watching that approach, he would ignore all others. Wheeling the weary buckskin, he retraced his tracks to the foot of the mountain and pushed on.

He reached the town proper—COOPERSVILLE, a faded sign on the roof of a livery stable informed him—and guided the gelding into the deep shadow behind the saloon. Glancing about he saw a small barn located near the base of the mountain, and angled the buckskin toward it.

Keenly alert, he dismounted, and stood for a full minute, tense, listening. Music started up again within the bulky, two-floored structure. A man shouted and then there was laughter. Nevada could see no one outside, either around the building or in the narrow strip of street that separated the saloon from the remaining structures.

Moving silently, he led the buckskin into the barn, and again paused to listen. There were horses; he could hear the crunching of grain, an occasional stamp of a hoof. No human appeared to be present. Still leading the gelding, he continued down the runway until he came to a side entrance. Ground-reining the buckskin, he pulled the door open, and propped it with an empty keg. An emergency exit was always a handy thing to have at one's disposal.

He guided the gelding into the stall nearest the door, forked a quantity of hay into the manger, and looked around until he found a sack of oats. Dipping out a quart, he added it to the buckskin's meal and then turned to leave. He would have liked to remove his tack from the horse, but decided it would be better to wait

41

until he was sure of his ground. If all went well, he'd return, relieve the buckskin of the bridle and saddle, and permit him to get the complete rest he'd earned.

Removing his spurs, he hooded them over the horn and doubled back to the doorway, again cocking his ear into the cool night. The racket inside the saloon seemed to have increased. Everyone in town would be there, he guessed, along with all those who were making a stop-over. Only the sentry delegated by Richardson to watch the road would be elsewhere. Probably he would be some distance away.

He swung his attention to the rear of the looming structure. There was a back door, and a back stairway leading to the upper floor. Ignoring the first, he crossed a narrow strip of ground to the steps. Without hesitation he mounted them quickly.

At the upper door he halted, and placed his ear to the crack along the frame. The noise coming from the lower level was so loud he could not tell whether or not there was anyone beyond the panel. He'd have to gamble on it. Twisting the knob, he opened the door, and stepped inside.

A blast of heated, stale air, heavy with the odor of liquor, sweat and smoke, and throbbing with sound, met him head-on. Closing the warped panel, he stepped up against the wall. He was in a small entry area. Three strides in front of him there appeared to be a hallway running at right angles, and dimly lit by a lamp somewhere farther down.

Quietly, he eased forward until he reached the cross corridor, and paused. The hall was long. Several doors opened off it on both sides. At its south end he could see posts indicating the location of the stairway leading to the lower floor. From there he should be able to see what was happening below as well as all of the saloon's occupants.

Nevada reached for his gun, drew it, and made certain the cylinder was fully loaded. Then, sliding it back into its holster, he turned the corner into the hallway. The click of a door lock brought him up short.

"You lookin' for me, cowboy?"

Lacy turned slowly to face the speaker—a girl. She was not young, but far from old in years. Her hair was a straw-yellow, and there were thick daubs of rouge on her cheeks, and a brighter red heightened the color of her lips. Here eyes were deepset and a discoloration was spreading below the left one. Managing a tired smile, she cocked her head, smoothed the garish red-and-yellow spangled dress she wore and spoke again.

"I said—are you lookin' for me?"

Nevada shook his head, realizing how important it was to be careful and not give away his presence to those below. "Not right now," he said. "I'm hunting a pard of mine. Figured he came up here."

The girl shrugged, pushed at stray wisps hanging from her loosely gathered hair.

"Who is he?"

"Uh-name of Hank. Hank Beeman."

"Never heard of him," the girl said bluntly. She started to move on, then hesitated. "Kate's got some jasper in her room—end of the hall. Maybe that's where your friend is."

"Most likely," Lacy murmured and touched the brim of his hat with a forefinger. "Obliged."

The girl shrugged and waited until he had turned for the distant end of the corridor.

"Best you knock first," she advised. "Kate don't like folks bustin' in on her." She shrugged agian, and continued on toward the stairway.

Nevada walked on slowly, stalling until he was certain she had reached the lower floor. Then, wheeling, he followed her swiftly. If the girl intended to report his presence, the quicker he got out of the hallway, the better.

He halted again, cautiously, at the top of the stairs. He stopped the girl instantly through a thick haze of smoke. She was making her way leisurely among the patrons, and he saw with relief that her brief encounter with him was far from her mind.

He turned his attention to the confusion below, searching the smoke-blurred faces of the men standing at the bar, and those sitting at the tables.

One almost had to be Cud Richardson.

VI

Nevada's searching glance finally picked up the man in the fringed buckskin coat. Instantly he came to attention. There were four others with him, scattered around a circular table playing cards. He stared intently, endeavoring to penetrate the haze. One of the five could be Cud Richardson. Carefully he examined each shadowed face. After a moment he shrugged, and gave it up. Even if the outlaw chief resembled his brother it would have been impossible to tell from that distance.

But Richardson was there in the crowd. The presence of the man in the fringed jacket assured that.

The piano struck up a tune. A huge woman whose

44

bulk overflowed the stool upon which she sat had begun to hammer mercilessly at the keys. The girl with whom Nevada had spoken in the hallway emerged from a corner of the room, paused beside the table occupied by the outlaws and spoke to them.

Men began to shout, and after a few moments she smiled and made her way to the piano. Taking up a position at one end, she began to sing, rendering an unrecognizable ballad in a rasping, dry nasal tone that could scarcely be heard above the music and the loud hum of conversation.

Suddenly a table overturned with a crash, and a hoarse voice shouted an oath. Abruptly pandemonium broke loose. A fight began at one of the tables and the music and singing halted abruptly. Chairs skittered across the bare floor, and another table splintered. There was a quick flare of fire as a wall lamp fell with a crash. More yelling arose as three men leapt out from the bar, and began to stamp out the tongues of flame which were now licking hungrily at an overturned table.

Someone dashed a pitcher of water, or perhaps it was beer, on the growing conflagration. Immediately a pillar of dense smoke spiraled upward, fusing with the thick haze clinging to the ceiling. A dozen men joined in the scuffle, cursing and shouting. Three more fist fights started up almost simultaneously. One of the bartenders began to wave madly at the piano player. The music started up again and the girl singer climbed into a chair and resumed her ballad in a voice that rose higher in volume.

Then, gradually, the turmoil began to diminish, and the fighting ceased, except for two cowpunchers who continued to trade blows in the center of the room.

Finally they, too, called a truce, and allowed themselves to be pulled apart by friends, who crowded in and herded them into separate areas. As soon as the tables had been righted and there was no more shooting, Nevada turned his attention again to where the five outlaws had been sitting.

A frown crossed his face. The fringe-jacketed man and another were missing. Swiftly his eyes swept the room. They were nowhere about. At some time during the turmoil they had apparently slipped out the door. He swore impatiently at his own carelessness, and then a disturbing thought occured to him.

Was Cud Richardson aware of his presence? Had the outlaw somehow discovered that he was in the building? How? He'd been careful, had remained well back and out of sight on the small landing at the head of the stairs.

The girl. . .That had to be the answer. She had recognized him for a stranger and Richardson had probably dropped the word that he was expecting the arrival of someone who might attempt to keep his identity concealed by telling some hard-to-believe story.

Again Nevada swore. If his hand had been tipped, it was necessary for him to make his move now, at once. But against whom? Which one was Richardson? The man in the fringed jacket? Or the man who had disappeared with him? Was it one of the three who were sitting at the table? Or could it be someone entirely different?

It irked him to stand in the shadows, prevented from acting by his own lack of knowledge. It was even more galling to be unable to simply walk down into the crowd and confront Cud Richardson, his voice raised in a challenge. That was the way he would have preferred to handle it. But there was too much at stake now. The odds were stacked high against him. Not only was Richardson on his guard against that kind of challenge, he was making sure it wouldn't happen—by having four men at his side. He'd never get the chance to face the outlaw leader alone. He'd simply throw away his life, accomplish nothing—and the Mogollon country would again become the private preserve of the lawless. Yet there must be a way to single out Richardson. There had to be.

The solution came to him suddenly. Women such as Kate would do anything for a price. If he had thought, he probably could have bribed the other girl into pointing the outlaw to him. But it was only now that he was faced with that particular problem.

He glanced back along the dimly-lit hall. Kate's door was still closed. He had no choice except to wait, and take careful stock of the situation. Richardson had three men siding him, there could be no doubt about that—four, if you counted the extra man who'd been at the table. And there could be more. But it was best not to worry about odds at the moment.

It was knowing who the opposition was that mattered —the leader and the riders who actually would be backing his play, and not merely bystanders. He'd try to find that out from Kate, too. He had nothing against walking through the doors of the saloon, and calling Richardson out, provided he had the outlaw's men spotted.

A door-lock clicked, and someone stumbled against the panel, cursing. Nevada turned, and glanced swiftly down the corridor. A cowpuncher, in range clothing

47

and very drunk, was coming from Kate's room. Drawing back into the shadows, Nevada watched the man approach. He was walking unsteadily from side to side, ricocheting off the walls as he made slow progress for the stairs.

He passed Nevada unseeing, reached the steps, and stumbled. But he caught himself in time, and, clinging to the rickety banister, fought his way downward.

Nevada turned and, hurried down the hall. Kate's door was still open. He stepped quickly inside, and closed it. The woman, large, dark-haired, with jet-black eyes was rubbing rouge into her cheeks. She almost ignored Nevada's entrance, merely touched him with a reflected glance through the mirror she was facing.

"I need a drink," she said.

Nevada reached into his pocket for a double-eagle, and flipped it onto the dresser before her. "That'll buy a few," he drawled.

Kate picked up the coin, and turned slowly, a look of bewilderment in her eyes. "What—"

"I need a favor."

"You mean you ain't here to—"

Nevada shook his head. "All I'm after is a favor, a small one. I'm looking for a man. I want you to go downstairs, and put your hand on his shoulder. I'll be watching from the landing."

Kate dropped the gold coin into the crevice of her ample bosom. "Who's this man you're looking for?"

"Cud Richardson."

The woman's eyes widened. "What do you want him for?"

Lacy shook his head. "That gold doesn't entitle you to any details. It happens to be a personal matter. I want

48

you to point out the men siding him, too."

Kate continued to stare at him, her lower lip slack, almost petulant. "You some kind of law officer?"

"No."

The woman remained silent for a moment longer, and then shrugged. "Why not? Cud Richardson's tight-fisted and women like me are just dirt to him. You want me to do it now?"

Nevada nodded. "I'll be at the head of the stairs."

Kate turned, picked up a lace scarf, and clutching it in her hand, walked by Lacy into the hallway. As she passed she gave him a faint smile.

"This ain't going to get me killed, is it?"

"Not you," he replied, and followed her down the corridor.

Reaching the landing, Nevada resumed his position in the darker corner as Kate started down the steps slowly, making her entrance as dramatic as possible. Several heads turned, voices shouted to her.

The saloon had quieted considerably. It was filled now with only the drone of conversation and the occasional scrape of a chair. The piano was silent, and the girl singer sat at one of the tables with several men.

Kate reached the foot of the stairs, and paused on the last step. Casually she looked out over the scatter of patrons, then moved on, swinging her hips. This immediately evoked a few more appreciative shouts from the seated patrons and the dozen men lining the bar. Lacy scarcely heard them. His attention was on the woman's hands. The instant she touched—

Nevada stiffened as the hard, round muzzle of a revolver was jammed with abrupt violence into the small of his back.

"Don't you move, mister," a voice coming from directly behind him ordered quietly. "Lift his iron, Dude."

VII

Lacy raised his hands slowly. It was sure that it had been the girl, dropping a warning to Cud Richardson when she had paused at the outlaw's table. He was just as quick to realize that a moment after the brawl had started—a fortunate accident or possibly an incident deliberately staged to create confusion—two of the renegades must have slipped out the door, circled the building and entered by the same route he had earlier used.

He felt the lessening of weight at his side as his .45 was yanked from its holster. From the tail of his eye he glimpsed the man standing close to him. It was the one who wore the fringed jacket.

"Now start backing up," the outlaw with the pistol said quietly. "No ruckus—unless you want to have your skull bashed in."

Moving slowly, Nevada began to retreat into the dark hallway. He reached the short passage that led to the outside door and stairway. Dude pushed by him, opened the panel, and held it wide.

"Get going," the other outlaw commanded.

Lacy started for the exist, self-directed anger now pushing at him. *Sure messed this one up*, he thought bitterly. *Reckon I should have taken my chances and waded right in on them*.

He stepped out into the moonlit night, and came face to face with Dude. He was a slightly built, clean-shaven man of about twenty-five. His hat, pushed to the back of his head, revealed sandy, or perhaps, red, hair. In the weak light Nevada could not be certain. Dude's eyes were dark and piercing.

"I'll keep in front of him, Clint," he said, and started down the steps.

"Yeah, you do that," the man with the gun said. "Only don't go getting too close. He's a real stem-winding curly wolf, they tell me."

They reached the foot of the stairway. Nevada halted, uncertainly. Clint jabbed savagely with his gun barrel.

"What the hell you want me to do?" Lacy asked.

"Just keep trailing after Dude. He'll show you."

The outlaw crossed behind the building, turned right at the corner and led the way to the street. Without hesitation, he contined on to a low-roofed structured on the opposite side. At one time it had apparently been a livery barn. Abandoned now, it stood in sagging neglect, doors missing, windows shattered and littered with an accumulation of wind-blown weeds and trash. Through this dismal rubbish patch Dude led the way to a small room at the rear.

"Stand easy," Clint murmured, pressing hard with his weapon. "Dude'll get us a light going."

A match flared in the half-dark. Shortly the dusty cubicle came alive with a yellow glow from a lantern. Clint laid his hand on Nevada's shoulder, and pushed him roughly toward a bench in one corner.

"Make yourself to home, Mr. Lacy. Cud'll be coming along in a few minutes."

Nevada eyed the outlaw coldly. Clint was a big, raw-boned man, wide across the shoulders and with a thick bull neck. Clint had been one of the five at the table but

Nevada's glimpse of the party back in Winthrop had been too fleeting to be sure the big man had been there also.

He shifted his attention to Dude. Clint appeared to regard the younger man with faint contempt, tinged with an amused tolerance. He did seem to have little in common with the hardened outlaw, being cleaner, better dressed and with an air of near-refinement about him. But that was no sure guide as to a man's character, Nevada knew. He'd encountered many a hardened killer who had the looks and mannerisms of a Sunday School teacher. It was what lay beneath the veneer that made the difference. Due was a greenhorn taking lessons from a hardened old-timer, he finally concluded.

Boots thudded on the old stable runway. Clint straightened, looked around. Two men were moving up through the murky light. They reached the door to the small back room, and stepped quickly inside. One was a short, red-faced man, the other tall, dark with pale eyes and a sharp hook for a nose. Nevada was sure that he was Cud Richardson. There was a faint but unmistakable resemblance to his brother Ed.

"Got him, eh?"

Clint grinned, exposing his broad, tobacco-stained teeth. "It was as easy as eatin' apple pie."

Richardson swung his piercing glance to Dude. "Seems you'll do," he said, and stepped nearer to Lacy. He leaned forward, staring intently at Nevada's face, then settled back.

"Had me a hunch I'd know you. Jim Lacy . . . Name rung a bell when I heard it was you that cut Ed down. Made you the big muckety-muck down Mogollon way, I take it."

"Ed got what he asked for," Nevada said coolly. "You're headed down the same road."

Cud Richardson laughed. "That wouldn't surprise me none—only you won't be there when it happens."

"Don't be surprised if I am," Nevada replied.

He was studying the outlaws narrowly, searching for an opportunity, an unguarded moment during which he could make a quick break. Clint had relaxed his vigilance somewhat, but Dude, his arms folded across his chest, was standing off to one side. Nevada was sure any move he attempted would place the man in the fringed buckskin jacket at his back—a fatal mistake for certain.

"What are you aiming to do with him?" Clint asked. "I mean, besides making buzzard bait out of him," He added with a laugh.

"We're taking him out a ways into the hills," Richardson answered.

The outlaw stared. "Now, why the hell should we do that?" he said.

"Cooper don't want any trouble around here. He says people'll get so jittery they won't stop over. We'll just drop Mr. Lacy here down a hole with a couple of rocks on him, and there's no fuss and no questions."

"They didn't pay no mind to that ruckus in the saloon?"

"That was different. Cowpunchers are always blowing off steam, anywhere you go. But killings—that's something else. It could cause the law to come poking around—and I reckon he does make a heap of gold for himself with folks trotting back and forth on their way to the Fort or Prescott.

"Anyway, we're listening to Cooper. I want to keep

on his good side. It's smart to have us a place to come to where we can lay low when there's need."

Richardson glanced to Nevada. "Where's your nag?"

Nevada remained silent, considered refusing to answer, and then decided it would serve no good purpose. Any move he might make in an attempt to escape would have to come later and his chances would be better with the buckskin under him, instead of a horse he didn't know or trust.

"I tied my horse in the barn—behind the saloon," he said.

Immediately Dude joined the heavy-set man Richardson had called Drawson, and together they left the stable. Cud watched them for a moment and then moved deeper into the room. Placing his shoulders against a wall, he studied Nevada.

Cud Richardson, Nevada saw, was a harder, tougher customer than Ed Richardson. He lacked his brother's smoothness and polish. Ed had been a handsome man with a knack for making friends, and a winning way with women. There were none of these qualities in Cud Richardson—only a cold ruthlessnes that shone in his eyes, and was evident, as well, in the cruel set of his mouth.

The muted thud of horses' hooves sounded in the runway. Richardson swung about and stared through the opening.

"Here they are," he said. "Let's get moving."

Clint, his gun again ready, reached for Nevada's arm. Nevada jerked his elbow away and stood up. Walking slow, he crossed in front of Richardson, and strode to where Dude was holding the buckskin. Silently, he swung to the saddle.

54

"He got a rifle?" Cud asked from the shadows.

"We looked," Dawson said shaking his head. "Reckon he only totes a handgun."

"What about them saddlebags. There could be a spare iron in one of them."

"Nothing but grub—and some duds."

"Won't make no difference, anyway," the outlaw chief said. "Here's some rawhide, Dude. Tie his hands behind his back."

The outlaw in the fringed jacket stepped forward, and took the length of leather cord. He glanced up to Nevada.

"You heard him. Hold out your hands."

Nevada shrugged, and did as he was directed. He felt the tough, narrow strips of leather encircle his wrists, and cupped his palms to their fullest.

"None of that!" Dude snapped. "You're not tricking me that way."

Richardson laughed. "What's he up to—trying to get some slack so's he can work himself loose?"

"He's trying," Dude answered, giving the rawhide a sharp jerk, "but he's not having any luck."

Lacy grunted as the cord bit into his flesh and locked his wrists together. Dude worked with the ends of the string briefly, and stepped back.

"That'll hold him," he said.

"All right, mount up," Richardson ordered, moving toward his horse.

"What about some grub?" Dawson asked. "We'll be a while getting this done."

"We'll live," Richardson said. "Anyway, didn't you just say he had some grub in his saddlebags?"

"A little. Ain't hardly enough for all of us."

"We'll stretch it," Cud Richardson said, and swung to the doorway.

Clint fell in behind him. Someone—Dude or Dawson—slapped the buckskin on the rump, prompting him to be next in line, and then those two, riding abreast, followed.

They entered the street, and turned right. The hubbub in Cooper's saloon had not slackened, and the piano was again lending its support to the general din. Up ahead Clint's plaintive voice sounded above the soft *tunk-a-tunk* of the walking horses.

"Sure hate to be leaving—"

Nevada Lacy barely heard. A sharp tingling was racing through his body. He had moved his arms, and felt the cord that bound his wrists give slightly. Dude, obviously inexperienced in such matters, had secured the leather strips with a greenhorn's knot.

VIII

"What was you saying to do with grub, Dawson?" Clint's voice was a whine. "I'm getting hungrier than a wolf pup with his throat cut." Clint's complaining words faded as Richardson twisted about on his saddle, his face flushed.

"We'd better get something straight, right now. If you want to head back for Cooper's, nobody's stopping you. Only, when you get your gut full, don't come looking for me. Just find yourself some other place to roost."

Clint shook his head. "I'll be staying. All I was saying was that—"

Cud Richardson sighed, and settled himself again on

56

his saddle. Nevada, working carefully to avoid drawing attention from Dude, gradually freed his wrists to the point where he could pull his hands apart when a favorable opportunity presented itself. It would have to come later. At the moment they were crossing a high shoulder with little brush and no trees at all into which he could bolt.

He dug into his memory, endeavored to recall the area. The arroyo was to his right, a good quarter-mile distant. Farther ahead the trail veered closer. The banks of the wash, he thought, were six or seven feet high at that particular point—a dangerous leap for a horse running full speed in the dark. But if any horse could manage it, the tough little buckskin was the one.

But if he made it to the arroyo—then what? Lacy rolled that through his mind. With no weapon he could not fight off pursuit. He could only run—and keep running. To where?

Slowly, refusing to be hurried, he began to shape a plan that would get him out of the desperate situation in which he found himself. It would be fatal to go down the arroyo; for the outlaws would simply race alongside the sandy-floored gash, with their own horses on firmer ground, and pick him off with ease.

Suddenly he remembered the small, brushy wash coming in from the opposite side—the one that he'd used earlier to climb out of the arroyo. If he could make his break below it, and turn back up—which the outlaws would hardly be expecting him to do—he could employ the gully as a means for gaining the other bank. On beyond that lay the mountain with its rocks and dense timber.

But after that?

Nevada stirred restlessly. He'd make that final, important decision when he came to it. First things first. He'd have to manage somehow to break away from the outlaws and gain the comparative safety of the arroyo without stopping a bullet. Assuming he managed that, and the buckskin didn't snap a leg bone in the downward plunge, the problem of finding the gully and gaining the opposite side could wait. He might not even be alive at that stage.

He began to slow the buckskin, doing it imperceptibly, to avoid the watchful scrutiny which Dawson was keeping almost constantly trained on him. There was nothing he could do where Dude was concerned. He'd be trusting wholly on luck there, hoping the greenhorn would be so taken by surprise that his reaction would be slow.

The most important thing at the moment was to pick the proper place for the break. It must be below the side gully—not above it. And he should be as near to it as possible. He couldn't risk a lengthy race with the outlaws above him on solid footing.

He looked ahead. A gnarled cedar tree looked familiar, and a mound of rock also evoked a stir of recognition. They were swinging in nearer to the arroyo. Tension began to build within Nevada. He stirred again, striving to settle his nerves, and glanced warily at Dawson.

The outlaw was now slightly ahead of him, half the length of his horse—a little more, perhaps. He wished the heavy-set man had decided to ride on his left flank rather than on the right. There would then be no one between him and arroyo. No, he decided suddenly. It was better this way. When he made his break, he'd try to drag Dawson off the saddle as he raced by. That would create confusion, and temporarily block the use of one gun. If Dawson had been riding on his left, the big man would be in position to open up instantly.

Dude was the one who could give him the most trouble. Riding behind, he'd be sure to detect the start of an escape attempt instantly, and be in line to bring it to a halt almost immediately. Head down, Nevada stole a backward look. Dude's face was tipped forward. He appeared to be dozing in the saddle.

Lacy could see the edge of the arroyo now, less than twenty yards away. There was little brush in between—a few clumps of sage, large stands of rabbitbush, and a row of snakeweed thriving in the sterile soil, hedgelike, along the rim of the big wash. The gully was above him. He was pleased with what he saw for the position of the growths was in just the right relation to the mountain.

Nevada bunched his muscles, tested his wrists, and made certain the rawhide would fall free when he exerted pressure. The hindquarters of Dawson's horse were now even with the nose of the buckskin. He risked another covert glance at Dude. This outlaw rode as before—head bowed, face slanted as if sleeping. Ahead Clint and Cud Richardson slumped on their saddles as their horses slogged on wearily. They, too, could be catching a few winks of sleep.

It was now—or perhaps never. Once deeper into the hills he'd find no opportunity at all.

Abruptly he jerked his arms apart. Seizing the reins, he jammed his heels into the buckskin's flanks, and swung sharply to the right. The horse responded instantly. With his left hand, Nevada grabbed for Dawson. His fingers caught the collar of the outlaw's jacket, and locked about the fabric. The buckskin's momentum lent strength to Lacy's grip. The startled man yelled, and tried to save himself by clawing for the horn. He missed, and fell heavily to the ground as Nevada rushed off into the pale darkness.

More yells sounded as Richardson and the others realized what was taking place. A gunshot ripped through the night. Two more followed in quick succession. Lacy began to swerve the buckskin from side to side, making good use of the training for roundup work the horse had received.

"Get after him!"

Cud Richardson's voice was an exasperated, infuriated bellow rising above the confusion.

The arroyo was in front of Nevada before he realized it. The buckskin did not hesitate. He simply sailed over the rim, and struck solidly on all fours with bone-jarring force. He went to his knees for an instant, then recovered and staggered on. Lacy cut right, up the broad gash as the horse gathered his balance and regained his forward momentum. Dust arose in a great swirl beneath the animal's clattering hooves.

Nevada squinted into the murky night before him. To the rear the pound of hooves above and directly behind him sounderd uncomfortably close. One of the outlaws had followed him down into the arroyo. He hadn't expected that.

Ten yards—twenty. Where was that side gully? Had he misjudged the distance? Thirty yards. Gunshots were blasting through the night again, but now the bullets were striking behind him. apparently they were shooting blind, not sure of his exact location.

Fifty yards. Clearly he'd made a mistake, waited too

60

long to make his try. In a matter of minutes the outlaws would overtake him, and have him at their mercy again. He grinned tightly. It was a good try—one that had almost succeeded.

A long, gusty breath of relief came whistling up from his lungs, and out between his lips, making his entire body shake. The gully at last! He veered the buckskin toward it. There's be no time, he realized, to dismount and lead the horse up the rough course again. He'd have to make it, rider and all.

They plunged into the narrow, brush-choked opening. The buckskin faltered, bunched his hindquarters, and then leaped swiftly ahead. His front hooves dug in, caught. He heaved again, stumbled plowed on through the losoe rock and clawing undergrowth.

Abruptly he gained the top, muscles quivering, wheezing for wind. Nevada, crouched low, hammered at his flanks again, and set him rushing for a dense clump of brush a dozen strides distant.

Harsh voices arose from high above, whipped by the wind.

"He's pulled out of here!"

"Where?" Richardson's voice was taut with anger.

"Wash, on the side."

"Well, follow him, damn it! We'll circle, try crossing below."

"I am trying," Clint shouted back. "Blamed jughead's balking. He's afeared to climb—"

Lacy reached the cedars, allowed the buckskin to slacken his dead run. But he did not halt. Keeping the brush between himself and the point where the gully led out of the arroyo, he pushed steadily on for the towering, black mass of the mountain.

He had the jump on Richardson and the others. They would lose a good ten minutes trying to find a place where they could cross over. And Clint would finally be forced to dismount, and lead his balky mount up the steep and treacherous wash.

A decision as to his next move was now urgent. He couldn't turn south to the plains, for that, he knew, would lead him straight into the outlaws. Neither could he get up on the mountain, and lose himself in the thick pines, the oak brush and rock. With no weapon of any sort he could do nothing but lie low for the time being.

A quarter of an hour later he reached the first outcropping of boulders at the foot of the mountain, and began to search for a trail that would lead him to the crest. A sheer wall faced him here. But he rode on, seeking a break, an arroyo, a crevice—even an old game trail. The solid granite slab shining dully in the starlight ran on indefinitely, offering no relief.

Faintly, considerably to the rear, he could hear the thud of oncoming horses. The outlaws had crossed over, and by this time Clint had probably managed to climb out of the gully. All four men would be together. But at least they could not see him, he was certain of that. They would have no way of knowing which way he had chosen to go—back to the arroyo, directly up the center of the small mesa, or into the mountains.

He topped a slight ridge and came to an abrupt halt. A half-mile ahead a scatter of lights broke the darkness of the night. It had to be Coopersville.

Nevada swore softly, scanning the face of the mountain anxiously. Nothing but palisades—steep, vertical cliff walls of solid granite. He was trapped at the base, with no way to go except straight on. The drumming of the oncoming horses was growing louder. Abruptly he came to a decision.

Urging the winded buckskin to a faster lope, he bore directly for the twinkling lights. If he had to make a stand, his chances would be better in the town. And maybe he could figure out some way to get his hands on a gun.

IX

They saw him as he topped the last ridge at the edge of the settlement, and immediately opened up. The burst of gunfire was deafening, but the bullets fell short. Had they been using rifles, their luck might have been better.

Nevada rode into the town, again from the rear. The barn in which he had earlier stabled the buckskin was to his left. He ignored it, and continued on. It was sure to be the first place the outlaws would look when they started a search for him.

The racket within the saloon had not decreased to any extent. He was grateful for that, for it almost ruled out the likelihood that anyone had heard the gunshots and emerged into the open to see what it was all about. Walking the buckskin, nevada circled the building, came to the street, and crossed. The abandoned barn where he had awaited Cud Richardson was directly in front of him.

Avoiding that weathered structure also, he pushed on, pointing his horse for a dark, brush-filled hollow a short distance beyond. Swiftly he dismounted and tied the horse to a scrub cedar. Then, crouching low, he trotted back to the old barn.

Approaching from the rear this time, he snatched up

an empty crate, climbed upon it, and pulled himself onto the building's roof. The timbers beneath him creaked and groaned in protest as he worked his way forward. But he minimized the danger of their collapsing by keeping close to the wall where the studding could support his weight. Reaching the forward end, he crawled in behind the six-foot-tall false front to wait.

There was no movement in the street below. He turned his eyes to the hitchrack of the saloon, and tried to locate a rifle still in the boot of some rider's saddle. The light was too poor, and he could make out nothing at that distance. Odds were against his finding a weapon, for most punchers, leaving their mounts, took their long guns with them. But he refused to give up all hope in that respect. He'd make a closer inspection as soon as he learned what Richardson intended to do.

Apparently there was another stable somewhere along the short street. There weren't enough horses at the saloon's rack to account for the number of patrons he had seen in the saloon, and there had been only two or three tied up in the barn where he had first left the buckskin. If he failed to find a rifle on one of the saddles in the street, there was nothing to prevent him from locating the other livery stable, and trying his luck there.

He saw movement at that moment—a dark shadow slipping quietly along the side of the saloon. The figure came to the corner of the building, and halted. For a full minute he remained motionless, and then advanced farther into the open.

It was Cud Richardson.

The outlaw chief was alone. That could only mean that the rest of the party had separated, and taken up positions around the edge of the town. Apparently they had decided to work their way in, toward the center, hoping to pocket him. Nevada grinned tightly. It was not pleasant to find himself backed into a corner—with no weapon. But there was one thing in his favor. He was almost sure he knew what they had in mind.

Richardson, walking slowly, almost indolently, but taking care to remain in the shadows, rounded the end of the saloon, and crossed in front of it. He stopped again, this time at the edge of the landing. Leaning back against the wall, protected by the darkness, he simply waited. Lacy could see his head swing back and forth as his eyes maintained a continuous watch along the street.

They knew he was there, somewhere—that he had few choices in the selection of a hiding place. Sooner or later he would be compelled to move, to show himself, and Cud Richardson was clearly determined to finish up the chore he'd undertaken.

"It's not going to be that easy, mister," Lacy murmured into the night.

Dawson and the others might work their way in, and tighten the noose. But they wouldn't find him in it—at least not down where they could see him. But the time would come, he knew, when he'd be forced to do something. And at any moment one of them could stumble on the hidden buckskin.

He had no intention of worrying about that, however —not so long as there were other mounts standing nearby. It wouldn't be the first time he'd been tabbed a horse thief when an emergency had called for borrowing the mount nearest at hand. He could always return, explain an exchange the animal he had taken for his own.

Richardson continued to wait in the darkness fronting the saloon. Piano music, the girl's off-key singing, shouts, laughter, and an occasional crash as a chair or table overturned were the only sounds riding the cool night air.

Once the three missing outlaws reached the street, gathered to report their failure to flush him from hiding, it would be a simple matter to drop back off the roof, make his way to the buckskin and depart. There would be another day, another time when, under more favorable circumstances, he could settle with Cud Richardson.

But no such thought was in Nevada Jim Lacy's mind. The man he sought was here, standing no more than fifty feet away. He'd not pull out until he'd settled up in full.

"Cud?"

The carefully hushed voice came from somewhere below Nevada, and to his right, in the street. Standing absolutely motionless, so as to cause no creaking of the rotting planks beneath him, Nevada listened. There could be little doubt that the owner of the voice was standing in front of the building adjoining the old barn.

"Over here," he heard Richardson reply. "Any sign of him?"

"None."

A moment later the heavy-set, square-shouldered form of Dawson moved into Lacy's line of vision as he crossed over.

"You think he may have kept right on going? He could have taken the road to Prescot, or maybe the Fort?"

"No—get rid of that idea. He's here, just setting

66

tight. I'd bet on it."

"Funny we can't find that buckskin he was forkin'."

"He's made sure we wouldn't. Lacy's plenty smart."

Another figure appeared, this time along the dust-covered brush at the edge of the street north of the saloon. A tall, gangling shape—Clint. Ignoring all precautions, the outlaw strode into the open, revealing himself fully in the flare of lamplight coming through the saloon's doorway. He halted directly in front of Richardson and Dawson.

"Well, he sure ain't around here nowheres," Clint announced flatly.

There was a short run of silence and then Cud Richardson, his voice thick with disgust, said: "If he is—one thing's dead certain. He sure as hell knows where we are, with you bulling around in the street that way."

"I can't see as it makes any difference," Clint replied. "He ain't here. My guess is he's high-tailed it for home."

"You'd be guessing wrong. Lacy won't run. See the Dude anywhere?"

"Sure ain't, but I reckon he'll be showing up pretty quick. He feels powerful bad about that chewing you done on him."

"He's got more than that coming to him."

"Claims he put that rawhide on good. Lacy must've had a knife tucked up his sleeve or somewheres."

"Maybe. All I know is he got loose—and we're right back where we started from."

Dawson removed his hat, and rubbed at his head. "You going to run Dude off?"

"Ain't made up my mind yet. A jasper like him is

mighty risky to have around. All right, he's trying. But a mistake like he made can hurt like hell. That him coming?"

There was a brief silence, and then Dawson said: "It's him. Over here, Dude."

The outlaw appeared at the edge of the light, the fringe on his jacket swaying gently as he walked. "No luck," he announced.

"Us either," Clint said. "I figure he kept right on going. We'd have spotted that horse of his, is he still around. Place just ain't big enough for a man to plain drop out of sight."

"You could be right," Richardson said suddenly. "Maybe that's what he's done—kept going."

Dawson jerked off his hat again, scrubbed at his head. "I thought you said—"

"Been thinking it over. Maybe this Lacy ain't such big shakes after all. Could be I figured him wrong. Let's go on in and get a drink. Are you ready to eat now, Clint?"

"I sure am!" the tall outlaw said at once.

"All right. Come on then."

A faint smile on his lips, Nevada watched the four men emerge from the shadows, mount the steps to the landing and cross noisily to the saloon's entrance. In single file, they entered, and disappeared into the smoky haze.

Cud Richardson was fooling nobody. Failing to turn up his intended victim by combing the town area, he was making a noisy show of giving up, fully aware that the man he sought was hiding somewhere nearby, watching.

"Obliged to you, Cud, old hoss," Nevada murmured, and worked his way to the back of the roof.

68

Two could play at the game as well as one.

Reaching the edge, he dropped lightly to the ground. He'd have, he realized, only a few minutes in which to act. Richardson and the others were probably on their way to the rear door of the saloon, and in another moment would be doubling back to the street.

He hesitated, considering the wisdom of looking over the horses at the saloon's hitchrack for a rifle, instead of trying to locate the stable he felt certain was somewhere nearby. But he decided against that. Not only would conducting a search further away involve less of a risk, he would be afforded more time.

Wheeling, Nevada ran along the rear walls of the structures lining that side of the street, listening, testing the still night air for the familiar odor that would indicate the location of a livery barn. He found it at the extreme end of the alley.

The door was open. He slipped inside, and remained for a long moment motionless, getting his bearings in the gloom. Gradually, he was able to make out the vague outlines of five or six horses, all of them occupying separate stalls. He could see the hump of the saddles still on their backs.

Pressing forward, he entered the first compartment. A scabbard—but no rifle. The result was the same in the next. But in the third stall his heart skipped a beat, and the strain and uncertainty under which he'd been laboring became less oppressive and much easier to bear. The stock of a rifle protruded from beneath a dangling stirrup. He jerked it clear, and stepped back.

The gun was an old seven-shot Spencer. Rust scarred the mechanism in places, and the stock was cracked. But the action seemed tight. Hopefully, he checked the next two saddles but found no other weapons. There were no more horses in the stable. The Spencer would have to do. He looked then at the rifle's magazine. It contained five cartridges.

His spirits rising. Nevada returned to the alley, deciding he'd be better off on the opposite side of the street, since that would place him behind the outlaws, and his movements would be less likely to attract their attention. He needed all the advantages he could muster.

Turning, he trotted to the corner of the livery stable, and followed along its south wall until he came to the street. There was no one in sight, but it would be a mistake, he knew, to draw any comfort from that. The outlaws could have returned, and be waiting again, unseen in the shadows.

He'd have to risk it. He still believed his best chances lay on the opposite side. Crouched low, he sprinted across the dusty strip of roadway, and ducked into a deep pool of blackness behind a clump of rabbitbush. No gunshots had challenged him; perhaps Richardson and his crew were still inside.

Nevada, still crouching low, moved forward, toward the corner of the bulky structure. The shadows Richardson had made use of would serve well for his own purpose. He drew near the wall of the building, and paused to study the surrounding area. No one was visible. Moving on, he gained the wall near the center, and began to edge cautiously along its dark bulk.

"Right there, mister! Hold it!" Clint's voice lashed at him from the darkness. "Make a move and I'll blow your head off!"

X

Nevada Jim Lacy's reaction was instinctive and instantaneous. He bobbed, lunged to one side. Clint's gun smashed through the night as the lean rider hit the ground, went full length, and rolled fast. The outlaw's bullet thudded into the wall of the building. The blast was still echoing through the darkness when Nevada stopped rolling, triggered his weapon and took aim.

The old Spencer bucked in his hands. Clint's jaw fell open and his shoulders jerked as a glistening redness spread across his chest. But reflex action enabled him to press off a second shot as he fell, the bullet digging into the ground at his feet. Lacy continued to hug the ground, striving to keep clear of the light, knowing that the other outlaws would be somewhere near.

"That was Clint! He's found him!"

The shout came from a passageway on the opposite side of the street. Men were pouring out of the saloon now, gathering on the porch, shouting questions. Nevada lay sprawled on his stomach under a small cedar, his eyes sweeping over the ground ahead of him for a glimpse of Dawson, Richardson and Dude. A dark shape moved near the old stable. Richardson, he thought.

Instantly he bounded to his feet and darted into the blackness alongside the saloon. A gun cracked sharply, the sound coming from the opposite end of the street. A breath of hot wind plucked at his arm. Nevada whirled, fired the Spencer from the hip, aiming only at the flash of the outlaw's weapon. Then he raced for the other side of the street.

"There he goes!" someone on the saloon porch yelled.

Gunshots racketed through the night again. Lacy ignored the blasts. It has been Cud Richardson he'd seen near the abandoned stable—and Cud Richardson was the one he wanted. Gaining the darkness just below that building, he pulled up short. If the outlaw leader was hiding somewhere beyond the dilapidated structure it would be foolhardy—suicidal in fact—to approach from the street.

Spinning about, he raced back toward the livery stable where he had obtained the rifle, having decided to circle the line of business houses and come in on Richardson from behind.

Drawing abreast of the stable the figure of a man lying half in the roadway, half in a clump of brush, caught his eye. It was the outlaw who fired at him after he downed Clint. He flung a glance at the sprawled shape. Dude or Dawson?

It was Dawson. Nevada moved silently past the man toward the near corner of the livery barn. He came to that point, plunged suddenly to one side as the unexpected blast of a gun, almost at his heels, rocked the night. He spun about, the older Spencer up and ready.

Dude, revolver in hand, was motioning to him from the doorway of the building. A short distance away Dawson, on his knees was falling forward.

"He was about to pot you from behind," the man in the fringed jacket shouted.

Lacy stared. "You're not—"

Dude shook his head. "Here," he said, pulling Nevada's .45 from his belt and tossing it.

"Expect you're handier with this than you are with that old thunder gun."

Lacy caught the revolver, tossed the Spencer aside. Straightening, he stepped back to the corner of the building.

"Don't know what's going on," he said. "But I'm obliged to you."

"We'll talk about it later," Dude replied. "We both want Richardson. I prefer him alive."

"Don't count on that," Nevada said. "I'll circle the buildings. You—"

"I'll work toward the end of the street," Dude said, cutting him short. "Luck."

Lacy hurried on, checking his gun as he moved, making certain that it was loaded. He was stunned by the change in Dude. Perhaps, he thought, it was all some kind of a trick, and he was being led into a trap. But the cylinder of the .45 was full and the revolver was in perfect working order. Dude would hardly have handed him a loaded gun if they were hoping to bushwhack him.

Dude almost had to be some sort of lawman. He said he wanted Richardson alive, but Cud, Nevada knew, was not the kind to let himself be taken. Dude should have known that, too. But a government lawman, a Deputy United States Marshal perhaps, could have some peculiar ideas. U.S. Marshals had a code no one could talk them into abandoning. They always wanted to capture the man they sought, haul him up before a judge. It was a fine idea. Only it didn't usually work out right. A lot of dead lawmen were proof of that.

Nevada reached the end of the alley and halted in the darkness behind the abandoned barn. He was sure that

Cud would be near, either inside the building, or in the adjacent brush. He considered climbing again onto the roof, but almost instantly rejected the thought. It would be impossible to do so quietly, and the noise created would attract the outlaw, put him at his mercy.

A shadow crossed the passageway alongside the structure. Instantly Lacy hunched low and catfooted his way silently up the weed-littered corridor to the street. Halting, gun ready, he peered around the corner. Stray light from the saloon touched a figure only an arm's length away—a man in a fringed buckskin jacket. Dude again.

In that same instant there was a quick hammer of hooves off to the right. Dude swore violently, having evidently been quick to realize that Richardson was making a run for it.

"It's me behind you," Nevada said, stepping out into the sagging board sidewalk. Further down the street several men had collected around the body of Dawson. Others were bringing the limp form of Clint from where he had fallen near the rear of the saloon.

"Reckon he got away from us," Nevada drawled, eyeing Dude keenly. "You mind telling me now just who you are?"

Dude holstered his weapon, swung about and offered his hand. "Name's Drake. Harlan Drake."

Nevada accepted the man's hand, "I'm Jim Lacy."

"I know," Dude said, smiling. "Fact is, I've heard a lot about you in the last few years."

"Nothing too good, I take it."

"Not all bad, anyway," Drake said. "I know that gun of yours is fast—too fast maybe at times—but that you've made use of it plenty often."

"I always had a good reason," Nevada said coolly.

"Don't doubt it."

Lacy glanced toward the saloon. The bodies of the outlaws had been carried to the porch and placed side by side for all to see. Suddenly, there was a stir among the onlookers. One of the bartenders came into the open, shouldering his way through the crowd. He stared briefly at the dead men, then motioned impatiently to several others standing close by. At once they stepped forward, lifting the bodies and started around the building with them.

The white-aproned man faced the remaining crowd, said something Nevada couldn't catch and started making an effort to herd his patrons back into the saloon. Several obeyed and the gathering began to thin. About a half a dozen men, ranged along the outer edge of the porch, made no effort to comply. Instead they continued to talk, now and then glancing across the street to Nevada and Harlan Drake.

Lacy considered them absently. "Looks like Richardson's got some friends here who don't exactly like the way things turned out," he said.

"They figure I doublecrossed him," Dude replied. "Makes no difference to me. Expect we ought to get on his trail."

Nevada shook his head. "That would be playing it his way. It's just what he's hoping we'll do. Best we wait for daylight."

Drake frowned. "He'll be plenty far from here by then."

"Not likely. I'm almost sure he's sitting in the dark a couple of miles up the trail right now, just waiting to pick us off when we come riding past. Let him sweat out a wait. Meantime, I'm feeling a bit hollow. Let's get a bite to eat.''

"Saloon's the only place.''

Nevada's shoulders lifted. "So?''

Drake nodded at the men on the landing. "We're not going to be very popular in there.''

Nevada grinned. "I can't recollect ever losing much sleep over something like that.'' Taking a step out into the street, he paused, his expression serious again. "And I can't recollect you answering the rest of my question. What are you—some kind of a lawman?''

Harlan Drake brushed at the stubble of beard beginning to show on his chin. "Not the kind you're thinking of, maybe. I'm with the Pinkerton Agency.''

XI

Nevada Jim Lacy said nothing for a moment. Finally he murmured, "A detective.''

"In a way. But it would be better to say that I'm a special government agent. Explains the jobs I do more accurately.'' It was Drake's turn to be silent. After a time, he said, "Why? You have something against detectives?''

Nevada laughed. "Not me. Man's got a right to be what he wants to be. But I'll admit it surprised me some. Come on, let's get those vittles.''

Drake fell in beside him, and together they crossed the street. Reaching the saloon landing, they ascended it in silence, Lacy's cool, challenging glance raking the men standing there, stifling any comment. Continuing, they entered the building, which was still clouded with smoke but considerably quieter than before the shooting.

Spotting a table in a far corner that gave them a complete view of the room and both front and rear doors, as well as the stair to the upper floor, Lacy led the way to it. Drawing out a chair for himself, he motioned to Drake to take the one on his left.

A hush settled gradually over the place. Lacy beckoned to one of the bartenders. The man came quickly.

"Yes, sir," he said, centering his attention on Nevada.

"Something to eat. Whatever you've got that's ready."

"Steak. Boiled spuds. Biscuits."

Nevada glanced at Drake. "Suit you?"

"Be fine."

The bartender frowned, fidgeted nervously. "Well, I ain't so sure we got enough for two plates—"

Lacy straightened in his chair slowly. "There'd better be," he said softly. "Maybe you'd like us to go have a look-see for ourselves."

"No need for that! I'll try."

The man bobbed his head, and scurried away. Lacy watched him for a moment, "That Cooper?" he asked.

Drake shook his head. "No, the other bartender standing at the end of the counter's Cooper. They call this one Cary." Drake studied Lacy with a half-smile. "No call for you to stand up for me. I can look out for myself."

"Expect you can. Only I don't like weasels. If he'd come out and said he didn't want to serve you—either one of us—I wouldn't have thought much about it. But squirming around, lying like that—"

"A man in my business runs into that problem a lot of times," Drake said. "You learn to live with it."

77

His eyes shifted to the doorway. The men who had gathered on the porch were just entering. Their faces were set in grim lines and there was a belligerency to their manner. "Looks like it's one of those times," Harlan Drake added dryly.

Nevada watched the group pause to scan the room before moving forward. Folding his arms across his chest, he awaited their arrival.

"Something bothering you gentlemen?" he asked as they came to a stop in front of the table. Getting in the first lick at such times was a way with Nevada, who believed firmly that a strong offense was the best defense.

"Not you, mister," the spokesman for the party said. He was a large, square-shouldered man with a stubble of red beard. "It's that there back-stabber you got setting with you."

Nevada's pistol was suddenly in his hand. Thumb hooked over the hammer, he lazily recrossed his arms again.

"Sure," he drawled. "You go right ahead, speak your piece. Don't mind me."

A long minute of complete silence followed. Then another member spoke up. "We just don't cotton to doublecrossers," he said, looking straight at Dude. "We figured you was a friend of Cud and the men who ride with him. Then you turn around and shoot Dawson dead. We're wanting to know why."

"No business of yours," Drake said evenly.

"Could be, we're making it our business—"

The Pinkerton man shook his head. "My advice to you is forget it."

Nevada nodded approvingly. "That's mighty good

advice, gents. I strongly urge you to take it. Now, if you'll step aside I'll be obliged to you. Man's bringing us some grub. We're both a mite on the hungry side—and you know how ornery being hungry can make a man."

The group parted, allowed the bartender, carrying two heaped platters, to reach the table, and place the dishes before Lacy and Drake.

"Coffee," Nevada said. He glanced at Drake. "That all right with you, pard?"

"Fine," Dude replied, a faint smile again tugging at his lips.

The bartender turned away. Nevada laid his .45 alongside his plate, took up his knife and fork and began to eat. Drake also fell to. The red-bearded man and his companions stirred uncertainly. One worked his way to the foreground, his eyes on Nevada.

"Seems I ought to know you—" he began.

Nevada continued with his meal. "That's not surprising. I've met a lot of people I just can't recall to mind straight off."

"Ain't you Jim Lacy the gunslinger?"

"I'm Lacy," Nevada cut in coldly.

A murmur ran though the party, spread across the saloon. And then again there was a hush.

"You two working together?" the red-bearded man asked.

"Could be."

"Then I reckon that makes you what I just said he was—a backshooting doublecrosser!"

Nevada set his fork down very quietly. Slowly he raised his eyes to meet those of the speaker.

"You've got a big mouth to match your size, Red,"

79

he said with a tinge of sadness in his voice. "It could get you in trouble."

From somewhere in the saloon a voice said: "Let it go, Tom. You don't know how fast he can draw. There ain't another gun—"

"His gun is in plain sight," the red-bearded man snapped. "Maybe he's buffaloin' the rest of you, but he sure ain't me! I'm not scared."

"If you had any sense, you would be," Nevada said. "I figured you for a fool. Otherwise you'd be dead right now, after calling me what you did."

The words seemed to bring courage to the big man instead of serving as a warning. He shrugged his massive shoulders.

"Ain't it like I've always said? Man stands up to such as this pair, and right away they start talking loud—and backing off."

"Ease off, friend," Harlan Drake said. "This man is Jim Lacy—and everything you've heard about him is true, I *know*."

"Only thing I ever heard about him was that he'd killed plenty of men. I'm wondering how—by shooting them when they looked the other way?"

Nevada kept his eyes on the table before him. He was tyring to ignore the man, but his temper was getting out of control. It was nothing new. He'd been through the same situation man times in the past—a man, like the red-bearded giant seeking to prove his own courage, and build a reputation for himself.

There appeared to be a slight difference here, however. The man called Tom evidently thought he was in the right. He could actually be sincere. They were the worst kind—the stupid ones. They usually ended up

80

dead because of poor judgment.

"Move on, Red," Nevada murmured, settling back in his chair. "I don't want any trouble with you."

The bartender appeared at the end of the half circle, a small pot of coffee in one hand, two mugs in the other. He set them on the table, spun about, and hurried back into the hushed crowd.

"Maybe I ain't of a mind to move on," Tom said. "Maybe I would just rather stand here, and—"

Nevada Lacy was on his feet, gun in hand—all in a single, blurred motion. The muzzle of the .45 was suddenly pressing against the red bearded man's throat.

"Listen good," Lacy said in a harsh, dry voice. "I'm not saying it again. Get the hell away from me—and stay away!"

Tom gagged as the barrel dug into his windpipe. Eyes spread wide, he managed to bob his head. "All right," he got out. "I guess—I made a mistake."

"Goes for everybody else," Nevada said, drawing back, and sweeping the remaining men with an angry glance. He then swung his attention to Cooper, still at the end of the bar. "If you don't want somebody hurt in here, keep them backed off."

Cooper started forward, but the group was already breaking up, melting into the crowd. Nevada continued to stand until they had all disappeared. Then he holstered his weapon, sat down, and resumed his eating.

Drake said softly, "I thought for a minute he was a dead man."

"His kind usually end up that way," Nevada said, "Never seem to learn. I guess they plain don't get the chance."

"You gave him some good advice. Let's hope he

profits form it."

Nevada grunted. "Yeah, I'm downright surprising at doing good turns. One thing you'd better understand, however."

Drake's brows lifted. "What's that?"

You said something about wanting Richardson, alive. I aim to track him down myself, and I give you fair warning I expect it will wind up in a killing."

XII

The Pinkerton man looked at Nevada steadily for a moment, his eyes troubled, almost accusing. "Sorry to hear that. I need him alive."

"It's not that easy," Nevada said impatiently. "You don't take a man like Cud Richardson without a fight. And in his kind of fight you either win—or you're dead yourself."

"It doesn't have to be that way," Drake protested. "I figure if you give a man a chance to quit, he'll likely take it. Nobody wants to die."

"They don't look at it that way. All they're thinking about is staying alive—no matter how. Fact is, I doubt if any of the owlhoots I went up against would have listened to sensible advice. Chances are you'd never live long enough to make them an offer."

"I've been around a few years," Dude said stiffly. "And I'm still breathing."

"How many gunslingers like Cud Richardson—the tough ones who figured themselves for dead years ago and are living now on borrowed time—have you hauled in alive?"

"Well, I can't say there's been any exactly like him—"

"Here's what I'm driving at. Their kind just don't give in. They'll fight you down to the last breath—and if you don't watch them close, they'll kill you after they're dead. Like Dawson. I got careless out there in the street. He almost got me—and would have, if it hadn't been for you. What are you after Cud for?"

"Robbing the United States mail—and murder. Cud and two others were in on it. We got the two. I've been on Richardson's trial ever since—almost a year."

Drake told of how, after the robbery and killings in Kansas, Cud Richardson had vanished from sight, very likely taking refuge in Mexico. About three months ago, the Pinkerton agent had had news of him in Arizona, and had made his own way there.

Posing as a tenderfoot from the East, looking for a quick way to make a lot of money, he had gained Cud Richardson's confidence, and been taken into the gang as a recruit.

The first order of business had been to get rid of Jim Lacy—in revenge for Ed Richardson's slaying, and, more practically, to eliminate the strongest obstacle to the rustler's plans.

"That man who tried to warn you, Cash Burridge," Drake said, "was to take care of the business end of it. The gang would rustle the stock, he'd dispose of it. Was Cash a friend of yours?"

"More of a friend than I knew," Nevada said moodily.

"I liked him," Drake said. "I was around him only short while, but I liked him. He didn't seem to be of the same stripe as Richardson and the others."

"He wasn't. Cash got himself into a few shady deals, but never anything real bad. He was more on the slicker—"

"Confidence men, we call them in our business."

Lacy grinned. "Fits. That was Cash all right." He leaned back, and toyed with the handle of his coffee mug. "How'd you plan to take Cud, with his bunch always around close? You sure couldn't have been loco enough to just walk up to him some day, and tell him you aimed to arrest him."

"Hardly. After I'd finally got myself set with him and the others, I began to look for a way to manage it. Law wanted him real bad, so, that a trial could be held and an example made of him. They figured a show of strength on the part of the Law would have a good effect on other renegades—prove that it was big enough to lay the best of them by the heels."

"It meant taking him alive," Drake went on, after a pause. "Dead he'd be just another outlaw to bury. I had to come up with some long-range scheming. When he got the idea of bushwhacking you in Winthrop, it fitted right in. The town had a marshal and a good jail, something the places we'd been hanging around in—like Cooperville here—didn't have."

"Winthrop's the only town that does in the whole county."

Dude nodded. "Had to have those two things—a lawman and a jail where I could keep Richardson until I could get help to take him back to Kansas. Plan was simple. I'd get Richardson off alone while he was setting up the ambush for you, throw a gun on him, and lock him up before the others knew what was going on. Once he was behind bars I didn't think Dawson and the rest would try hard to break him out."

"You're probably right," Nevada admitted. "They'd figure it was Cud's hard luck, and go on their way. Cash doing what he did must have spoiled the play for you.''

"It sure did," Drake said. "Broke it wide open. We got there a little late—or maybe you were early. Anyway, there wasn't time to do things the way Richardson wanted. He was going to scatter the men all along the street. As it was, we'd no more than got off our horses when Cash made a run for that church, yelling at you to look out.''

Drake tightened his lips. "After that, there wasn't anything I could do but go along with the way the cards had fallen, and hope for another chance in another town where I could get help.''

"One thing bothered me—why did you all pull out? The odds were with you. Why didn't Cud stay and finish what he'd started?''

"He thought the town would come swarming out to help you. He said it would be smart to high-tail it, and let you come looking for him. And that was just what you did.''

Nevada nodded. "Cud knew I was playing his game—something I try not to do. But I had no choice, leastwise not until I found him." Nevada paused, added, "Forgot to say I'm obliged to you, too, for leaving that rawhide loose.''

"I took a chance on one of them looking the job over," Drake said. "But I guess by then they figured I was all right.''

"Did it cause you any trouble with Richardson?''

"Cud had himself a fine time cussing me out, but nothing worse." The Pinkerton man hesitated, then said: "You really think he's waiting for us somewhere up the road north of town? Seems more logical to believe he'd ride on, and try to reach another settlement."

"He'll be waiting," Nevada assured him. "All the cards are on the table. He knows I'm after him, and that you are, too. He's probably trying to figure what your angle is, but he's damned sure you're not the prize tenderfoot you made out. He'll be there, all right."

"I've got to find a way to talk to him."

"Forget it," Nevada broke in roughly. "Your chances of taking him alive are less than ever now."

"I suppose so, but it's still up to me to try." The lawman stopped, faced Lacy squarely. "I'd like to ask a favor of you, Jim. I know I can't persuade you to give up going after him. But I'd like the opportunity of talking to him first. There's just a chance he might be willing to surrender if he knows he'll be riddled with bullets otherwise."

Nevada studied his empty cup. "It fair goes against my grain," he said finally. "But you did me a couple of mighty big favors. I can't say no."

His face was somber as he studied Drake, and he wondered if the Pinkerton man realized that the undertaking he had just given had lengthened the odds aginst them dangerously. But he had given his word now and would play the cards as they came, new rules and all.

XIII

They rode out of Coopersville shortly after dawn the next morning. The air was brisk and both men sat in their saddles with their hands tucked in their armpits, and reins hanging from the horn, while the horses followed the distinct ruts of the road.

Silence hung between them like a thick blanket, as

each, filled with his own thoughts and turned quiet by the cold, found nothing to say. A half-hour or so later, when the pearl of the eastern sky began to lighten, and change gradually to pale gold shot with fingers of color, the reserve broke.

"You making any guess where he'll be?" Harlan Drake asked, chafing his palms.

Nevada shrugged. "It was mighty cold last night. He could have looked for a shack or cabin to hole up in. He won't be far off the trial, however."

Dude looked ahead, hs eyes following the course of the trail running almost due north through the wooded hills.

"Expect you're right. But I'm still wondering if he didn't keep going.

"And be looking back over his shoulder every minute, knowing we were on his trail? Not Richardson. He'd pick a hiding place, wait and settle things."

They lapsed into silence as the riding grew worse. They were into rough forest, trending generally up, but often descending into precipitous ravines.

Cedar, oak, pinon, and pine surrounded them, giving way from time to time to sandy flats that slowed their horses, as the glare of the early sun, now well up, struck them. Though occasional small streams, limestone outcroppings gleaming from their banks, impeded them, they were grateful for the cooling water, not least the refreshing music of its splashing.

As they rode on, Nevada told Harlan Drake something of he background of Cud Richardson's emnity for him: of how, when working on a ranch in the Mogollon Brakes, he had determined to break up the

Pine Tree rustling outfit which was ruining most of the nearby ranchers, including his old friend Ben Ide.

He had worked his way into to the Pine Tree gang—much as Harlan Drake had done with Cud Richardson's—and soon discovered that Ben Ide's trusted foreman was Ed Richardson, leader of the outlaw band.

"I called him on it," Nevada said, "and that was the end of it."

"You outdrew him."

Nevada shrugged. "As I recollect," he drawled, "the drawing was a tie. I put my bullet where it counted."

"Wouldn't it have been better to disarm him, and turn him over to the law?" Drake asked, staring off into the hills. "Hanging him might have stopped the rustling in the Mogollon country for years to come. The way it turns out, you not only brought another killer into the area, but you got the gang started again."

"Maybe," Nevada said, "but there just wasn't any way to arrest Ed. You could have a Gatling gun trained on him from ten feet away, and he'd still draw and fire. You didn't grow up around men like Cud Richardson— or me. I can see that."

"You mean if you were—" Drake hesitated uncertainly.

"Go on, say it. It won't hurt my feelings any. I was one of the worst when it came to using my gun—or maybe you'd say one of the best since I'm still alive to talk about it. Law was looking for me plenty of times."

"But the men you killed were outlaws—renegades every lawman was after. It made you a sort of lawman yourself, outside the law."

"An excuse-seeking way of putting it," Nevada said drily.

"All right. What I meant to ask was—if you were in Cud Richardson's boots, and two lawmen had you backed up with the odds against you, would you turn down a chance to surrender, and take your chances on a trial? You wouldn't feel that things might still go in your favor, that a judge might sentence you to a long term in prison instead of a hanging? You'd not see a little hope there, knowing you'd be sure to die if you tried to shoot it out?"

"No," Jim Lacy said, "I wouldn't. I'd take my chances with a gun. So will Cud Richardson and all the others like him. You've got a fine idea there. Only this country's not ready for it yet."

"You have to start somewhere—sometime—"

"You've said that before. But if you'll take my advice you won't try beginning with Richardson. You won't—" Nevada broke off abruptly. "Smoke ahead," he said, pointing, and rising slightly in the saddle.

Harlan Drake pulled to a halt, and swung his eyes to the trail, where a pale blue streamer was twisting its way into the cloudless sky.

"You think that's him?"

"It could be a trapper—or a miner," Nevada replied. "It's a little hard to believe it's Cud. He's not fool enough to advertise his presence with a fire."

The pressed on, keeping to the road until they reached the rise beyond which the smoke was rising.

"We'd better split here and keep to the brush until we have a look," Nevada said, pulling away from the ruts.

Drake immediately cut to the opposite side of the road, and together they crossed the ridge. The instant they reached the other side they could see, in a cleared hollow below the crumbling, time-ravaged remainder of a cabin. The roof was half-gone, forming no more than a slanting, lean-to affair with it upper end resting upon the only wall which was still intact. The smoke they had seen from the other side of the bridge was issuing from the stone chimney.

"It must be him," Drake said. "Nobody would be living in that place."

Lacy nodded in agreement. But a strong current of suspicion and dissatisfaction was running through him. He no longer doubted that it was Richardson—but why would a man waiting in ambush build a fire and create smoke that would reveal his hiding place? Something else troubled him. Why hadn't they seen the smoke earlier?

A man bulding a fire for warmth or comfrot would have done so hours ago. Why had he waited until they were fairly close. So near, in fact, where they could not have failed to notice it?

"It has to be a trap," he said aloud. "Cud's got something up his sleeve."

"A sign of some kind is right in line with what we were hoping to find," Drake said, turning to face Nevada straight on. "We'll get nowhere if we're too suspicious. I'll take over from here."

Lacy stared at the Pinkerton man. "If you try riding down there, you'll be making a mistake—perhaps your last one," he warned.

"I don't think so. This is a good time to prove that everything I've been trying to tell you makes sense."

Nevada was silent for a long minute, his eyes again on the cabin. Finally he shrugged. "All right, you're dealing. We'll see how the cards fall. I'll stay in the game as I promised, but I don't like it. What do you want me to do?"

"Stay back in the brush at the edge of the clearing, out of sight. I'll shout when I want you to move in."

"You're not aiming to ride—" Nevada began, and stopped when Drake made a motion wit his hand.

"Not exactly," Dude said, and moved on.

In full view of the shack, he crossed the road to Nevada's side, and angling through the brush, approached the ruined cabin slowly. Reaching the edge of the clearing, he halted.

"Richardson!" he called in a strong, clear voice. "This is Drake—Dude. You in there?"

"I'm here." The outlaw's reply was muffled, and came from somewhere at the rear of the structure.

"I'm a Government lawman. Pinkerton Agency. Jim Lacy's waiting in the brush. You haven't got a chance. I want you to throw your guns down, and come out."

There was no answer. After a time Drake yelled. "You hear me?"

"I hear you. What're you dogging me for?"

"That Kansas train robbery. You come with me and you'll get a fair trial."

"Sure—I'll just bet."

"You have my word on it."

Again their was that dragging silence, broken this time by the outlaw. "You ain't fooling me. I show my head, you'll blow it off."

"No. It won't be like that."

"How do I know?"

"We'll have to trust each other. There's no other way."

Once more there was quiet, once again broken by Cud Richardson.

"I ain't so sure. You crossed me once. It could be

you're figuring to do it again. Come on down—we'll do some talking.''

"No!"

The word exploded involuntarily from Jim Lacy's lips as he spurred forward. Richardson was giving nothing; Drake was accepting all the risk.

The Pinkerton man twisted hurriedly on his saddle, and halted Nevada by lifting his hand, palm outward.

"My way—" he said.

Swearing in helpless anger, Lacy pulled up, watched Dude move on, saw him break from the fringe of brush into the open, and head directly for the cabin. He covered half the distance. Two-thirds.

Abruptly the small valley echoed with two quick gunshots. They came not from the cabin but from the trees a short distance to its right. Harlan Drake jolted on his saddle, buckled forward.

Roweling the buckskin, Nevada swept out his gun, and started down the slope on a swerving, erratic course. Richardson had run true to form.

XIV

The outlaw broke from the trees, reining in his horse so abruptly that the animal reared. The weapon in his hand bucked, puffs of smoke lifting from its muzzle. Nevada, steadying himself as best he could on the plunging buckskin, returned the fire. But accuracy on the part of either man was impossible.

It was clear what Richardson had done. He had allowed Drake to think he was still inside the cabin, but had slipped out after talking to him circled, and waited in the brush until the Pinkerton man was in range. From that side vantage point it had been easy to cut the lawman down.

Suddenly Richardson flinched. Bent low, he wheeled his horse around, and headed for the road that led on into the country beyond the Mogollon Rim. Nevada, dull fury beating at him, triggered another shot at the outlaw. But just as the shot rang out, the buckskin veered to avoid a rotting log, and he knew that the bullet had gone wild.

"Run, damn you!" he grated through clenched teeth. "I'll hunt you down wherever you go!"

Drake lay sprawled beside his black horse when Nevada reached him. Leaving the saddle in a hurried leap, the lean rider hunched beside the lawman. A broad crimson stain had spread across the Pinkerton man's chest. There was a slackness to his features, but his eyes were bright, alert.

"You—figured him right," he murmured. "Should have listened."

"Don't try to talk," Nevada snapped. "I've got to get you to a doctor."

Drake shook his head. "Waste of time. You know I won't make it—same as I know."

Lacy glanced toward the cabin. Someone had bridged two rocks with planks to form a crude bench. Slipping his arms under Drake, he carried him inside, and eased him down on the rough pine boards, feeling it would be warmer and a little more comfortable close to the fire that was still smoldering.

Harlan Drake looked around, his lips twisting in a faint smile. "Not a bad place to die."

"It's a hell of a place!" Lacy said harshly. "And for no good reason."

Drake checked him with a raised hand. "Too late now for regrets. You were right, and I was wrong, but it does no good to hash it over. We've still got a long way to go before we get the respect for law we need. But like I said—we have to make a start."

Drake paused slightly and took a bubbling breath. "Day's gone when one man, like yourself, can be jury, judge and executioner—all rolled into one. Has to be that way. Country will never amount to anything until there's law . . . every place."

Nevada said, "The Pinkertons are about as important to you as anything—I can see that. But I don't know much about them. Sort of a private law force, is that it?"

Harlan Drake nodded. "It's more than that," he said, his voice suddenly stronger, more intense. "The Agency got started about ten years before the was broke out. Pinkerton was a Scotsman, and he opened his first company office in Chicago. Did mostly railroad work.

"Did such a good job that when the trouble between the states started, Washington asked him to set up a Government secret service. It was the Pinkerton agents who smuggled President Lincoln through Baltimore to the Capital right after the trouble at Charleston Harbor that set off the war."

Drake paused, breathing heavily. He brushed at his lips, glanced around. "Could you get me some water? Throat's mighty dry."

Nevada obtained his canteen from the buckskin's saddle, returned and held it to Drake's lips. The lawman took it in his own hands. He showed amazing strength, considering his wound. But to have loaded him on a horse would only have hastened the end, and Nevada knew that the dying man had been right in refusing to let himself be moved.

Lowering the canteen, Drake smiled faintly. "Much better. Where was I? Oh—President Lincoln issued blanket authority to us, gave Pinkerton agents the right to go anywhere in the country, and arrest a man for breaking the law. That's why I was sent here. I was in Pennsylvania on another case. Head office ordered me to Kansas, to get Richardson. I'm ending up in Arizona."

Drake paused, his voice faltering again. "That shooting—Richardson—get away?"

Nevada nodded. "Could be I winged him. But he won't go far. I'll find him. Today, next week, sometime. But I'll find him."

"Know you will—Jim."

Nevada looked more closely at Drake. "Better just lay there, take it easy."

"Why? I feel like talking. And when I shut up this time—it'll be for good."

Drake turned his head and gazed out over the gently rolling hills dark with pines. The sun was well on its way and a warmness was spreading over the land.

Suddenly the change came. Drake was going fast and with his last strength he caught at Jim's arm. His voice was a hoarse mutter: "Take the leather packet inside my shirt. Papers."

Drake made a feeble attempt to brush his eyes, swallowed hard. "Take to Bern Jensen—Prescott, chief agent—tell what happened."

The stillness was suddenly absolute in the decaying shack. Somewhere across the road a meadowlark trilled cheerfully. A man dies, a bird sings, and the world continues to spin through space.

For a long minute Nevada Jim Lacy stared at Harlan Drake's slack features, and then he rose stiffly, angrily. Yes, a man dies. But another man would pay for the dying. That was the way it had to be—the code of retribution, of vengeance.

Grimly, he moved to the edge of the lean-to roof, and stood for a long moment staring up the road. Cud Richardson was out there, somewhere, waiting, no doubt planning another ambush with some slight variation. His mind worked that way.

Like a kill-crazed, hunted animal, he'd run, stop to fight, and failing in his efforts to down the man on his trail, would run again. And thus it would go until he had destroyed his pursuer—or himself. Kill or be killed. That was the rule Cud Richardson lived by—and would die by.

Stepping out into the open, Lacy gathered in the reins of Drake's black, and led him back to the cabin. Bending over, he found the papers that Drake had mentioned, sewed to the fabric at the dead man's shield-type shirt just below the left armpit. Without examining the packet's contents, he thrust it into the inner pocket of his own shirt, and finished loading Drake's body on the black, securing it firmly to the saddle with a double lashing of leather strings.

Mounting his buckskin, Nevada returned to the ridge, and pointed Drake's horse down the road for Coopersville. He slapped the animal smartly on the rump, and sent him trotting for the settlement. The black, he knew, wouldn't stop until he got there—and Cooper would see that Dude was buried. He would have liked to be there for the funeral, but there wasn't time.

Cud Richardson was waiting, and he had no intention

of disappointing the outlaw. Dude would want him to keep that appointment.

XV

Ahead the trail curved slightly westward on its way to join the Prescott-Fort Apache road. The valley was not wide here, and trees and brush crowded in close on either side, creating an almost channel-like course.

Nevada didn't like it. He was pursuing Richardson on the outlaw's own terms again, and that was the surest way he could think of to get a bullet in the head. He must get off the road as soon as possible, and do his traveling through the trees where he would not be so conspicuous. But he must also stay in the open for a time—long enough for Richardson to see him, and become convinced that he was being followed.

The problem was to decide how far he would have to ride in the open to mislead the outlaw—one mile or ten? Much depended, of course, on how great a lead Richardson had.

Lacy endeavored to put himself in Richardson's position. How would he have figured it? Probably, after shooting down Harlan Drake, and knowing that the lawman was not alone, he had ridden hard for the first few minutes, not certain whether pursuit would be immediate or come later.

Within five miles or less, he would have become fairly sure that no one was on his heels. He would have slowed his place to spare his horse as much as possible, and have started making plans for a second ambush.

Maybe Richardson would spot another deserted cabin, but the outlaw was smart enough to realize he could not work that ruse twice. Most surely he would look for a narrow place in the trail where rocks would provide good self-protection, and take his stand there.

Nevada was sure no hard-pressed man would make a stand in an area similar to the one through which he was now passing. Not if he had any sense. There was too much brush, and vision was limited. Cud would seek open country that would enable him to see an approaching rider for a considerable distance, while he crouched in a well-concealed vantage point.

The trail ran on. Now and then, in mud turned soft by recent showers, Lacy saw the hoof prints of the outlaw's horse. He did not stop to examine them closely, for only the knowledge that Richardson was ahead of him was important while they both remained on the road. Near noon the trees and brush began to think out and the country became broken and rough.

Nevada began to rein in his horse occasionally and sit motionless in the saddle, searching the far distance for signs of movement. He could see nothing but that was understandable. Cud had a full hour's start on him, barring the possibility that he had stopped on the way.

The road slashed across a wide, grass-covered swale, and for a long mile Nevada knew he was visible from all directions to anyone who might be watching.

It was just such a point in the trail which Nevada had been hoping to encounter. In all probability, Richardson had by now seen him and the hunt would take a different turn.

The buckskin, loping tirelessly, crossed the swale; and entered a small grove of stalwart pines that followed a ridge extending down from the higher hills to the west. It would be a good place for an ambush, Nevada thought, probing the dark shadows beneath the trees with a sharp eye. But he reached the grove without incident, and there pulled to a halt.

That Richardson had some specific location along the trail in mind seemed a certainty now. Otherwise, Nevada told himself, the outlaw would have made use of this particular section of the road. And there had been two or three other spots that would have served him almost equally well.

The lean rider glanced at the sun. In three or four hours it would be setting and there was a distinct possibility that Richardson could be stalling, waiting until he had the added advantage of darkness. A hunted man strives to build the odds in his favor.

But permitting the outlaw to grasp the whip handle was far from Nevada's mind. Up to the present moment, he'd been forced to play the game Richardson's way, to let him know that he was being pursued. Now everything would change.

The grove was a good place to make the break. Cutting the buckskin sharp left, he held the horse to a due west course, keeping deep within the trees where his passage would go unseen. Richardson, having seen him enter the dense grove, would be watching the point where the road emerged. When no one appeared, he could hardly fail to conclude the man following him had paused to rest.

For a full hour Nevada pushed on and came finally to the foothills which rose gradually to melt into the high bluffs and ridges of the mountain range proper.

He found a trail after paralleling the base of the ragged formation for a mile and a half and began at once to ascend the steep slope. A few minutes later he broke out onto a small, flinty, roundtop, and continued on.

The road was below him and he knew that he could look down from it by moving to the edge if and when he desired. But that was not an immediate part of his plan. Later when darkness closed in over the land, he would take that look.

Sometime before sunset he reached the crest of a high bluff and halted. Leaving his horse to graze he prowled the edge of the rim—taking care to avoid becoming visible from the valley below—and succeeded in locating a point where he could descend. That fixed in his mind, he doubled back to the buckskin to await total darkness.

He became conscious of hunger and, digging into his saddlebags, pulled out the sandwiches which Hettie had prepared. They were dry and had lost their flavor. But he ate them gratefully and took a long drink of water from his canteen.

The last trace of sunset glow had gone when he finished. Restoring the remainder of the food to the leather pouches, he moved to the rim of the bluff, sprawled out flat, and began a slow, methodical search of the country below.

Darkness all but obscured the road. But a pale glimmer of moonlight made it possible to see it in a few separated places. He could detect no signs of life. There was only the long stillness broken by the occasional bark of a coyote, high up on the slopes behind him.

He did not change position, simply waited, patient, almost sure the moment could come when his search would be rewarded. And eventually it was, two dragging hours later. A tiny red eye sprang to life a short distance from the road—a small camp fire, well hidden, to his right.

A grim smile pulled at Nevada's lips. He'd overshot Richardson and the ambush, and was now behind the outlaw. It was a stroke of luck he hadn't counted on. Establishing the location of the outlaw's camp by noting adjacent landmarks in his mind, he returned to the gelding, took up the reins and led the horse down the steep trial he had discovered.

As soon as he reached the floor of the valley again, he cut sraight across, walking the buckskin to avoid the warning sound which clattering hoofbeats would have made, and in less than three minutes emerged on the road. Halting, he took stock of the landmarks. Richardson would be a mile, perhaps two, below him. He swung right and, holding the gelding on the hardpack of the road, then quietly and with finality, closed in.

Cud Richardson had chosen the location well—a low, rock-strewn hogback through which the trail cut a narrow pass. The outlaw had dropped back a short distance from the gash and built his fire in a deep pocket that would prevent the flames from being seen from the valley to the south.

Standing behind a climp of juniper, Nevada watched Richardson moving about, mistakenly confident that his intended victim was still somewhere below him. His movements were unhampered and Lacy guessed he had not wounded him, even slightly, back at the cabin.

Suddenly a faint stir of movement on the opposite side of the pass caught Nevada's attention. By staring hard he was able to make out the outlaw's horse, tied to a tree and standing unsaddled in the moonlight. And there was something else— a hat perched on a stake near the front of the ridge where it could be seen from the road. Nevada grinned. Richardson had evidently gone to great lengths to fool him. The plan was easy to fathom. The instant his attention was drawn to the decoy that the outlaw, crouching in the rocks fifty feet away, would blast him down in cold blood.

Cud Richardson would have no qualms about shooting him in the back. Yet, to Harlan Drake's way of thinking, for a lawman to meet such a man as Cud with matching coldbloodedness couldn't be more wrong. The law and only the law should deal out the punishment for those vicious men who have no regard for the law.

Maybe Drake was right. Maybe there was no other way to establish law and order, to advance civilization. But Nevada refused to let himself dwell on that as he continued to watch the outlaw. Richardson was boiling up a can of coffee but apparently had no other provisions with him. Every few moments he would move to the ridge, stare off down the road for a time, and then return to his fire. Plainly, he expected his pursuer to appear at any moment.

Removing his spurs, Lacy cut silently to his left and made his way through the brush and rocks until he was slightly above and to the east of Richardson's fire. There, gun in hand, he crept in to a point where he was at the edge of the pale flare cast by the flames.

Richardson was crouched by the fire, absently stirring the coffee with a twig. Nevada knew he had only to rise and speak the outlaw's name to bring Cud whirling about, weapon in hand, for the showdown. He studied the hunched figure of the man for a brief time, and then came to a decision.

All right, Dude, I'm trying it your way.

The words formed soundlessly on Nevada Lacy's lips as he rose suddenly and lunged at the outlaw.

XVI

Three days Later Nevada pulled into Prescott, a black stubble covering his cheeks and chin, sweat clinging to his clothing, Cud Richardson's horse trailing behind him at the end of a short rope.

The outlaw himself was slumped on the saddle, morose and somber with his hands tied behind his back and his legs linked together with rope stretched taut under his horse's belly.

Both riders bore witness to the changes which could be brought about in a man's physical appearance by no more than a minute of harsh violence on the trail. A long red gash lay across Nevada's forehead. Cud Richardson's eyes were swollen, his mouth crushed, nose slightly askew. He was a thoroughly beaten and cowed man.

He had wheeled that night by the fire, just as Lacy lunged. The two had come together in a bone-crackling collision. Nevada's rock-hard fists smashed into Cud's jaw as they sprawled, and the outlaw had countered, using his sixgun as a club.

Nevada had jerked away. The barrel of the weapon had grazed and left its mark, but had done no more. A flurry of punishing blows to Cud Richardson's head— and the man had given up, raising both hands as a gesture of total surrender.

Oblivious to the curious standing|passersby, Nevada made his way into the business center of the settlement halting finally before a small, narrow building which bore the neatly lettered sign *THE PINKERTON AGENCY* on the window.

Pulling in to the hitchrack, Nevada looped the buckskin's reins over the rail, and turned to anchor Richardson's mount more securely alongside. A man appeared in the office doorway, and stared wonderingly at the operation. From farther down the street a tall individual wearing a star was approaching at a fast walk.

Satisfied that the outlaw's horse could not jerk free, Nevada faced the man in the doorway. "You Jensen?" he asked.

The graying man, his pin-point blue eyes veiled with reserve, nodded. "That's me."

Lacy gestured toward the outlaw. "Here's a little present for you," he said. "Name's Cud Richardson."

"Richardson!" Jensen echoed.

"I brought him in for a friend of mine—Harlan Drake."

"Ah-h-h," Jensen said in a sighing voice. "I see."

"What's going on here, Bern?"

It was the tall lawman who had approached with just about the fastest and longest strides Nevada had ever seen. The Pinkerton agent pointed to the outlaw. "He's Cud Richardson, Tom. Wanted for murder, robbing the U.S. mail and a few other things. Tuck him away good. I'll bring the papers over in a few minutes."

The deputy freed Richardson's horse, moved back up the street. Bern Jensen studied Nevada for a few moments, then stepped back into his office.

"Like to know what happened, Mr.—"

"Name's Lacy. Jim Lacy."

Surprise again sharpened the Pinkerton man's eyes. But he recovered quickly, smiled, and waited for Nevada to enter.

"Is Drake dead?" he asked, as if sensing the truth in

Nevada's grim manner and slight reluctance to meet his gaze.

Nevada nodded, noting at that point the empty sleeve on Jensen's right side.

"Sit down," Jensen said, pointing to a chair. "Naturally—I'd like all of the details."

Nevada sat down on the padded cushion gratefully, and reaching inside his shirt, removed the packet of folded papers he'd taken from Drake and handed them to the lawman's superior.

"He asked me to give you this."

Jensen examined the creased sheets idly. "Was Cud Richardson the man who got him?"

"That's right. Place called Coopersville—or near it."

"I'm eternally grateful to you for finishing the job for him."

"It was what I started out to do—get Richardson, only it was for myself. We sort of joined forces." Nevada looked off into the street. "Dude would have been alive right nw if he'd listened to reason."

"Dude?" questioned Jensen.

"That's what Richardson and his bunch called Drake. He'd worked himself in as a member of Cud's outfit. He had it strong in his head to take Richardson alive—let the law punish him, it was the only way, he said—the only *right* way."

"You don't agree with that?"

"Not a hundred per cent. I figure it's all right to give a man the chance to quit. But you've got to know who you're talking to, and be ready to make your own move if it's a doublecross."

Bern Jensen nodded. "Exactly the way I feel about it. A man has to use good judgment—keep remembering you can't trust a killer very far."

Nevada frowned. "I thought I understood from Drake it was your company that wanted it that way."

"We do—if it's possible. We feel it's better for the courts to do the punishing. But with Harlan Drake it meant more than that. In fact, it was almost an obsession with him. He insisted every outlaw should be given a chance to surrender. I warned him several times he was sticking too close to the letter of the idea, that he was stretching things too far, and that it might get him killed someday."

"It did," Nevada said slowly. "But it works, if you handle it right. Richardson was all set to fill me full of holes when I went after him—and I had plenty of reason to cut him down when I caught up with him. But I tried it Dude's way. Only—I went about it real careful, knowing that Cud Richardson was the type who would kill me in a minute."

Jensen was plucking at his chin, his face wreathed in a deep frown. "You mean Drake was killed by Richardson, and then you went out after him, and brought him in?"

"It was what had to be done, and I sort of felt—well, that I owed it to Dude to finish the job."

Bern Jensen crossed to where Nevada was sitting. "I'd like to shake your hand, Jim Lacy. You did a fine thing, and made a right thorough job of it."

"Fine? I don't know about that," Nevada said slowly. "But the thing was, it had to be done, and I was the man who had to do it."

Both men were silent for a moment, thinking of the dead—the outlaws, and the lawman who had gambled his life in his masquerade as an outlaw. But there was a lightness in Jim _____ , too. For the first time in what seemed _____ it had been, in reality, only a few days, _____ d country he loved best were free from _____ riminal savagery. And he was free, too _____ to Hettie and to take up their new lif _____ interrupted before it had really started.

An _____ out time he was on his way to Hettie! Nev _____ acy swung into the saddle, gave a bid fa _____ Bern Jensen, and rode out of Prescott _____ home.

THE
TRACK OF BLOOD

I

A fluffy cloud puff obscuring the full moon scudded past, urged on by a cool breeze off the northern Colorado mountains to the west.

In the silver light, the riders could be seen clearly. There were about fifty of them, superb horsemen controlling their barebacked ponies with strong knees and rope hackamores.

Naked torsos gleamed with bear grease; eagle feathers stuck from braided hair. The streaked war paint gave the faces of Sioux warriors a terrifying expression. The savages wore deerskin leggings, tassels hanging from their moccasin heels. Most carried bows and quivers of arrows, the usual long knife for scalping and close fighting, a coup stick with which a brave could count coup on an enemy in combat.

They bunched around their chief on a low rise overlooking a small settlement which lay across a little river winding down from the heights. No lights showed; the inhabitants were asleep.

Whites were crowding into this lovely country; ranchers, hoemen, tradesmen, miners. The Union Pacific had joined the great continent, and Cheyenne, in Wyoming Territory, a station on the railroad, lay a few hours ride to the north.

Many Teton Dakotas were large men, but the leader of this band was a tall, striking figure. His massive breast carried the scars of the sun dance, powerful muscles rippling in his mighty arms. He had a proud eagle beak—the broad face of the Sioux, streaked with war paint.

The Indians spoke in their guttural tongue.

"Here we wait," ordered the big chief. "If any warrior goes ahead of me in battle, or makes a loud sound before I give the word, I will cut out his liver and eat it."

No brave challenged this, they knew Flint Heart would do as he threatened, for they had seen him carry this out on an overeager youth who had rushed into the fight prematurely during a raid on a Crow village the previous autumn.

Two horsemen pushed slowly from a nearby spruce grove.

"Flint Heart!" called one softly.

"I am here," replied the chief. He turned his mount and went to face the pair. "*Hou, cola*," he greeted "Hello, friend."

His massed warriors waited as Flint Heart talked with the whites, who wore war bonnets and were disguised as savages, but were not Indians. They were "Gray Men," as the Sioux called renegades who masqueraded to hide their evil deeds.

"Talk English," said the white fellow who had hailed Flint Heart.

"Where are the guns?" demanded Flint Heart.

"You'll get 'em. Ammo, too. First listen. Take no prisoners. Leave no witnesses."

"Young women are good for the Sioux," argued Flint Heart.

"No. Spare none, kill girls, children, savvy? We got coal oil for you. Burn every house. Spare nothing."

"*Hou*. It is good. Give us the guns and the burning oil." Flint Heart's dark eyes had a bloodred glow in them.

The big-boned, lean white man's leather creaked as he pulled the rein of his black stallion, turning back toward the spruce grove. His companion followed, and Flint Heart, braves slowly trailing their chief, moved after the two Gray Men.

It was inky among the trees, and the lean fellow said, "Light that bull's-eye, Joe." He swung from his saddle, tied his rein to a low branch.

Flint Heart and Joe Cordell got down. The latter struck a match and in the rays of the little flame, Cordell's curly hair could be seen under the Indian headdress. He was younger, slimmer than his friend, who ordered:

"Keep the beam turned this way so it don't show in the town."

"Okay, Pate."

Joe Cordell raised the slide, adjusted the wick as he touched the match to it, and the yellowish light showed the bundles of repeating carbines, boxes of ammunition, a dozen small cans of oil. Also, there were plugs of tobacco, a roll of gingham cloth, a box of beads and other trinkets prized by the savages.

These items were the price the Gray Men were paying for the death massacre.

Pate's cheekbones were high as Flint Heart's; he was bronzed by sun and wind, and a crisp mustache grew under his long nose. One pale-blue eye fluttered a bit as he spoke to the Sioux chief.

"You sure you can handle your braves?" he

113

demanded.

"They are all warriors. They are young and eager for brave deeds to prove themselves. The Sioux hate all *wasichus*. They are ready to kill."

"Don't look at me like that," growled Pate. "Ain't I white? One move outa any of you and I'll show you who can kill, savvy?" Pate spoke icily.

"Friend. Yes, you are a friend of the Indian. We look on such as you as brothers."

"Keep it in mind. And young Joe Cordell here is the boss's son, and if you want more guns and trinkets, you'll do what we tell you."

Flint Heart nodded. He stared greedily at the fine carbines and ammunition, at the goods which would please any squaw.

Joe Cordell set the lantern on the smooth, brown-needled earth, assisting Pate as he began passing the weapons to Flint Heart. The chief armed his braves; the Indians quickly loaded, caressing their new guns. The Sioux never had enough rifles and ammunition. One older Indian grunted something as he accepted his weapon, and Pate asked, "What'd he say?"

"He wants burning water," replied the chief.

"Nothing doing. Not till you finish this job. I don't wany any drunk Injuns ravin' around."

Flint Heart nodded. "We leave the other goods here till we are done." He turned, giving orders to his followers, who started to their mustangs, carbines in hand.

Below, the hamlet slept in the night, unaware of the horrible fate in store. There were about a dozen buildings, one a store with a livery stable at the side, the rest cabins, all constructed from timber cut in the nearby mountains.

114

The two Gray Men, putting out the lantern, led their mounts to the edge of the spruce grove and stood, reins in hand, watching Flint Heart and his Sioux warriors move down the slope and stealthily fan out through the village.

Joe Cordell said, "I reckon they'll do it, George." There was a little quaver in his young voice which Pate didn't miss.

"You got to harden yourself more, boy. You travel with me a while and you'll learn. Your pop and me can tell you plenty and teach you what's what. Dog eat dog, every man for himself. That's what we say. Why worry about a few stupid cusses?"

"Well, let's get on home."

"No. Hold on. You watch. It'll be good for you." There was cold steel in George Pate's cruel tones. "I've seen plenty men die in front of my own guns and so's your pop. While we were in Leavenworth together we watched others get it from cold steel. You got to learn, I tell you. Wesleyville's a stumblin' block. Your old man and me got big plans and we don't aim to let a handful like those below stand in our way."

Flint Heart was most efficient. He'd led many raids on isolated cabins and tiny settlements as the Sioux savagely fought the white invaders of their hereditary hunting grounds.

Their *Pa Sapa*, the sacred Black Hills, had been taken from them despite the solemn treaties and promises made by the pale faces. The buffalo was being slaughtered, the iron roads—the white man's railroads—were being inexorably thrust into the great wilderness. The Union Pacific had joined the East and West, in 1869, and already there was another, called the Northern Pacific, stabbing into the heart of the

115

Dakotas. And small branch lines were being surveyed, crisscrossing and uniting the main ones.

A shiver, almost a shudder, passed through young Cordell. He was not yet as hardened to murder and horror.

The gunny gripped his arm.

"Hold on," Pate growled. "Watch!"

The peace of the Spring night was suddenly shattered by bloodcurdling war cries of the Sioux. Yellow flames quickly licked up around the bases of the log cabins, around the larger store.

A gun shot rang out, then a spattering volley. High-pitched screams of women joined hoarse shouts of men, awakened by the attack. From the rise on which they stood, the two Gray Men saw figures running from the buildings, already burning hungrily with the oil thrown on the pine and spruce walls.

As the whites rushed outside to escape the choking smoke and heat, Indians shot them down, shouting in triumph at each victim who crashed in the dirt street. Women, children, were riddled with carbine lead. A few males got off a few retaliatory volleys, but they were against the yellowish-red light of the fires, the attackers in the semi-darkness beyond. Three females carrying children in arms fell in the road. There was no mercy.

Flint Heart was carrying out Pate's orders.

The two on the rise could hear the increasing crackling of the licking flames consuming the structures of the settlement.

Now there were no more outcries from the victims; they were dead, men, women, children. . .

The bronzed figures of the Sioux could be seen as braves hurried from corpse to corpse, lifting scalps, raising them high as they whooped in victory.

116

Joe Cordell gasped, turning away from the horror below. Several Indians were driving off some horses they had run from stables and corrals; others were picking up weapons dropped by the whites, searching them for loot.

Pate remarked in a satisfied voice, "They done a good job."

Joe Cordell began to retch. Pate laughed, said, "Here, take a swig, brace up." He held out a flask.

Cordell downed a long pull, then said apologetically, "This—well, this ain't like downin' some hombre you're mad at."

"It had to be done," replied Pate, in a practical voice. "Forget it. C'mon, let's ride home. You can see that little blonde filly Penny tomorrow. Think how rich you'll be! Why, she'll fall over for you, boy." Pate laughed coarsely.

Young Cordell had drunk several ounces of burning liquor. He turned to pick up his handsome pinto's rein, swung into the saddle. "Dammit, George, my horse started limpin' a while back. This paint horse is the finest money can buy and I don't like ridin' anything else."

"Probably picked up a little pebble. You can have a new shoe put on when we get back"

George Pate led off, glancing back over a hunched shoulder as they rode away. The ghastly massacre seemed to fascinate and please him.

"Yeah," he said satisfiedly, "that Flint Heart's a good boy. I'll use him again, when I need a job done."

They skirted south of what had been Wesleyville, hitting a trck which led through rising, wooded hills from which jagged rocks thrust serrated formations.

And they heard the long, mournful howl of a lobo

117

wolf in the beautiful night.

II

Al Slingerland rode easily along the trail winding near the crystal-clear mountain stream.

The early morning air was bracing with the aromatic odor of conifers, which dominated the slopes. In meadows alders grew and cottonwoods lined the creek; in season, there were wild grapes, raspberries, bear cherries, gooseberries, currants, buffalo berries, the pink flowers marking the rattlesnake root. Wild turnips were good eating, too, for Nature's bounty furnished the knowing man with many fine things.

Tall and raw-boned, Slingerland had no spare suet on him; his sinews were whipcords and his muscles were hard as steel. In one huge hand he held the rein controlling his handsome bay stallion; his piercing gray eyes missed not the slightest sign in range of his vision.

In the boot rode a long-range hunting rifle, a Sharps Creedmore which could bring down big game, while he also had a carbine, a Colt revolver, and the indispensable long knife, sharpened to razor edge.

He had breakfasted at dawn in his log cabin, set on a pleasant rise by the little river. This wild valley was his home. He had built the place himself and furnished it comfortably. An expert trapper, he could earn more than enough to satsify his needs. All along the eastern slopes of the Rockies game was still plentiful, though it was threatened by the encroaching whites who pushed into the land of the Tetons, the mighty Western Sioux.

Slingerland didn't fear the Indians. They were his friends; he spoke their tongue and was versed in the universal sign language. As a youth he had lived with the Oglala Sioux, hunted and caroused with them, as had other trappers and mountain men. The savages would not harm a comrade.

On a lead-rope behind the bay trudged a long-eared, sleek mule, the packs on his sturdy back holding traps and other gear.

Jays, squirrels, butterfies abounded in this lovely valley. But like the Indian, Slingerland killed nothing save what was required for food, and for pelts which he sold to earn his living. He wore soft buckskin, with a coonskin hat on his thick hair. A beard protected his bronzed cheeks from sun and icy winds. Contented with his lonely life, he could take care of himself.

But he wasn't a hermit who disliked other humans. His nature was open, expansive, and he was always glad to help anyone in distress. He often thought of Warren Neale, the young engineer he'd assisted when Neale was helping lay out the U.P. Trail, the Union Pacific Railroad which had joined East and West. When he'd met Neale, Slingerland had been living in a wild Wyoming Territory valley, but other settlers had spoiled the hunting there, so he'd moved south into the northeast quadrant of Colorado.

Neale had opened a consulting engineering firm in Cheyenne. The nation was now railroad-minded. The Northern Pacific would pierce the very heart of the Sioux's traditional hunting grounds. So naturally the Indians were infuriated and were ready to fight to the death.

Connecting and branch lines were being laid or planned all through the land, so Neale had plenty of work. He and his pretty wife, Allie Lee, sole survivor of an Indian attack on an east-bound wagon train, lived with their two small children in a spacious home south of Cheyenne, which, like so many new settlements, was growing by leaps and bounds.

But Al Slingerland felt as the Indians did. The rapid expansion of civilization saddened him. How much longer would a trapper be able to operate? The forests were being systematically destroyed. The hordes of bears, elk, deer, martens and minks, skunks and foxes, beaver, and, most vital to the savages, the bison, which furnished them with food, shelter, and clothing, were being killed off with the same ruthless abandon by white hunters.

The bay stallion snorted, ripped his sleek hide, and Slingerland alerted instantly. The horse had told him something, and his keen gray eyes swept every inch around. He glimpsed a small paint horse, with a rope hackamore, as the mustang showed for a moment as it retreated up the slope, covered with balsams. He knew it was an Indian pony.

Where was the Indian? He made sure his carbine was loose in its socket by his hip. Then he decided to dismount, and swung a long leg off, fastening the bay's rein to a handy limb and pulling the light rifle out.

It was something he must check. While the Indians were his friends, there were bad ones, sometimes outcasts, or it might be a member of some tribe which didn't know who the tall trapper was.

Carbine in one hand, he flitted along the trail. He paused several times to listen intently. Birds trilled to the new dawn, the creek murmured over a rocky stretch not far away.

He came on fresh, unshod hoof tracks, no doubt left by the paint pony. To his left, toward the river, was a dense thicket, and several stalks of grass at one side were slowly coming back into position after having been crushed down. Nor did he miss a small twig, broken off low on one of the bushes. Somebody had just crept off the path at this point.

Slingerland threw a cartridge into his carbine. If a brave was crouched in there, waiting for him, the savage might kill without warning.

"*Hou, cola*," he said softly, tentatively.

There was no reply. As he squatted, listening, watching, a sudden raucous scolding began, jays in a dither at being disturbed, closer to the creek. Jays were constantly scolding, but the pitch told Slingerland's trained ear the birds were alarmed about an intruder.

This was all he needed. He moved that way.

He found her huddled beside a huge gray boulder on the bank.

Light glinted from the butcher knife in her left hand. She wore soft, bleached doeskin on her slender body. Dark braids hung over her swelling bosoms, telling him she was a maiden. He could guess that, anyone; she must have just gone through the Sioux ceremony making her a woman, ready for marriage. Her full cheeks were smooth save for a dark bruise on one. Large, long-lashed eyes, fearful, wide open, watched him.

Slingerland almost gasped at her loveliness.

"*Wasichu!*" The Indian girl was terrified, and she raised her knife to defend herself.

She kept her right arm bent up, pressed to her side.

He leaned forward to put down his carbine. She misinterpreted this, thinking he was reaching for her, and with a faint cry, slashed at him with her knife. He caught her wrist so the point only ripped his shirt. He disarmed her easy and stepped back, speaking in Sioux.

"I'm your friend, the Indians' friend, Slingerland,

the trapper. I have lived with your people. I won't harm you. Let me help you."

Her breast was heaving. She dropped her eyes and he saw tears, unusual in an Indian.

Finally she began to talk, her voice low and musical. She was an Oglala, as he'd believed.

The English equivalent of her name was Mountain Flower. She'd run away. Though she was a good rider, she had fainted. And her pony had thrown her off. Next, she found she was lying on the ground. When she heard someone coming, she'd crawled off to hide.

"I won't hurt you, Flower," he said again, gently. "What's wrong with your right arm? Is it broken?"

Flower shook her head; she kept the arm crooked up.

When he touched it, she tried not to wince. He couldn't be sure about her injury without a closer examination. "My cabin's not far off. There I'll fix your hurt."

He held out his hand but when she tried to get up, she fell back. She was in a state of shock.

The fact he spoke her tongue, the look in the big trapper's eyes, his kind manner, had reassured her. When he stopped to pick her up, she put her left arm around his neck, relaxing against him.

He felt a sudden, deep emotion, the thrill of a strong man for a young, lovely female, soft and womanly, most desirable.

Slingerland spoke soothingly as he carried her back to his horse. He set her up befor ehim, swung aboard, and turned the bay. The mule trailed along as they moved toward his camp.

The cabin had two rooms, with a porch where the trapper might sit, enjoying the view across the beaver pond below. High racks, out of reach of wolves, coyotes and other predators, were strung with drying pelts and meats. There was an open shed where his two horses and the mule could shelter, though usually they preferred to stay outside. His second mount, a chestnut gelding, whinnied and started toward him.

Mountain Flower now seemed to trust him fully. Again she put her arm around his neck as he carried her into his home, and once more, the man felt her soft body against his. He found she was looking up at him, studying his face, but when he smiled at her, she dropped her pretty eyes.

The main room was comfortably furnished; he'd fashioned benches, tables and other conveniences; animal skins served as rugs. Through an open door could be seen the second chamber, filled with trappings and other gear, a gun rack, a stove and cooking utensils, a frame where hung spare clothing, boots beneath it.

He set Flower down on his bed. Rawhide strips stretched between the pine-limb sides held a mattress stuffed with fragrant mountain hay, and soft furs were laid on top, making a most comfortable couch.

"I'll fetch you a drink, Flower. Then I'll heat up some coffee and broth. You look piqued."

He was aware of her large, dark eyes following him as he went about his tasks.

She drank gratefully of cool water he brought her. Then he lit tinder and kindling in the stove and set the coffee pot and a pan of bear-meat soup, with pieces of liver in it, to warm over the fire.

Returning to Mountain Flower, he pulled up a low stool, and sat before her. "Now we must see about your arm. I'll be careful."

If he removed her deerskin blouse, her full bosoms would be exposed; and she was a modest girl, he could tell that. The sleeves were side, in Sioux fashion, so he fetched a pair of scissors and carefully cut off the right one at the shoulder. Now he could see her pretty arm; it was discolored.

But it looked in line, and he began to check the bones with long, gentle fingers, seeking a possible break. This hurt but she didn't wince or whimper. An Indian woman could withstand pain.

"I don't believe any bones are cracked, Flower. It's a strain, a terrible wrench."

Again, as he looked into her sweet face, she dropped her long lashes. She'd been studying him again.

Slingerland rose and went into the kitchen. The coffee and soup were bubbling hot. He poured two mugs of coffee, and ladled out the broth into a bowl. He put a horn spoon in the bowl, and carried it to her, with a mug of steaming coffee, set it on the stool so she could easily reach it.

When he returned with his own drink, she was sipping the soup. He sat on a chair, enjoying his coffee, while the girl ate. He was glad to see her finish her meal, and then her coffee. And she kept covertly glancing at the big trapper.

"When you're well, Flower," he said, "I'll take you back to your village."

But at this, she looked alarmed, and shook her head.

This puzzled him. He'd believed the girl had been hurt in a fall. But he began to wonder about it. His curiosity aroused, he asked, "Why don't you want to go back to your tribe?"

He had to repeat the question but finally she told him. A chief, one of her people, had struck her in the face and brutally twisted her arm.

This surprised Slingerland, for a Sioux seldom struck

a squaw, no matter what the provocation. Their women were honored as keepers of the tepees, owners of the lodge and all within it save for the man's weapons of war. The children belonged to the mother, and if a wife so wished, she might turn her husband out, refuse to serve him any longer.

Patiently he led her on, learning her unhappy story. The suitor who desired her had slain two rivals and seized their ponies and other valuables, using them to buy her, according to Sioux custom, since a daughter's duty was to bring wealth to her father, and Mountain Flower was his only child.

Her mother had died when she was born, her father was elderly and ill with the white man's coughing sickness, and when Flint Heart had paid him for Flower, her father had gone to the hospital on the reservation to see the medicine man there.

Flint Heart had already had two wives. One he had killed, for he had an evil temper. Flower feared him; he was cruel as well as very powerful, the leader of many young, reckless braves belonging to his warrior society, his *akacita*.

So Flower had run away into the forest as soon as her father left. But the chief who had bought her found her, struck her and beat her. He'd thrown her into his lodge with his other wife, an older squaw, to guard her. Before he lay with her, though, Flint Heart said he must go on a raid with his men, but would return. And when he had ridden off, Flower had mustered enough strength to slip out under the back of the tepee, while the squaw slept. She'd snatched a tethered pony and fled.

"Flint Heart, yes, I know him. He has a cruel name. I promise he will never hurt you again, Flower."

125

As they spoke on, he found she was a niece of Black Buffalo Woman, who carried power in her hands as she was related to Red Cloud. Al Slingerland knew Black Buffalo Woman had been sold to a Sioux named No Water, though she was the true love of Crazy Horse, paladin of the Tetons and the greatest warrior in tribal lore. His Indian name was Tasunke Witko.

The Sun was yellow as the trapper went out, unsaddled the stud, relieved the mule of the packs and turned both loose. He gave up his work that day so he could stay near Flower. If Flint Heart came along, Slingerland meant to protect her. Her pony had turned off and he'd brought her here on his bay, so there was no track of her mustang to his camp. Still, he would take no chances.

He looked through the doorway. Flower lay on his bed, her injured arm across her body, long lashes on her cheeks. She'd ridden all night and was exhausted. Now she slept, breathing easily.

He spent the morning around his home, checking pelts and traps, but kept his rifle handy.

When the sun was overhead he went inside and fixed another meal of meat, biscuits with wild honey, and coffee. As he carried this in, Flower opened her eyes and sat up. This time she looked fully at the man, a smile touching her soft face. He gave her a plate and mug, serving her.

Slingerland was astonished at how he felt.

He'd always lived alone. But now someone was by him, someone he felt strong attraction for, and suddenly he realized how lonely he'd been. A rare contentment swept over him as he watched the pretty girl.

And he knew that the Sioux were right when they said

it was bad for a man to be alone, without a mate.

The day passed swiftly. Sometimes, as he worked, he would glance over and see Flower standing in the doorway, watching him, and he'd smile and wave, and she would wave back. And again, during the evening meal, he experienced that wonderful contentment, the joy of looking at Flower.

That night he stretched on a pad at the barred door, his guns by him, ready for possible trouble. Flower lay quietly on his bed. He didn't fall asleep at once, for he was excited, and thoughts raced through his head. If Flower would marry him—

Up at dawn, Slingerland found the girl awake, and she rose, going toward the kitchen. Her hurt arm was at her side, so she could straighten it.

"Let me see," he said. He examined it, and now was sure it wasn't broken. "It'll get well in a few days," he told her. "Be careful of it."

She insisted on helping fix breakfast, using her left hand. They sat down together, and now she would smile whenever he looked at her.

After they'd eaten, he decided to get fresh water form the brook and picked up two pails, unbarred the door and went out into the crisp, cool morning air.

As he looked all around, as was his habit, he saw a pall of black smoke hanging in the sky to the northeast.

He knew every foot of the surrounding land and could place the smoke. It was over Wesleyville, a small settlement where he sometimes went for supplies, to sell his pelts, and for a bit of human company.

The smoke wasn't billowing up as if just generated. Wesleyville lay south of the usual Tetan range, but, desperate from the crowding of the whites, the bison and other game rapidly being wiped out, the Indians

127

had to cover more ground to find food.

The savages seldom fought after sundown. Evil spirits were abroad in the darkness, but there were practical reasons, too.

Falling dew softened bowstrings so arrows wouldn't fly true and a wet moccasin was easily penetrated by a thorn or sharp stone.

He had friends in Wesleyville and he felt worried. He didn't want to leave Flower, but there might be people who needed help. He fetched the fresh water and joined Flower.

"There is trouble in Wesleyville. I must go there. Wait. I'll come back. You have food and I'll leave you a gun. You can catch the chestnut horse or the mule but it will be best if you keep out of sight so Flint Heart can't find you. Hide if anyone approaches. You must be here when I return. Do you promise?"

She nodded, and he said, "I'll teach you to speak English, Flower. Say, 'Yes, Al.' That's my white man's name, Al."

Earnestly, she formed the words, her small, even teeth showing as she spoke: "Ye-ess, Al-al!"

"Good!" He patted her and rose, taking his guns; there was another carbine and belt of ammunition he left with Flower.

He waved to her at the doorway and she waved back.

Saddling the powerful bay stallion, Slingerland set off on the trail over the ridge which would lead him into the north-south valley in which Wesleyville stood.

A song was in his heart as he thought of the Indian girl. It was good to think of her in his home, that she'd be waiting for him when he returned.

III

Slingerland pushed the bay stallion across the shallows at the creek ford; the water flecked off the horse's legs as he reached the east bank.

The valley was unusual for the area. It ran for many miles generally in a north-south direction and was comparatively level, from Cheyenne on down the line. East and west, sharp-crested mountain ridges, steep slopes clothed in conifers, hemmed it in.

As the bay came up to the wagon road, Slingerland could take in what had been Wesleyvile, and he stifled a gasp of horror, though he had looked upon massacre scenes before. There was not one building left standing; all were smoldering ruins, just a few walls still upright. Even the stables and sheds had been fired. In the main street lay several longish objects and Slingerland knew exactly what they were: the scalped corpses of men, women, even some children.

A hound bayed mournfully somewhere past the blackened wrecks of homes, and as the trapper rode slowly along, a huge mastiff, standing by the twisted figure of what had been his master, bared his teeth, snarling as the stranger approached. But the dog didn't attack; he was simply guarding the remains of the man he had loved, and Slingerland passed without disturbing him. Raucous cries of vultures sounded; stray chickens scratched in the dirt, cows and a few mules grazed in nearby fields. Stray cats slunk uneasily through the ruins.

He glanced at another man's body; the face had collapsed when he'd been scalped. The shirt was bloody, and the victim had pulled on a pair of Levi's when he'd run outside at the night alarm. His trained eye noted the crisscrossing marks of unshod hoofs in softer spots, and he knew many Indians had been there.

There were few better trackers in the West than Al Slingerland. He had lived with the Sioux and could read sign with the savage's expert eye, as well as with that of a hunter and white trailer.

He swung off northwest as the welter of tracks came together near the river bank; now there were shod hoofs, too; the raiders had run off the horses found in the settlement. He splashed across the creek to the west side, easily picked up the trail. Without even dismounting, he decided the Indians had attacked around midnight and after wiping out the settlement, made off northwest with the stolen horses and whatever loot they might have picked up.

With Mountain Flower, the Sioux girl, in mind, he recalled what she'd told him: Flint Heart had hurried off with his warrior band, which had given her a chance to escape. He couldn't swear to it, but chances were the giant Sioux chief had led the raid.

He pulled up and started back, slowly; there was much to be done in Wesleyville's ruins. On the other side of the wide, cut-up trail, his alert, keen eye noticed something else. This was a second set of tracks, pointing toward the town, and he followed it; probably this was the way the savages had approached.

But soon he discovered they'd turned off, toward a spruce grove. He stopped the big stallion. Maybe the band had lurked in there until the time came to strike. Then his roving glance was diverted by the sheen of sunlight on a bit of metal, and he started toward the grove. The Indians had paused here. Now he grew very alert because he saw two sets of shod hoofs, coming to join the large group. They'd stopped, evidently for a parley, then the shod hoofs and some of the others had entered the grove.

Slingerland dismounted, dropped rein, and began to range about like a hunting dog seeking a scent.

The sun had glinted from a carbine cartridge, carelessly dropped there. Farther in, under the spruces, he came upon the spot where they'd got off their horses. He found a burnt match end in the needles, some indentations where he thought heavy objects had been set down. Slingerland squatted down, minutely examining every foot of the brown-needled ground.

There were a number of moccasin prints, but what most interested him were the high-heel dents; two men in riding boots had met the Indians. Several round marks gave him pause; he finally lay down and sniffed at them. Even with the aromatic scent of the needles he detected the faint odor of coal oil; there had been gallon cans of this set down.

"Huh!" He grunted aloud, pushed back his cap.

He never jumped to conclusions. He picked up his rein and began slowly moving toward the river. The shod hoofs led back that way, but didn't go into the settlement. No, the two on these horses must have sat their saddles for a time, perhaps watching, while the Sioux had crossed and struck in the night.

The needles in the grove and thick grass hadn't clearly retained marks. It wasn't until he reached the softer earth of the river bank that he found what he was hunting. The left forehoof of one horse had a shoe on it which had a slight crack on one side.

He was facing the smoking remains of Wesleyville now, and as he was about to remount and try to pick up

131

the sign of the two who'd been riding animals with shod hoofs, he sighed a saddle brown horse and a second one, a dun, with a lead-rope attached to the brown's horn. They'd been cut off from his range of vision when he'd started through the town because of a blackened house wall.

So he crossed the stream and headed that way. Closer, he noted the long, metal-footed legs of a tripod he recognized as a surveyor's transit in the bulky packs on the dun.

Warren Neale had had such equipment. When he came to the waiting animals, he saw the man huddled on a flat rock near the smoking ruins of the cabin. A woman, scalped, lay dead nearby and not far off were the bodies of two males.

"Hello," sang out Slingerland, but the man on the rock did not even look up.

The trapper dismounted and went to him. The warm breeze caught his flared nostrils, on it the sickening stench of burned flesh, wood, other smoldering things.

"Howdy," he said again.

The man had his face in his hands; he was either sobbing or retching, slim body drawn up in a knot. He wore whipcord pants and high-laced boots, a gray flannel shirt; his hair was auburn under the Army Stetson.

"Mister, who are you?" began Slingerland, reaching down, touching the young fellow's hunched shoulder.

At this, the other looked up, brown eyes dazed; his smooth cheeks and even features were convulsed with grief. "Lee! By golly. It's Lee Davis," cried Slingerland.

Lee Davis shook his head. After a time he said weakly, "My parents—and my only brother—"

132

Slingerland understood. This had been Lee's home. The dead, scarcely recognizable as they had been scalped and partially burned, were the youth's father, mother and elder brother Hal. The trapper was aware Lee had been away at school for two years, that Warren Neale, the engineer who'd helped build the Union Pacific, a close friend of Slingerland's, had taken a fancy to the bright Lee and given the lad money so he could study surveying and other engineering subjects.

Slingerland knelt, put an arm across Davis's shoulders.

"Take it easy, boy. I know it's awful. The Sioux struck last night. Your folks are gone, and you'll have to accept it. Pull yourself together. You'll have to be a man, pick yourself up and keep goin'."

He had a small flask of brandy in a pocket, and passed it to Lee. "Take a swig. It'll brace you. No sense sittin' like this.'

Lee's hand shook violently as he downed a gulp. Slingerland helped him rise and led him to the road. If he could start Davis talking, it might snap him out of his daze. "When'd you get back, Lee? Have you seen Warren Neale? That your rig?"

Davis gulped, but replied. "I reported to Mr. Neale—he gave me a job—survey, branch line—came to see my folks, and—"

"I savvy," nodded Slingerland, as Lee Davis broke off. "It's mighty hard but you're a good fellow. Now, there's lots to be done here. We better ride to Cordell City. We'll need help."

Davis glanced at the flapping buzzards.

"All right," agreed the trapper. We'll plant your people first."

They found two shovels in a partially burned shed out

133

back and set about the unhappy task.

By the time the sun was overhead, the two men, the pack horse coming behind, had crossed the rough trail over the mountain between the long north-south valley where Wesleyville had stood and the next town, Cordell City. From the heights they could see a magnificent sweep, a winding river, high peaks thrusting to an azure sky.

And below stood Cordell City, much larger than Wesleyville. The river was wide and clear, furnishing unlimited water. Cottonwoods and alders lined the banks, though this growth was kept cut near town. The panorama was pleasing, Main Street with stores and saloons, hotels and restaurants, a spacious plaza with a statue marking a watering fountain and a loop of rail-road track hanging from a frame, a sledgehammer by it, so fire alarms could be sounded. Smaller streets right-angled from Main, which bounded the square, the river just beyond. Private homes, smaller establishments, stables, barns and corrals showed. Curls of smoke issued from stone chimneys, as women prepared the noonday meal.

"Doc Cordell did a fine job layin' out this town," said Slingerland. "Most as good as Brigham Young did for Salt Lake City. Now, there's a farsighted hombre if ever there was one!"

Davis was still stricken but was recovering his poise.

"Jake Cordell is *it* here," he agreed. "This is his burg. He owns the Colorado Queen, biggest palace this side of Cheyenne, the best hotel."

"Not to mention the gun shop, handiest livery and top store! What Doc says goes. For an ex-con, he's come up in the world."

"They say he did ten years for armed robbery when

134

he was younger.''

"He did, but he's reformed, and it paid off. He hit it lucky here, settlers flockin' in for land and minin'. But between you'n me, I ain't too fond of Doc. He's too smooth, maybe oily. And I sure don't cotton to that strongarm gunny, George Pate. Cordell met Pate in prison. You must know Doc's son, Joe. He's about your age.''

"Yeah, I know Joe. He's got a mean temper. We tangled a couple of times when we were kids.''

They made rapid time downhill and headed for the closer of the two wide, railed bridges spanning the swift river.

The shale-covered track they'd been following held few impressions, and Slingerland was in a hurry. But as they reached the stream level, they came to softer under-footing, and Slingerland slowed, his gray eyes flicking this way and that.

"Hold on a jiffy, Lee," he said; and swung off the bay, squatted and studied the ground.

"What's up?" inquired Davis.

"Nothin'."

The trapper remounted and they pushed on, the thick planks of the bridge rumbling under the horses' weight.

Slingerland wasn't the sort who went off half-cocked. He kept his hunches to himself till he was sure of what he said.

But he'd found the imprint of a left forehoof with a slight crack on its side.

IV

The buildings were chiefly of wood. There was plenty of timber in the surrounding mountains, and Doc

Cordell's sawmill, powered by a race from the river, did a thriving business.

Slingerland made no attempt to pick up the cracked-shoe print, for there were hundreds of crisscrossing tracks in town as well as wheel marks of buggies and wagons. He knew the trail left by the two riders was many hours old, made during the night. It was impossible to examine the hoofs of every animal, some in corrals or stables, and besides, the unknown men who had rendezvoused with the Indians might have passed on through the settlement.

Most of the structures had been painted neatly. Homes had vegetable and flower gardens, with chicken coops and sheds or stables for horses, cows and goats. Barns held hay cut from the hills, while the feed store stocked oats, barley, wheat and seeds. Both men knew this also belonged to Jake Cordell.

"Yep," said Slingerland, "Cordell owns this burg, even the Law."

Davis knew what he meant. "There goes Stu now, headed for the Queen, Cordell's place."

"He gets free red-eye there. Stu Barrington does what Doc says. 'Course, with George Pate on deck, you won't see any real trouble here. Doc's all for law and order now, and has ordered Pate to plug any cuss who pulls a gun. He had Stu deputize Pate, so there ain't much work for the marshal, except to light the lanterns and sweep out the calaboose once a month. Say, that's a mighty pretty daughter he has!"

His eyes, narrowed to the bright light, flicked to Davis, and he knew he'd made a hit by the way the young fellow reacted. "Yes, that Penny's a beauty," went on Al Slingerland glibly. "Good girl, too, keeps house for her dad and sees to him since her ma died. A

136

shame Stu's a drunkard. Penny deserves better."

Men and women were on the wooden walks and around the stores. Wagons and buggies, saddle animals waited in the street; two cowboys were watering their mustangs at the big stone trough at one side of the square. A stream flowed into this by gravity from a higher elevation upriver, and spilling over, found its way through a narrow ditch back to the creek.

Cordell's Colorado Queen occupied a central position facing the wide plaza, with a magnificent view of the western mountains.

Its veranda was long, built of heavy pine, and there were two sets of batwings, side entries as well. A large sign over the center of the porch roof proclaimed, *The Colorado Queen, Jake Cordell, Prop.*" And another advertised *Finest Brandies and Liquors, Cigars, Dancing, Rooms*.

Davis and the trapper hooked rein over the continuous rail which kept horses from encroaching on the sidewalk, and stepping to the veranda, pushed through the nearer batwings. A smell of damp sawdust, whiskey, and tobacco smoke greeted them.

On the right was a long bar, large mirrors behind it with an array of bottles, glasses, boxes of cigars and plug tobacco. Two bartenders were on duty. Marshall Barrington was draining a tumbler of whiskey. He was stocky, vest loose over a flannel shirt, tucked into leather pants, half boots with runover heels, a sand-hued Stetson shoved back on his head. He was about fifty but drink was showing its effect. His unshaven jaws sagged and his nose was swollen, crisscrossed by tiny broken blood vessels. His deepset eyes were darkly underlined, his hair shot with white streaks. Seeing the newcomers in the mirror, he raised a fat hand but didn't turn around.

Several other men bellied to the bar. Damp sawdust had been freshly sprinkled. The hanging oil lamps and cuspidors were polished brass. A piano stood against the wall by a dance floor ringed with tables, but it was too early for the saloon girls to be one call. A free-lunch counter was laden with slabs of roast beef, hams, cheeses and breads, pickles, pretzels and other goodies.

The walls were sanded hardwoods, the chair, tables and such appointments the best that could be imported via the Union Pacific. Cheyenne was a station on the U.P., and within wagon haul of Cordell City, though there were steep mountains between. Past the dance space was a section dedicated to games of fhance: roulette, bird cage, dice, poker and monte tables, while in the rear were private rooms.

A lean man who had been dealing cold stud hands at a table got up and shoved back his chair. Large-boned shoulders pushed out his black silk shirt. His face was craggy, cheekbones high, long legs in dark pants tucked into halfboots decorated with the red lone star of Texas. His hair gleamed with pomade. A .45 Colt revolver rode in an oiled, open holster at one bony hip; the smooth-grained walnut stock and polished metal showed it was meticulously kept, a professional's weapon. He yawned, set his straight-brimmed black hat on his head, and sauntered toward the bar.

"Howdy, Slingerland. Howdy, Davis. Ain't seen either of you for a coon's age." His eyes were pale-blue, icy, a gun-fighter's orbs.

"Hello, Pate," nodded Slingerland. "Lee just got home from school. He's doin' a surveyin' job for Warren Neale."

"I hear a branch line's to be run from Cheyenne to Denver."

"Sure, Lee's on that. When he stopped to see his folks in Wesleyville, he found the settlement wiped out. Sioux, from the sign. His father, mother and brother scalped, dead, and not one sould left alive in the town."

"No!" Pate cleared his throat and the pale eyes shifted off the trapper's. "Cussed redskins are on the prod. Wipe 'em out, I say."

"We're here to see Doc. Men are needed over there."

"He's in back, eatin' dinner. C'mon."

Pate led them through a hall to a spacious salon. Two figures sat at a table laden with viands. One was slim, with curly hair, about Lee Davis's age; the other was about 45 and heavier. The latter was Jake "Doc" Cordell.

"Come in, gents," cried Cordell. "Siddown, have a bite."

Pate and the visitors took chairs. The boss of Cordell City beamed at his guests. His belly pushed out an expensive fawn-skin vest crossed by a thick gold watch chain from which hung an elk's-tooth fob. The hair on his large head was thinning and he kept it brushed across his pate to hide his balding. He was smooth-shaven; large ears stuck out, and the pointed nose was an acquisitive one over his tight-lipped mouth. The jaw was stubborn.

Al Slingerland and Lee Davis were hungry and helped themselves to the platters Cordell pushed at them, urging them to stoke up. Slingerland knew Doc Cordell had spent time in Leavenworth, but many others had come West for a new start. If a fellow behaved himself, the past would be forgotten.

"A horrible thing has happened, Mr. Cordell," began Davis. He'd taken a drink and begun to eat, but his mind was filled with the terrible tragedy. He described what he'd found in his home town.

"Why, that's awful, awful!" Doc Cordell acted appalled. "You ever hear the like, Pate? The whole settlement wiped out!"

"Mighty bad, Chief," agreed Pate. One pale eye fluttered.

"We need a crew to hustle over, bury the bodies and clean up Doc," said Slingerland. "The coyotes and wolves'll be in at dark."

"Right. I'll send a gang over pronto. See to it, George, and make sure they got plenty of shovels and all for the job."

Pate nodded, rose, glided soundlessly off.

Slingerland was watching Cordell's muddy eyes, seamed by crow's-feet at the corners.

Joe Cordell hadn't said a word except to mutter a greeting when they came in. When Slingerland glanced suddenly at him, Joe Cordell looked down at his plate. The trapper had a queer sensation. Nothing he could define; it was just a vague, uneasy feeling.

Doc Cordell was saying, "Look, Al, why don't you sell your pelts to me?"

"Well, Wesleyville was closer, and then, old Ed Turner and I were pards a good many years. But Ed's done in; his place was burned to ashes last night. I saw his scalped body when I rode by."

"Fetch 'em here. I'll pay you top prices."

"Maybe I will, at that." Slingerland knew Doc Cordell would have given more than Turner, who had had only a small turnover, but he'd never cottoned to Doc Cordell. He'd take his pelts to Cheyenne, though it

140

was much farther away than Cordell City. However, he saw no use in making an enemy of Cordell over this, at the moment.

"Reckon I'll step outside for a breath," said Joe Cordell, and as he rose, Slingerland saw a bandage on his left hand.

"Hurt your paw, Joe?" he asked.

"He ain't learned yet not to pick up a hot horseshoe," said Doc Cordell, a hint of sarcasm in his deep voice.

Joe Cordell said nothing but went out. Doc Cordell passed around cigars and lit one for himself.

"Warren Neale sent you off to college, Lee," he remarked. "You aim to work for him?"

"He already is," said Slingerland. "Lee's surveyin' the line from the U.P. south to Denver."

Cordell's broad face wreathed in a grin. "Why, that's great, son! Glad to hear it. You ought to run through this town. The territory's growin' fast, with stockmen, grangers, miners and all. Cordell City would be an ideal point for a station and railroad shops, too. We're ready to accommodate as many as come along."

Lee Davis's clear eyes fixed Cordell. "It would be, sir, but for the mountains hemmin' it in. The grades would be too steep, and far too many. Besides that, there are bottomless quicksands in the rivers just where we'd need to cross. I know all this terrain, which is one reason Mr. Neale picked me for the job."

Cordell stopped smiling, "Shucks, a top engineer like you could beat such small obstacles, Lee."

"They ain't so small. Mr. Neale knows that. You see, that valley Wesleyville is—was in—is unusual. It runs north-south for almost fifty miles and Mr. Neale aimed to locate the shops there, in my old town."

"But Wesleyville's done for, wiped out, boy."

Lee Davis shook his head. "I'll have to see what Mr. Neale says."

"You do that. And be sure to tell him I'll give the railroad free land for their shops."

Cordell was insistent, pressing, and Davis said uneasily. "I'm upset on account of my folks, Mr. Cordell. I'll think it over. Right now I am to see Penny Barrington."

"Sure, sure." Cordell smiled. "You're a fine boy, Lee, I always said so. Penny's growed up lately; she's a beauty. My Joe's chasin' her himself! Well, we'll talk more later. Don't you leave town without seein' me again."

"I won't. And thanks."

Slingerland and Davis went out to the sunlit main way. A bunch of riders were heading west across the lower ridge, leading pack animals with shovels, picks and other gear on them. This would be the crew on its way to the grisly task of cleaning up Wesleyville. Slingerland didn't see George Pate among them but there were several others he knew.

"I aim to buy something for Penny, Al."

"Good idea." Flower was on the trapper's mind, and he decided to pick up gifts that might please her.

Mounting, they rode over to Cordell's general store, Davis' pack horse bobbing behind. Inside, Davis bought a *Godey's Lady's Book*, a necklace, a box of sweets. "Al, if Penny asks me, I'll stay for supper. Maybe I'll spend the night in town. I told Doc Cordell I'd talk more with him 'fore I left. Tomorrow I'll head back to Cheyenne from here and see how the route looks. I know a lot more than I used to and will check it all out."

"*Bueno*, Lee. Long as you're okay, I'll mosey on home."

He hadn't mentioned Flower to Davis or to anyone else. It was safer to keep such information to himself.

Lee Davis thanked him deeply, and took his leave. Slingerland watched from a window as Davis mounted and rode off toward the north end of town, the pack horse trotting behind.

Slingerland spent some time in the emporium, choosing items he thought Flower would enjoy, a swatch of bright cloth, a small sewing kit, pretty beads he knew Indian girls fancied.

V

Stu Barrington's small cabin stood off by itself; the paint on the walls was peeling. There was a garden, probably planted by Penny. Chickens clucked in a pen; the stable door sagged on leather hinges, wide open. The marshal would have ridden to work.

Davis secured his horses to a post near the rear stoop. He could hear a woman singing in the kitchen. Taking his packages, he rapped on the back door. Penny Barrington opened up, and stared up at him for a moment; she cried, "Oh, Lee! Come in." There was a lilt of delight in her voice.

"Penny, I can't tell you how happy I am to see you!" he told her.

As a virile young male would, Lee Davis couldn't help appraising the lovely girl. She took off her apron, smoothing back her golden hair, pinned on her trim head. She had matured since Davis had last seen her, and as all said, she was a beauty, brown eyes sparkling, full red lips inviting, swelling bosoms pushing out her blouse.

"Sit down, Lee. I'll fetch you a bite."

"I ate at Cordell's. I'd rather sit and look at you."

She dropped her eyes, but smiled, apparently pleased. "Well, shall we go into the parlor?"

"Let's stay here, it's homey. I fetched these for you." He pushed the parcels toward her.

She exclaimed with pleasure over the gifts. "You shouldn't have spent so much, Lee."

"I've a good job, surveyin' for Warren Neale."

They sat together and he told her about Wesleyville. Tears sprang to her eyes and impulsively she patted his hand. "I'm sorry Lee. This is terrible for you." She watched him anxiously.

"It hit me mighty hard. But the hope of seeing you held me up, Penny. I got your letters."

"I've kept every one you wrote me, Lee."

Davis seized her hand; he pushed on faster than he might have, had he not been away so long. Over and over, he'd thought of what he would do when he returned to her.

"Penny, I worked mighty hard at school. There were other girls but I never saw one like you. You been in my mind day and night. I love you. Will you marry me?" He almost blurted it out, he'd rehearsed it so often.

And then she was in his arms, and he was kissing her soft lips, pressing her body tightly to him.

After a time, he felt in his pocket and brought out the ring. "I bought it in Cheyenne, Penny. It ain't as big a diamond as you deserve, but later I'll get you another."

She smiled, holding out her left hand, and he sipped the ring on her finger; she gazed at it delightedly. "It's beautiful, Lee!"

The time flew magically by as the two lovers planned

for their future together. "I'm worried about my father, Lee. I take care of him, you know. And he won't quit drinking. I must tell you this, that Joe Cordell has asked me to marry him, again and again. He just won't take no for an answer. Be careful of him, will you? He has a hot temper."

"I know that, Penny. I'm not afraid of him, though."

"Joe will make Doc fire my Dad when he hears you and I are engaged, I'm sure. Joe says if he can't have me, nobody else can, either. He's a lot tougher than he used to be, Lee. He hangs around with that awful George Pate, I—I don't know what my father will do if he loses his job."

Davis took her in his arms, saying, "My work means we'll travel a lot, Penny. We'll live in Cheyenne till this branch line is finished; then Mr. Neale may send me way off, and I'll sure take you with me. But I promise your dad will be taken care of; I can afford to pay his expenses somewhere."

This was a great relief to her. Later, she asked him to stay for supper, when Barrington would be home and they would break the news.

"I sure will, Penny. Now, I promised to see Doc Cordell again before I left town. But I won't be gone long."

"You go ahead, then, but hurry back. Dad killed a chicken this morning and I need to pluck it and get things ready."

After leaving the store with the things he'd bought for Flower, Al Slingerland rode his bay stallion to the livery near the Queen. Nest to it was a blacksmith's, and the sound of a hammer clanging on iron came from the forge.

The bay needed a rubdown, and a grain feed, before starting the run back across the mountain. Slingerland unsaddled him and removed the blanket pad, examining the animal's sleek back carefully, as was his wont. There was a slight rub and he smeared some dope on it to keep it from getting any worse. He paid fifty cents for a nose-bag of oats, and while the bay was eating, stepped over to the open door of the smithy.

As he stepped in, the familiar odor of smoking hoofs, seared as the hot shoes were pressed home, greeted his nostrils. A hammer clanged. The blacksmith, torso naked except for the leather protective apron, was driving fresh nails into a shoe he'd just set on the rear hoof of a draft horse.

The man was a friend. For a time, the blacksmith had tried trapping before he'd gone to work for Doc Cordell. He was a burly fellow, with a wiry black beard and tousled hair, great muscles standing out in his arms.

He had nails in his mouth so he nodded at Slingerland. The trapper waved back, and looked around as he waited. There was a small heap of discarded horseshoes nearby, and Slingerland, who seldom missed small details, glanced at them idly.

He suddenly became interested, and stooping, picked up a shoe which had a bad crack on one side. The split was wider than that in the left forehoof he'd come on close to Wesleyville and again on the river bank outside Cordell City. But it was in the same place. There was a pebbled wedged in the crak; that would have caused the metal to keep on splitting when the horse's weight was on it, as the hard little stone worked farther and farther in.

Slingerland waited, with a purpose now. In a few

minutes Vince Farley, the blacksmith, finished the docile draft animal and tied him near the front door to wait fo rhis owner to claim him. He wiped sweat from his brow with the hairy back of his brawny arm and grinned through is beard as he came to shake hands with Slingerland.

"You old so-and-so!" he swore affectionately. "What fetches you over this way? Ain't seen you for a year."

"I been busy, Vince. I just rode over today with Lee Davis. You heard about Wesleyville, I reckon."

Farley had. The news had spread quickly through town. He shifted his cud and spat a brown stream of tobacco juice at a corner, swearing a blue streak as he vented his opinion of the Sioux.

Slingerland held up the cracked shoe and asked casually, "Horse go lame?"

"Sure it went lame! I don't think much of a man who stays on a horse when it begins limpin'." Farley cursed again. "Lucky the sprain ain't bad. In a week or two, if that gelding's rested, he'll be good as new. Doc's young whelp is stupid; danged if he didn't grab holt of a shoe while it was still smokin'!"

Slingerland didn't have to ask questions, for Farley was telling him what he wanted to know. "You mean Joe Cordell?"

"Sure. He thinks he's Gawdamighty 'cause his pop's top dog here. Well, I told Doc he spoiled Joe, rotten-spoiled, that's what!" Joe Cordell had irritated Farley and he was letting off steam. "So he busts in 'fore I even had my fire up and orders me to hustle and take care of that pet pinto of his'n. He don't like to ride anything else. Told him to keep his pants on, and he give me lip, said he'd have his old man discharge me!"

"Early this morning', eh? He must've been out last night."

"Yeah. Chasin' some female, I reckon. He's been after Stu's daughter, but that don't stop him from buzzin' around other gals like a fly after honey. So when I warned him not to use the pinto till the leg was sound, he called me a liar. I near took my sledge to him! But finally he said he'd let the pore critter rest up."

"Was Joe out alone last night?"

"Dunno. But I think he was with George Pate. The young jackass follers that gunny around like a cussed hound dawg."

Farley hadn't the slightest idea of what grave information he'd given Slingerland, who showed no sign of his inner thoughts as he tossed the cracked shoe back onto the pile. After telling the blacksmith about what luck he'd had in trapping, Slingerland took leave of his friend.

The fact that Joe Cordell, and probably George Pate, had been the two who'd armed the Indians outside Wesleyville, was a soul-chilling, horrible thing. Slingerland felt he must think it over most carefully before taking any action. He couldn't make any accusation on the slight clue he'd uncovered. It was his word against young Cordell's and Pate's, and the trapper knew he'd never get out of Cordell City alive if he even hinted at his suspicions. The motive certainly wasn't clear to him as to why the pair might have done such a ghastly thing which had resulted in the death of many men, women and children and left Wesleyville a smoking ruins.

Bearded face set, keen gray eyes slitted, he strolled back to the livery and called the wrangler.

"I won't be ridin' out for a while, Billy. Turn my

horse into the corral and pitch in some hay." He stowed the presents for Flower in his blanket roll, leaving it with his saddle gear, and went into the main street.

People were around, at the stores; a few dedicated drinkers were in the saloons. Slingerland took a chair at the end of the Queen's long veranda and filled his pipe, lit up, leaned back, his mind busy with what he'd uncovered. He could hardly go to Cordell with such deadly accusations against Doc's only son.

He was puzzled. While Joe Cordell was mean of temper and unpredictable, why should he arm a band of savages and egg them on to wipe out Wesleyville? Then he recalled that George Pate had probably been along; the Texas killer would think nothing of instigating such a massacre if there was profit in it for him. Suffering and death for others wouldn't bother Pate.

Yet Pate was Doc Cordell's chief of staff. Would he carry out such a grave enterprise without Cordell's consent?

Slingerland shook his head. He was up against the same problem: why would Doc Cordell want Wesleyville obliterated?

His brown study was interrupted as Lee Davis rode up on his brown gelding and got down at the Queen. He didn't have the dun and his gear with him. Seeing Slingerland, he hurried to him, crying, "Al, congratulate me! Penny says she'll marry me!"

"Great," said Al, slapping him on the back.

"I'm goin' in to see Doc Cordell as I promised. Then I'll have supper with Penny. I left my pack horse at her place."

Slingerland was relieved to see the youth cheerier, after the awful shock Lee had experienced. He watched Davis enter the Queen, and then resumed his seat, sucking on a cold pipe.

An hour later, the surveyor emerged. Davis almost ran to his horse, and he jumped aboard without touching the stirrup. He didn't seem even to see Slingerland, and the trapper thought his face was set, red with some inner emotion. Lee Davis rode swiftly away.

Davis was out of sight when the batwings down the porch banged open and Joe Cordell catapulted out. Doc's son looked infuriated, also, as had Lee Davis. He was flushed, and his lips writhed as he cursed. Apparently he didn't notice Slingerland hunched in a chair down the veranda, but stepped into the gutter, staring in the direction Lee Davis had taken. His fists were clenched and he was breathing hard.

Finally he swung, muttering to himself. He scowled at the trapper but gave no sign of recognition as he went back inside.

Interested in this exhibition, Slingerland rose and peeked over the nearer batwings. Joe Cordell was at the bar and began talking animatedly with Stu Barrington. The marshal heard him out, then shrugged and spread his hands in the classic gesture of impotence. This disgusted Joe Cordell, who waved the officer off, looking as though he'd whiffed a rotten fish. Cordell crossed the big saloon to a table where George Pate sat, playing solitaire.

Intrigued, Slingerland watched. Pate listened to Joe Cordell who was obviously making an impassioned plea. The gun boss shook his head, but as Joe Cordell argued on, Pate finally seemed to agree, for he nodded. Joe Cordell sat down beside his mentor, and for several minutes the pair spoke earnestly together. Then the younger Cordell left Pate and disappeared through a corridor to the rear of the big structure, where he had his quarters. Pate resumed his game.

Slingerland strode down the long porch and entered the other batwings which were nearer the bar. He shuffled up beside Barrington. "Howdy, Stu, glad to see you."

Barrington turned bleary, worried eyes on him.

"Howdy, Al," he said, dispiritedly, and downed a swig of redeye.

A bartender came up and Slingerland ordered a beer. "Say, Joe Cordell looks peaked. You reckon the whippersnapper's sick?"

The marshal slowly shook his head. "Well, no, not exactly. But he just now heard my Penny aims to hitch up with Lee Davis. What can I do? I can't stop her. She's got a mind of her own, like her maw had. Scolds me all the time 'cause I take a snifter or two, till I wonder who wears the pants in my own home!"

The marshal was aggrieved, but was afraid of losing his job. Joe Cordell might prevail on his father to fire Barrington, and Stu was voicing his anxiety.

"See," he continued, "Joe's been stuck on Penny a long while but she won't have him. I've begged her to take him, but she says she'd rather be dead. I'm done for, I reckon. If Doc takes away my badge, I'll starve." He was wallowing in his misery. Pouring another three fingers, he tossed it off at a gulp.

Lee Davis must have told Jake Cordell of his engagement to Penny. After the young surveyor had left, the father had passed on the tidings to his son.

Joe Cordell's violent temper was notorious. He considered himself the crown prince of the Cordell empire, and he wasn't used to being balked.

And Joe Cordell had enlisted George Pate in the deal. Much as Slingerland yearned to get back to Mountain

151

Flower, he couldn't leave Davis in the lurch. He could only conclude that Joe Cordell, infuriated at losing Penny, had talked George Pate into some plan to get rid of Lee.

And if, as Slingerland suspected, the two had sparked the Wesleyville massacre, one more killing would mean nothing to them. The hot-tempered Joe Cordell would revel in his rival's death.

VI

So Slingerland hung around, trying to make himself inconspicuous, until dark. Marshall Barrington touched off the street lanterns with a taper attached to a long stick and then rode off home to supper.

The town picked up steam. The day's work done, men flocked to the Queen. Music could be heard. Saloon girls and dealers, other employes had come on duty. Saddle horses and buggies crowded the hitch rails. Stores had been shuttered for the night. A cool west wind sprang up, blowing over the river from the mountains, and myriad insects piped in the brush along the stream; moths and smaller flying things circled thickly around the yellow lights hanging from their posts beside the street.

Slingerland was devoted to Warren Neale and his wife, Allie, whom he'd helped so much in the U.P. Trail, when Neale had solved knotty engineering problems for the transcontinental road. And Lee Davis was Neale's protege. Besides this, the kind-hearted trapper liked the young surveyor, and was sorry for him because of the terrible tragedy which had struck him when the Davis family had been killed in Wesleyville.

Yet there was more to it, something bigger than Lee's

152

personal fate. Slingerland had grown convinced that George Pate would not have armed the Sioux and set them upon Wesleyville without Doc Cordell's consent. He felt compelled to check this out.

He kept peeking in over the batwings at Pate, who stood at the lower end of the long bar. Joe Cordell wasn't in sight but he was probably eating dinner in back with his father. The way Joe had acted up that afternoon, after Davis had left the Queen, forced Slingerland to believe he'd enlisted George Pate in some scheme to dispose of his rival for Penny's hand. Pate had agreed to whatever it was Joe Cordell had suggested.

It was time to make ready. Slingerland's long legs took him quickly back to the corral in which his bay stallion was penned. The horse scented his friend, whinned and trotted to the gate. Slingerland led him out, closed the barrier so other animals couldn't follow.

There were lanterns around, and some light from the rear windows. The trapper belted on the blanket, and setting his high-pronged saddle, tightened the cinches carefully. Due to the presents he'd bought for Flower, the roll was a bit bulky but wouldn't bother him in riding. As was his habit, he checked his carbine and the heavy Creedmore, made sure his Colt was loaded, that his long shining knife was in its sheath at his hip. Leaving the rifles in their boots, he led the bay off behind a barn, tethering him in dense shadow.

Returning to his watch, he waited around. Pate was still at the bar. Slingerland had an Indian's patience. At last, this was rewarded as Joe Cordell came from the back of the roomy building and skirted the dance floor.

Joe Cordell joined George Pate, who signaled. Two men in cowboy garb got up from a table and slouched

153

over. Slinglerland knew one, Lew Ince, as a tough who rode for Pate; the second would be a new member of the Texan's killer gang.

Pate led the way to a rear corridor, trailed by Joe Cordell and the two gunnies.

Convinced his diagnosis had been correct, Slingerland loped back to Tin Can Alley. A brass lantern burned over the Queen's rear exit.

Crouched in shadow, the trapper watched the quartet emerge and cross the alley to the stable. Music and voices from the front of the Colorado Queen came to him, but he could hear the four talking together as they saddled up.

They brought out their mounts, got aboard and started off, swinging through a lane to the plaza.

Slingerland took his time. He knew exactly where they were headed. He picked up Reddy, his bay stud, and let the four have a long start so they wouldn't see him as he trailed.

He hit the north road. Dust still hung in the air, raised by the riders ahead. Cabins along the way were lighted, families in them enjoying the evening meal.

He soon left the beaten track and made a wide circle. There, from a rise, he watched the four horsemen dismount well out from Stu Barrington's little house. One man stayed behind, holding the mounts. Slingerland glimpsed three stealthy figures flitting to the rear of Barrington's. The moon was up and there was enough light to glint on the barrels of their carbines.

He untied his bandanna and knotted it around the bay's snout, so his pet wouldn't sound off. Reddy would sometimes whinny to him if left for a time.

In Barrington's back yard was a post with a flickering lantern hanging from it, and the kitchen windows were lighted. A saddled horse waited by the rear stoop.

Before long the stocky marshal came forth and mounted his plug. Barrington rode off, headed back for the center of town and the Colorado Queen, where he would hang around and drink until late in the night.

Tethered outside the stable were Lee Davis's brown and the dun pack horse. Davis had unsaddled them, relieving them of their loads as they waited; he would have watered and fed them before going into the cabin.

Slingerland went way around and tethered the bay in darkness near a pine grove. He left the heavy Sharps, but took his repeating carbine with extra loads he shoved into his pockets. Stealthy and silent as a stalking Indian, he kept low, always in shadow, and approached the Barrington yard.

A thick spruce grew several yards out from the perimeter of light cast by the post lantern. Slingerland bellied the last stretch of its protective cover, and flattened out, the carbine laid in front of him.

The armed trio had also hidden themselves. With inexhaustible patience, Al Slingerland watched. Again this paid off. Men waiting under such conditions would shift slightly to ease cramped muscles, or from boredom. He finally caught a faint glint on the far side of the yard; that would mark one. In a few minutes, a second moved a bit, and at last, the third. Now Slingerland had all three positions marked in his mind.

They evidently didn't believe Lee Davis would remain here overnight.

And they were right about this. About an hour after Barrington had left, the kitchen door opened. Slingerland saw Penny's feminine figure, and Lee's taller one. Davis kissed her, held her for a time, and the girl stood in the lighted doorway, watching as her sweetheart

155

started outside, meaning to pick up his horses. Slingerland figured Davis would ride north, in the moonlight, for a time, then camp on his way back to Cheyenne, where he would report to Warren Neale.

But the trapper no longer watched Davis and the doorway, where Penny stood. He raised his carbine, a cartridge in its breech, ready to fire. And a breath later, he caught the telltale glint as one of the three threw his rifle into position, then a second and a third—

Slingerland opened fire, aiming at the points he'd spotted. His carbine crackled, once, twice, three times, as he moved his accurate rifle. Somebody over there screeched; a gun flamed from the brush but Slingerland could tell by the flash it was high, thrown off as he dusted them, peppering them as fast as he could shoot.

Penny screamed, and Lee Davis, frozen for an instant in his tracks, turned and ran back inside, slamming the door.

A high-pitched wail sounded. "I'm hit—I'm hit—my face—" Slingerland thought it was Joe Cordell's voice.

As he ceased firing and rapidly reloaded, a hoarse order rang out from the ambushers' spot.

"Hustle, get on back, you fools!" That must be Pate, Slingerland decided.

They were running for it. Slingerland glimpsed three figures, one staggering, the other pair close together; maybe a wounded man was being supported by another. Slingerland let them go. They reached their horses and climbed aboard, and he heard the beat of hoofs as the four, including the holder, retreated back to town.

When he was sure they were gone, Slingerland loped to the kitchen door. "Lee—Penny!" he called, softly but urgently. "It's Al Slingerland. Open up, pronto."

After a moment the door was unbolted and pulled

back a few inches; Davis peeked out. "That you, Al?"

"Sure." He shoved inside. Penny stood, eyes wide, frightened, a hand on her sweetheart's arm.

They watched the trapper's bearded face as he said grimly, "Get away fast as you can. Take Penny with you if you want to see her again, Lee. Pate and Joe Cordell just tried to drygulch you."

"I was afraid something like this would happen," Penny said to Slingerland. "Joe's made threats."

"This is Doc Cordell's town. He'll cover his son."

Davis seemed hesitant. "But it's dark, Al, and Penny can't very well—"

Slingerland broke in, "There's no time to talk, Lee. George Pate won't give up so easy. He'll be back in a jiffy with a big enough crew to do the job. I know that Texas gunny!"

"What should we do?" asked the girl.

"You grab a few things you need, Penny. Lee, leave your gear. Penny can ride your pack horse."

"I—I have only one saddle. I don't see how Penny can—"

"There's an old one of father's in the stable," the girl said quickly. "I'll get ready."

"Good girl," said Slingerland. Sometimes, he thought, a woman saw things quicker than a man did.

"I'll put on Levis, and ride astride. I'll be there by the time you've saddled up." The girl turned and ran into the other room.

"Hustle, Lee. Pate'll be back and this time we can't beat him off. He's got a dozen gunnies workin' for him."

The two men hurried outside, and Al Slingerland found the old saddle on a wooden peg inside the stable. Davis had his brown gelding ready, and the two cinched

157

Barrington's worn saddle on the dun. The pack horse wasn't made for speed; he was sturdy but no runner.

Penny ran out, carrying a small bundle, and Davis helped her mount; the tight Levis accentuated her rounded feminine thighs.

"Listen, Lee! Now, you can't go through town, they'll spot you sure. Hit the track north, this side of the river. You savvy this country. When you reach Beaver Ford, five miles upstream, cross there and go over the mountain, and get on the Cheyenne road in the Wesleyville valley. Neale and Allie'll shelter you. Do like I say. Don't turn off course."

"Ain't you coming?" asked Davis.

"Never mind me. I'll take care of myself. Ride fast as you can and don't stop 'less you have to."

Slingerland watched the lovers start for the wagon road winding northward. The moon was rising, well up over the brooding heights.

When he was sure the two were on their way, Al Slingerland hurried into the house, loped to the parlor and bolted the front door. Back in the kitchen, he turned the lamp down but left it burning, shot the bolt on the kitchen door and eased out a side window, shutting it after him. He trotted to the point where he'd left his horse.

He shoved his carbine into its boot and removed the bandanna muzzle; the bay stallion sniffed and nuzzled his big hand. Swinging a long leg over his mount, he rode off but pulled up after a short run, and turned to wait on a wooded rise from which he could look back and watch Barrington's.

Cordell City's glow dominated the south sky as he sat his saddle in the darkness. It wasn't long befor ehe saw his conclusion verified. Horsemen's figures showed, hurrying from town, sifting around Barrington's house. From this distance, he couldn't tell exactly how many there were, and was unable to identify individuals, but he was sure George Pate was the leader, and the other were his gunslingers.

A faint grin touched his bearded lips as he observed the stealthy, careful approach as Pate threw a death cordon around the place. Pate was taking no chances this time; the Texas killer knew very well he'd been made a jackass of, and such a man had his pride. It was an evil pride, perhaps, with the overweening ego of a notorious gun boss.

Slingerland patted his handsome bay's neck.

"Look at 'em, Reddy," he murmured, chuckling. "It's perfect! That is, if there was anybody inside!"

The bay rippled his hide; he liked it when the trapper talked to him.

Pate had left the mounts back in shadow. Afoot, the armed stalkers flitted around, trying the doors, finding them locked.

Slingerland had figured on this. It would give Lee Davis and Penny a few minutes start on their desperate night run. The trapper was aware that Pate's string of horses consisted only of the fastest, best mounts available. Davis' pack horse, even his riding critter, couldn't outdistance such runners. The bay stallion was probably superior to them, but that was a question only a race could settle.

Noises came from town, strains of music, a whoopee now and again as some over-exhilarated drunk sounded off, dimmed by distance.

Next there was an interval; Slingerland figured they were consulting with Pate on what to do, as the entrances were bolted. He knew that they'd finally get in

159

through a window; that was obvious. Pate would also check the point from which Slingerland had fired his shots; the flashes of the carbine would have marked the spruce for that.

He allowed a few more minutes; they'd search the house carefully, hoping to root out Davis and Penny.

Failing to find them, Pate would make sure Davis's horses were gone, too. Then he'd start after them, aware they could have gone only one way, northward. Had they passed through the settlement, they'd have been seen, and rugged mountains loomed to the west and east, impassable to riders and difficult even for a man afoot. Only a few steep paths could be used to cross over to the long valley in which Wesleyville had stood.

Slingerland did not underestimate George Pate. He was well aware the Texas was a master tracker, as trained and keen as Slingerland and most Indians were.

Feeling he'd stayed there long enough, he rode down the slope and sat his saddle at the edge of the road, silver moonlight slanting down on the rutted way.

To the west lay the deep, swift river, the serrated black shapes of cottonwoods and brush outlining its course. Across it was a high, rocky ridge. Familiar with the terrain, for he'd hunted and trapped all through it, he was aware that not far above Beaver Ford the vale came to an abrupt end, a mountain blocking off the route to Cheyenne. The wagon road climbed it by switchbacks, a slow, difficult feat, while the river cut through a deep gorge with perpendicular granite walls, then, on the other flank, in a dip between heights, the stream widened in a swale abounding with quicksand. To cross the swamp a corduroy road of rocks and great tree trunks had been laid over which sturdy freight

160

wagons and horses could maneuver.

He drew his carbine, making sure a cartridge was in the firing chamber, eased one leg up, staring intently at the moonlit road.

He heard them before he saw them. Swinging the bay, he trotted to a bend where the track veered with the winding river's course. Again he pulled up. They were coming fast, for Pate would be sure the fugitives were ahead, though he wasn't aware Slingerland was in between.

Here they came, two-by-two, low over the withers of their swift mustangs, ready for a fast run and certain of success.

He raised the carbine and threw two shots close to the van. The leaders, hearing the vicious whine of the bullets, jerked hard on their resins, turning off into the brush. Moments later a mass volley ripped the space where they'd noted the rifle flashes, but Slingerland was galloping toward the next turn.

But they wouldn't know he'd shifted, and would work around to make sure the drygulcher wasn't still there. So he'd gained a few more minutes for Penny and Lee.

When they finally came out they moved slower and more carefully, in a single file, a man out front with carbine at the ready. Slingerland let go, a couple, but did not linger, for they were on the prod and instantly replied.

It was expert delaying tactics. Of course, there was always a chance one of the blind bullets would find either Slingerland or the bay, in which case that would spell the end for the trapper and no doubt for Lee Davis and his sweetheart.

VII

Slingerland bedeviled them for five miles but George Pate doggedly hung on.

The road was now close to the river and he heard the low sound of rapids. Beaver Ford was an upthrust of hard rock where the stream shallowed and widened. There were quicksands at either side, and he put the bay carefully into the hock-deep, swift current. A wooded mountain loomed over there but he could make out the break marking the west gap and kept the stallion directed toward it.

Davis and Penny must have come this way had they obeyed his directions, as he was sure they would. He knew this trail over the mountain wall wasn't as easy as the one he and Davis had followed from Wesleyville to Cordell City; wheeled vehicles couldn't negotiate it, and it was hard even for horses or mules, slow going.

He started up the narrow, shale-strewn path, the stallion straining at the grade, pebbles sliding under his digging hoofs. When he'd made enough headway, he dismounted and stood, rein in hand, looking down at the moonlit crossing.

Before long, the pursuers began splashing over; and as the next fifty yards was unusually steep, Al Slingerland led his horse. Pausing, listening, he heard them coming, stones rattling down as they were disturbed. He couldn't see much now but fired several shots back blindly to give them pause.

He was near the summit when the trail passed between two brutal granite shoulders which almost closed it in. He led the bay through the gap, and tethered him to a stubby spruce. Taking his carbine, he returned to the gap and crouched at one side, listening, watching.

After a while the first one arrived, a dark blob against the sky. The gunny was leading his mustang, straining up the slope. Slingerland opened fire, and the man uttered a high-pitched shriek and fell down. The others behind him began shouting, hurriedly throwing lead at him. The metal slugs spattered against the stones, breaking off bits that sounded like hail.

He knew they'd have a tough time working around behind him, even on foot. Still, it could be done, and Pate would try.

Then he had an idea. There were some large, roundish boulders close at hand, poised on the shale. He couldn't possibly lift them, but by putting his shoulders to a couple, managed to start them rolling. They were stopped short by the narrow slot, and he pushed down as many as he could, forming a crude barrier, blocking the trail.

Eventually, Pate's boys would clear the way, but that would take an hour, anyhow; they wouldn't keep coming without their horses.

He led the stallion over the summit, hit leather, and started down the western slope into the next valley, sure he'd gained the time Davis and Penny needed to escape.

From a low rise, the exhausted Lee Davis and Penny Barrington looked ahead over the endless, dusty plain on which Cheyenne stood. The sun had risen an hour before and was beginning to heat the air.

Davis glanced at his sweetheart. During the hard, frightening night ride, the young woman hadn't uttered a word of complaint. He could see she was suffering, that she was completely drained. Lather had dried on the horses and the animals were almost completely played out.

"We'll be at Warren Neale's in half an hour, Penny. Hold on."

She tried to smile at him. Her face was drawn, caked with fine dust, her hair matted to her head.

North of the U.P. tracks, a wood-burning locomotive with a brass bell stack puffed toward Cheyenne station, drawing a long string of freight and cattle cars. Cheyenne really owed its existence now to the railroad; it was said to be a God-forsaken, God-forgotten place. Uneven lines of frame houses and shanties, some painted a glaring white, other unpainted, sheltered the permanent population of some 5000 souls. Some of these "souls" were white enough but many were evil, for the scum of advancing civilization had flocked in, rowdies and desperadoes. Stabbings and shoots were a commonplace. A vigilante committee had been organized recently to try and stem the violence. Several outlaws had been strung up.

Few homes had gardens or even trees by them; huge rubbish heaps, some as high as the buildings, were everywhere. In the distance a cattle herd was being held on the outskirts of the town, and there were numerous freight wagons. Far off, three peaks like immense teeth thrust to the sky.

Neale's ranch stood on the southern edge of the city. It was built of mountain timber, chinked logs, with two stone chimneys. There was a stable, beyond this a hay barn for the few cattle and horses the engineer kept. Allie had chickens and geese, a milch cow. Neal had his office in his home; he was very busy now with his work.

Smoke came from the kitchen chimney. The couple

had two children, a girl about three, a baby boy starting to toddle.

As the bedraggled pair rode slowly up, Warren Neale waved at them from his low front veranda; he'd stepped out for a breath of air before breakfast. Lee Davis slid from his sweated saddle, turned to lift Penny down, and Neale came toward them, staring at them, keen eyes questioning.

A New Englander of poor family, Neale had come West as an eager young fellow, wild for adventure, intrigued by the engineering problems of the U.P. Trail. His face was bronzed by sun and wind. He was just under six feet, built like a wedge; though not heavy, he'd taken on a few pounds with the years and a few lines in his brown showed how deeply he took his work to heart.

"Lee!" he cried, shaking hands. "What's wrong?" He glanced inquiringly at Penny.

"Mr. Neale, this is my fiancee, Penny Barrington, from Cordell City. She—I, too—well, we're both frazzled. We've had to ride all night to escape. We'd never have got clear if Al Slingerland hadn't saved us."

Neale saw the straits the two were in. "Tell me all about it later, Lee. Now, come in, and Allie will give you breakfast. It's about ready. I'll have a man see to your horses."

He put a fathering arm around Davis' shoulders, and smiled at Penny, escorting them into the house and through to the roomy kitchen. Allie had just set a large pot of coffee on the table, and there were fried eggs and bacon, biscuits and syrup. The baby was in a high chair, banging on the tray with a spoon. The little girl, who had her mother's large, violet eyes, sat demurely at the table.

Allie Neale was slight, with rich chestnut hair. She had been the sole survivor of a Sioux attack on a wagon train before Neale had met her and later married her. But had it not been for Al Slingerland's help, Allie and Neale would have lost each other forever.

Allie greeted Lee Davis and Penny; she could see what straits the girl was in, and quickly led her off so Penny could wash up, catch her breath. Neale poured coffee for Davis and himself and they sat down together, Lee Davis giving a quick account of the massacre at his home, how Wesleyville had been destroyed, of the events in Cordell City.

"Mr. Neale, Doc Cordell's determined the branch line be run through his town. He wants the shops located there, too. He offered me a big bribe if I'd recommend this, but I can't. The grades over the mountains, the swamps and quicksands, would bankrupt the company."

Warren Neale frowned as he nodded. "I know that. I've been through there, Lee, and I'd never okay such a route. I meant to use Wesleyville. Since it's gone, we'll have to think up an alternative, but Cordell City is entirely unsatisfactory."

Allie fetched Penny back into the kitchen. She'd loaned the girl a fresh pink gown, and Penny had washed up, fixed her hair. Tired as Lee Davis and his sweetheart were, they needed food and drink first of all, and both ate heartily as Allie pressed them to fill up.

Once they'd eaten, the two younger people couldn't keep their eyes open. Allie led Penny to a bedroom where she could turn in, while Neale, who had ordered his hired man to take care of the horses, showed Davis where to sleep . . . .

Slingerland, in the meantime, had swung south,

picking up speed on the good road which led past Wesleyville. He made a detour when he neared the site, believing Cordell's crew would still be there, cleaning up. Crossing the river, he threaded through forest trails toward his valley home. He'd been gone longer than he'd expected.

He was most eager to see Flower again, recapture the enchanting magic of her presence.

"I'll marry her if she'll have me, Reddy," he told the stallion, and the bay flicked his ears.

The moon was high, offering plenty of light for a rider who knew the territory as well as Slingerland did. He was planning what he'd say to the Sioux girl as he crossed the divide and swung down along the path to his cabin.

Dawn wasn't far off. There was a west wind, and as Al Slingerland rode on, the creek on his left hand, a worrisome odor suddenly struck his nostrils. It was a smell of burning, not clean smoke from a wood fire which Flower might have going in the fireplace, but more like what he'd whiffed around Wesleyville, though it had been stronger there.

He slowed, and a troubled emotion clutched at him; he loosened his carbine in its boot. A moment later the bay gave him warning, snuffling, jerking his head to veer off. This was more than enough for such a man as Slingerland. He drew up, got down, muzzled Reddy, and tied him off in a pine grove. Carbine in one big hand, he began his approach, not a direct one, but a stealthy, studied circling so as to reach the camp from the far side.

He made scarcely a sound as he flitted from tree to tree, bush to bush, pausing to listen. Once on the west edge of his clearing, he crouched beside a clump of wild raspberry shrubs.

Moonlight bathed the cleared space. There was a black mass where his cabin had stood. The fire was nearly out but faint curls of smoke still rose slowly from the ruins. The shed had been razed, too. He heard the piping of frogs form the beaver pond, the incessant chirp of innumerable insects. Far off, a lobo wolf howled mournfully.

Slingerland was not a man to panic easily but as he thought of Flower, he felt as though a knife had been thrust into his vitals. Flint Heart must have tracked her, recaptured her! Generous to a fault, slow to anger, his strong hands tightened on his rifle. If he ever got them on Flint Heart's throat—

As the pounding blood eased a bit and his heart steadied its beat, he caught a "thud-thud" nearby, knew it was a horse stamping as it stood in the woods. He was on the point of creeping toward this, but the infinite patience he'd acquired from the Indians, his long experience as a top scout, stopped him. He would wait until there was enough daylight so he could make his maneuver properly.

If Flint Heart and his hotheads had burned his camp, the chief would have left two or three warriors to kill him when he returned home. That was the way of the Sioux.

So he waited, difficult as it was. At last the gray dawn came over the beautiful land.

He'd heard the first mustang twice, and knew about where the Indian pony would be tethered; and he'd caught faint wounds beyond, that of a second animal. So there would be two watching for him, at least.

Now he began his stalk. Inch by inch, never making even a faint noise, Slingerland bellied along. The

168

Indians wouldn't be far from their mounts. The daylight have overcome the moon's glow, stabbing into the shadowed forest. He lay flat, peeping through a narrow gap in the brush, seeing the dark outline of a horse.

After a long, painful study, he realized that what looked like a log lying on the needled earth was a man. The Sioux would have his mustang's rope attached to his ankle or wrist as he slept.

Slingerland carefully laid his carbine down, soundlessly. He had his Colt, and he drew his long, razor-sharp skinning knife.

He started across the several yards of open space toward the Sioux; he'd finish the Indian silently, then deal with the other one. The brave he was watching hadn't stirred.

He was almost upon his enemy when faint noises stopped him; he had to glance back. A large jackrabbit came hopping through the forest aisle. The animal's labored movements showed he was almost run out, close to the end, and a short way behind, Al Slingerland saw two small fiery red dots, knew they were a weasel's eyes. The snaky, low predator, intent on his prey, seemed like a shadow, and with a great bound, the weasel leaped, catching the rabbit's neck in his sharp death grip. The rabbit gave one last, high-pitched scream as he fell.

And the Sioux suddenly sat up, alerted by the sound.

There was only one thing to do, for Slingerland was in the open. Knife raised, the trapper launched himself at the Indian.

The weasel dropped his catch and scooted off into the bushes.

Slingerland could see his opponent clearly now. The Sioux wore a single eagle feather in his black hair, bound with a snake band. He was naked to the waist, deerskin leggings on his strong legs. The black eyes gleamed as he saw the white man upon him; he had to disengage the rope holding his startled mustang, which had jerked back as Al Slingerland attacked.

But he managed to kick up and knock the descending knife out of line. An instant later Slingerland was on top of him, the sinewy Sioux getting his strong arms into play. He had hold of Slingerland's wrist, fighting for his life, seeking to keep the deadly point from slashing into his belly. The savage had a knife in his belt and a repeating carbine lay close by, but he had no time to snatch at his weapons.

The struggle was silent, the only sounds the breathing of the two fighting men.

Slingerland sat astride of the Sioux, holding him down; slowly but surely, he was breaking the Indian's grip, and then—

Al Slingerland would never have lived long in this land had he not been possessed of survival instincts as strong as that of an Indian. He'd known there was a second savage nearby, and suddenly he ripped his wrist from the Sioux he held, and rolled frantically off across the needles in the small clearing.

The Sioux hadn't been expecting this, so Slingerland broke clear. The man he'd had down sat up, just in time to catch an arrow through his breast.

The second Sioux had heard the sounds, stolen around, aimed to kill the white man.

He was kneeling there, and as Slingerland pulled his Colt, the Indian had whipped another arrow from his quiver and fitted it to his bow. An Indian could send them as fast as a gun could fire. The bow was already well-bent as Slingerland fired, once, twice.

The second arrow flew from the string but drilled into the earth a yard in front of the trapper, who was curled on his left side.

Without a sound, the Sioux let go of his bow and fell over, two .45 slugs in his black-haired, feathered head.

Slingerland wasted no time. There might be more where these came from.

He crawled a long time. Neither Sioux had moved; the man he'd shot lay on his back, while the first leaned half against a tree, the feathered end of the shaft sticking from his breast.

The eastern sky was a glorious red, the daylight full.

Slingerland padded around and retrieved his carbine. Checking carefully, he found no more sign of his enemies. To be sure, he had a look at the two bodies; the Sioux were dead. He removed the rope halter from the mustangs; the second stood not far off in the forest. The doughty ponies were nervous; this was a white man, and they didn't like it. He let them go free.

Finally he went to the creek and washed up, drank heavily. Hustling back, he took the bandanna off the bay's nose, mounted and rode close to the clearing, where the wreckage of his home smoldered.

The mule and his chestnut gelding weren't around. He hadn't expected to find them. The Indians would have taken them. He cast about, and in several soft spots, found numerous moccasin tracks. One was extra large.

"Flint Heart," he muttered aloud. His Sioux rival was almost as big as the great Minneconjou chief, Touch the Clouds, who was seven feet tall, and a close comrade of Crazy Horse. Flint Heart, the trapper knew, was a Hunkpapa, as was Sitting Bull, and also Gall, the field general of the tribal branch.

171

Slingerland had some jerked meat in his saddlebags, a couple of hardtack biscuits. With water, he made a meal of this. He had no appetite but he knew he would need all the strength he could muster.

The sun had turned golden as he rode off west of his valley trail. Before long, he passed the spot where he'd found Flower, and his heart turned leaden as he imagined Flint Heart having his way with the pretty girl. He ground his teeth, but tried to cool off. He'd need to be in full command of himself for what he meant to do.

He rode fast through the warming morning, climbing out of the beautiful valley, veering northwest with the sign. He'd lived with the Indians and knew how they left pointers to show friends the route to a camping ground. Two small bird legbones arranged in a V turned him onto a winding trail; next, he came on a small cairn and took the direction this indicated. And in midafternoon he rode into the Sioux village on the bank of a mountain stream.

The wigwams were properly arranged according to protocol; the pony herd gazed in a meadow. A pack of mongrels challenged him. They snarled but didn't bark; barking dogs might betray a camp to enemies, and a noisy canine didn't live long. Puppy stew was a favorite Indian delicacy.

Some squaws worked with awl and sinews, making moccasins; younger ones, faces vermilioned, beaded bands hanging from braids, brushed flies off sleeping papooses. Long-legged naked boys played along the brook, while old men sat in little circles, smoking red willow bark or tobacco. Cooking fires were banked by the lodges.

Slingerland's approach had been open, deliberate; he was known to the Sioux as a friend and comrade.

A frantic bray rang out and the trapper's mule, Longears, came running to greet his beloved leader, the bay stud. Reddy was twitching and sniffing uneasily; he didn't like the smell of the savages. Slingerland didn't see his chestnut; the gelding would have joined him had he been nearby and could do so.

A slim warrior emerged from a lodge. He was short for a Sioux brave, his hair and complexion lighter than average. A single eagle drooped from his fur-wrapped braids; behind one ear was a small red hawk, behind the other a pebble, his "medicine."

Slingerland dismounted, holdng his rein.

"Tasunke Witko," he said, respectfully saluting Crazy Horse, the mighty Sioux paladin, who came to welcome the guest.

Al Slingerland alerted as a large Indian came around a tepee, but then saw it was Touch the Clouds, the Minneconjou, who was seven feet tall. He was one of Crazy Horse's closes comrades. The Minneconjou chief's poweful breast showed scars of the sundance, where the rawhide thongs had ripped through flesh and tendons.

Slingerland spoke in Sioux to Crazy Horse. "Tasunke Witko, my brother. Is the Hunkpapa Flint Heart in this village?"

"No. But he will return. When, I can't say."

Slingerland greeted Touch the Clouds, and the three entered Crazy Horse's lodge, the Minneconjou ducking low as he came inside. Black Shawl, Crazy Horse's faithful squaw, was there. She had known, before Crazy Horse had married her, she was second in his heart to Black Buffalo Woman, his earlier love. But she was happy to serve him because he was such a great chief and defender of her people.

173

Black Shawl bought the guest spoon, the horn of a large mountain sheep containing soup and pieces of meat. She also set before them other viands, an antelope haunch, flat cakes she had baked. The three men squatted in the center of the lodge, and Crazy Horse offered a bit of food to the earth, to the sky, and to the four great directions, according to ritual, before they began to eat.

When they had finished their meal, the silent squaw brought the pipes for smoking.

Al Slingerland would wait. He would learn where Flower was, and he would be there when Flint Heart rode in.

VIII

Doc Cordell fumed in his chair behind the table, glowering at his son and his partner, George Pate.

"You're fools!" he snarled, "tryin' to drygulch Lee Davis. I need him. You've wrecked the cussed deal."

Pate reddened; he hadn't shaved for two days and black bristles stuck from his smudged cheeks. Deep lines around the cruel mouth and crow's-feet at his eye corners showed how exhausted he was.

"How was I to savvy that, Jake?" he snapped back, temper flaring. "You should've told me. Your whelp here begged me to get rid of Davis. Joe's got the hots for that Penny wench."

"To hell with that. One girl's good as another. I'd just promised Davis I'd see he got rich if he'd rout that branch line through here. You know what that'd mean. A railroad, probably their shops, would draw thousands of new settlers. What with the business and land we own, we'd rake in millions! But if the tracks are laid through the next valley, folks 'll desert us like rats, and Cordell City'll be a ghost town. It's happened again and again. That's why Wesleyville had to be destroyed. With it gone, the railroad would have to come here instead."

The Texas gunslinger shrugged. He was worn out, in a murderous fury. "Jake, you asked me to help Joe, didn't you, teach him and try to make a real man of him. It ain't been easy. So far I haven't even been able to teach the fool to keep his head down!"

There was an ugly but superficial bullet burn, scabbing over, the length of Joe Cordell's cheek. He was sullen, pouting; his father had been jawing him constantly since the fiasco at Barrington's place.

"How's Lew Ince?" asked Pate.

"Still livin' but he won't be much use any more. Slug caught him through the hip." Doc Cordell lit a cigar, blew out a puff of blue smoke. "I doubt if Lee Davis 'll be of help to us now, not after what happened. We'll have to figger what to do next. I don't aim to lose everything I got here."

Jake Cordell was the brains of the partnership. Pate the brawn. Pate was saying, "Trailed 'em to Bever Ford, but this cuss hung back and slowed us. Then, he blocked us on the mountain. Davis is back in Cheyenne with Warren Neale, safe and sound."

"Young Lee didn't stop you, though?"

"No, sir. I savvy just who it was, that white Indian, Slingerland! They tell me hung around here all day. It was Slingerland wounded Ince and Joe, and bedeviled us on the route that night. And if I ever killed man, so help me, I'll kill Slingerland. Slow, if I can. I know plenty Indian tricks to drag it out." In his rage, saliva drooled from Pate's lips, and he raved curses.

"Pop, I didn't understand—" began Joe Cordell.

"Dry up," snapped his father. "From here on, you do as I tell you and try to learn some sense."

"Did the boys come back from Wesleyvile yet?" asked Pate.

"Yeah, this afternoon. They buried the bodies and cleaned up some."

Pate yawned, swore again. "I ain't had any shuteye for two days. I'm goin' to turn in."

"All right. Now, George, there's only one thing we can do. Lee Davis didn't cotton to takin' a bribe, and Warren Neale's a stiffneck, too, so we probably couldn't make a deal with 'em. We'll have to get rid of Neale. I got political influence, and I'll pay to have another engineer outfit appointed to build that branch line, one I control."

Weary as he was, Pate was interested. "How you aim to dump Neale?"

"Neale lives south of Cheyenne. You savvy where his ranch stands. Contact Flint Heart and his braves. We'll use all our men, too, fix 'em up like Indians. You lead the attack, surprise Neale at night. And you know what's got to be done." Doc Cordell stared at his outlaw pard.

"Yeah, I know what to do!" Pate ground his teeth. "Maybe I can trap Davis and even Slingerland at Neale's. That'll be a pleasure!"

"You can make it look like another Sioux raid. They been strikin' far and wide."

"*Bueno*. Neale's wife is mighty pretty, the Indians 'll have a good time with her, and they can have that Penny female, too. We can't leave any witnesses. George, don't listen to anything Joe says."

Pate shrugged, stood up. "Suits me, fine. I'll get some shuteye and then we can lay out all the details."

176

The sun had warmed the beautiful wilderness.

In the Sioux village, Al Slingerland had bided his time, not asking direct questions, but steering the talk into channels from which he might discover what he needed to find out.

He learned that neither Crazy Horse nor Touch the Clouds had a high opinion of Flint Heart, though Flint Heart was a Sioux and couldn't be interfered with unless it was a strictly personal matter.

As for the warriors who followed Flint Heart like coyotes after rotten meat, said Crazy Horse, puffing at his short-stemmed pipe, they were hot-blooded young fools. "I do not like to lead such into battle, for they are hard to control and apt to strike before I give the signal. Yes, they have spoiled more than one trap by shooting too soon, killing a few when many might have been taken."

Slingerland knew Crazy Horse to be a master at decoy. The brilliant Oglala had engineered the Fort Fetterman massacre and other skillful engagements against both white and red foes.

"Flint Heart himself is a fool," said Touch the Clouds, blowing out bluish smoke. "It was he who shot the two Crow scouts leading the white soldiers into the clever pitfall arranged by my friend Crazy Horse, so we slew but seven instead of all. And I do not like men who beat their squaws. Had Flint Heart's wife, the one whose neck he broke in one of his rages, been my relative, he would have answered for it."

"*Hoye!*" agreed Crazy Horse. "But, like the Mountain Flower, she had no men to protect her. A runner just brought word that Flower's father will die. The white man's medicine cannot help him."

Burning with desire to know where Mountain Flower

was, Al at last found out when Touch the Clouds casually remarked, "I do not blame the girl for running away as she did. I hope Flint Heart never lays hands on her again. But he is a most skillful tracker, and where could such a woman go that Flint Heart cannot find her?"

Both chiefs glanced at the trapper with as much curiosity as was polite toward an honored guest. Slingerland had already guessed they were aware Flint Heart had tracked Flower to the cabin and had burned it in fury when he failed to recapture her.

He was relieved as he realized she must have escaped. This would explain what had happened to his chestnut gelding. Flower had heard or seen Flint Heart's band approaching and ridden off into the forest. He didn't mention the two braves he'd left dead near the ruins of his home; they were Flint Heart's men, but still they were Sioux.

The quiet, efficient Black Shawl had fastened back the tepee flaps, and Touch the Clouds, who was facing the entry, gave a snort. "Here comes Red Antelope, Flint Heart's heel-dog. Look at his pony! He has ridden another good horse to death."

Slingerland glanced over a hunched shoulder. A wide-bodied Sioux, eagle father drooped over his braids, face streaked with paint, naked torso caked with sweated dust, hopped off a heaving pinto just as the handsome animal collapsed. Without a backward glance, Red Antelope went to the creek, where he put down his weapons and then stretched on his belly to drink deeply of cold, clear water.

A dozen more braves straggled in from the north woods; they were weary, horses showing the effects of hard riding. Their squaws hurried over to take care of the ponies and gear, as their men drank from the brook, then stalked toward their tepees, worn out, hungry. They were lithe young Sioux for the most part; each had bow and quiver, a new repeating carbine, and ever one carried the usual long knife in his rawhide belt.

"*Pagh!*" exclaimed Touch the Clouds suddenly. "Here comes that mighty killer of women!"

Slingerland swung so he could see more of the clearing. A huge Sioux, who was almost the size of Touch the Clouds, came riding in on a powerful, lathered black stallion, a white man's horse he'd undoubtedly stolen in a raid. The stud's chest was heaving, and he stepped slowly, pushed to the limit.

The trapper could see the sundance scars on Flint Heart's barrel breast; the chief was naked to the waist, a feather in his black hair, deerskin leggings and moccasins, a snake belt holding a Colt revolver and his knife. He had bow-and-arrows, a fine carbine as well. The eagle-nosed, painted face was a fierce one.

And Slingerland's heart fell, for on a lead-rope behind the black stallion came his chestnut gelding, also scratched and sweated, head drooped. On the chestnut's back Flower clung to the mane. She almost lay over the withers, so completely exhausted she couldn't raise her head. Then Slingerland saw her wrists were tightly fastened, though she could use her hands to grip the chestnut's thick mane. He rose and stepped outside. Flower's face was stained, her cheeks were mottled, and Al Slingerland thought the marks were fresh bruises, for he could make out a long, bloody welt on one side.

Now, Crazy Horse emerged and stood just behind the trapper; a moment later, the towering Minneconjou joined them.

An almost insane fury seized upon Al Slingerland. It

was plain Flint Heart had been abusing the girl again, after capturing her. It had been a long, hard search before they'd managed to overtake her.

Flint Heart slipped from his horse's back, stepped to the chestnut's lathered, heaving side. Reached up, he roughly pulled Flower from the gelding and cut the cords on her wrists. He shoved her toward his lodge and she went down on her knees, saving herself from falling over by using her right hand. The sprain had evidently improved since Slingerland had first found her, though as she glanced back, her face was contorted with pain. But she did not cry out.

Flint Heart shouted angrily, calling her the worst of names. His first squaw, an older, heavier woman, waited at the entrance to the lodge, and reaching out, helped Flower inside.

All the Indians in the village watched this display, stoical faces never changing expression. If Flower had any close male relatives there, none dared defend her. They knew Flint Heart would kill them if interfered with.

Flint Heart went over to the creek, laid down his weapons, and washed the sweated grime from his powerful torso. His hotheads, most of them young braves, only a few as yet displaying the sundance scars, ultimate test of a warrior's ability to withstand torture, followed their savage leader's example, cleaning up after the long, hard chase engaged in as they combed the forests for the runaway.

Now Flint Heart took a long drink of the cool, crystal-clear water.

Refreshed, he rose to pick up his weapons and go to his lodge.

As he turned, he found his path blocked by the tall,

steel-muscled figure of Al Slingerland, huge hands at his lean hips.

IX

Flint heart was evidently surprised the trapper would dare come here, even more that Slingerland challenged him.

Slingerland figured Flint Heart had tracked Flower to the cabin, that she'd ridden off when she saw the band coming. So he'd destroyed the camp in his frustrated rage and left two tough killers to drygulch Al Slingerland when the trapper rode home.

"Go away, white-man spy," he said in guttural Sioux. "You are a *wasichu*, the Indian's enemy. I would kill you here but will wait for I don't wish to soil our village with your foul blood."

Slingerland answered coldly, deliberately, "Yes, Flint Heart, I will go. Gladly, since it makes me vomit to look on such as you. I will go—but my squaw must go with me!"

Flint Heart started, taken aback by the trapper's claim. He said, "The Mountain Flower is not your squaw. She is my property. I have bought her."

"I will give you what you paid her father. But I tell you, she is my woman, surely. She slept the night with me and freely gave herself to me. And the Teton law says that a wife may leave one husband for another if she chooses, provided she is a virtuous woman."

There was a low murmur of agreement from older Sioux behind Slingerland but he didn't turn, for he was watching Fint Heart's burning, furious eyes carefully. The chief held his carbine and bow and might attack at any instant.

"You are a liar, like all white men," growled Flint Heart.

Slingerland had lied when he'd claimed Flower had been his. But it was the only way he might save her from Flint Heart.

"Ask her, then," he replied coolly. "Ask the Mountain Flower if she is not my woman."

Flint Heart glanced toward his nearby lodge; in the V of the entrance, Flower squatted, listening, watching.

"Is what the white trapper says the truth?" he shouted at her.

The girl came out and stood, facing the village. Young and old, squaws, children, intently watched, listened.

"Yes," cried Flower. "Yes, I am his woman. I have never been yours, Flint Heart, and I will kill myself before I would!"

A murmur went through the interested gathering.

As Flint Heart's followers saw their chief facing the tall trapper, they had seized their weapons and strolled over to back him up. From the corner of his eye, Slingerland saw the towering figure of Touch the Clouds, who held a war axe in one mighty paw, and by him, Crazy Horse, fingering a razor-sharp knife. Several other Oglalas, who rode behind Crazy Horse, and a group of Minneconjou braves who had come to visit the Indian village with Touch the Clouds, had approached and waited silently, guns, bows and knives ready.

Flower's confession stunned Flint Heart but soon he recovered himself. "Then you must die, Slingerland. After that, I'll decide what to do with this faithless squaw. Perhaps I'll turn her over to my warriors for their pleasure, for she has dared defy the mightiest chief of the Dakotas."

"*Pagh!*" That was Touch the Clouds making the derisive sound as Flint Heart boasted of his prowess. "Someone who is talking has perhaps forgotten such as Tasunke Witko, Pizi, and possibly even a tall Minneconjou Sioux!"

But Crazy Horse was not so impulsive and always he had the good of his people at heart.

"It is not good for Sioux to fight Sioux," he declared. "This I do not like."

Never taking his eyes off Flint heart, Slingerland took a step back. He threw off his coonskin hat, unbuckled his gunbelt and dropped it with the heavy colt in its oiled holster. Removing his deerskin blouse, he stood naked to the waist, on his feet soft, laced moccasins.

Slowly, he drew his razor-sharp long skinning knife and raised it high over his bared head as he called Flint Heart the most insulting epithets known to the Sioux tongue.

An excited muttering came from the spectators. Knowing the customs of the Tetons, Slingerland had issued a personal challenge to Flint Heart. And in the tradition, this made it a man-to-man duel. Flint Heart knew this, as did all present.

"This *is* good," announced Crazy Horse loudly. "For it would be wrong that many die because two blood brothers do not agree."

The fascinated audience waited with bated breath.

Flint Heart's followers were heavily armed, ready to back up their chief.

But Touch the Clouds gripped a war axe in one large hand, idly swinging it, while Crazy Horse had a pistol and knife in his belt. A clot of Minneconjous, who had come here to visit along with Touch the Clouds, strolled over, waiting by their chief. There were older, seasoned Oglalas and Hunkpapas, warriors who rode always behind Crazy Horse.

In a general melee, Flint Heart's band would surely be defeated.

Acting as referee and *akicita* leader, those chosen to keep proper order in camp or in battle, Crazy Horse again spoke:

"I have said it is not good for Dakota to fight Dakota. So only these two enemies may take part in this struggle. It is our custom and must not be forgotten. Now, if either of these men turns away, refusing to continue, he is a coward and the squaws shall drive him from our tribe forever!"

The Oglala glanced around; none challenged him.

Flint Heart grunted. His black eyes shone with fire, his hand tight on his carbine. But he knew if he tried to use the rifle, he would be killed even though he slew his foe, the trapper. So he handed his carbine and bow, his belt with the revolver in it, to Red Antelope, keeping only his knife.

Crazy Horse motioned others to stand back so as to allow the antagonists plenty of space in which to maneuver. A silence fell as Slingerland and Flint Heart, long blades glinting, sized up one another.

The Hunkpapa outweighed the white man by fifty pounds. The great muscles in his arms and body were like steel bands, and all present knew that few could match him with the knife. Both men held their blades for slashing rather than for stabbing, flat in the palm of the hand, the needle-sharp point slightly raised.

It was Flint Heart who made the first move; he feinted left, and Slingerland easily avoided the quick movement, fast as a striking snake. He could see Flint

184

Heart was trying him out, to discover just how skillful and experienced Slingerland might be.

The Hunkpapa's set, savage face never changed expression as he watched the trapper's narrowed gray eyes. He tried again to the right, and once more Slingerland countered; this time, the trapper, expecting the move, sliced Flint Heart's left forearm, drawing a little blood, but the Indian took no notice of the superficial wound.

But from this and the way Slingerland handled himself, the white man's expert footwork, Flint Heart knew he was fighting a master, perhaps as good as himself. His deadly look did not flicker as he prepared for a difficult contest.

Slingerland, too, had no doubt he would be fortunate if he managed to defeat Flint Heart. Carefully, hoping the Indian wouldn't realize the trick, he slowly tried to switch position so that the sunlight, slanting in through the higher trees, would shine in the savage's eyes. But this nearly cost him a serious wound for Flint Heart knew exactly what he was doing and took advantage of it by crouching, whirling, his knife cutting through Slingerland's right trouser leg and gashing the flesh.

The tall, lean trapper felt blood flowing down into his laced moccasin but paid no heed to this.

Flint Heart, having found his enemy experienced, took no unnecessary chances. He had the Indian's patience, inexhaustible and calculating. And despite his training, Slingerland was a white man, and could not match this, though he knew a rash move might mean his death. As the minutes passed, the time seemed to drag out to Al Slingerland; he was eager, and his anxiety about Flower's fate was ever in the back of his alert mind.

His right moccasin sloshed now with his own blood. There was too much. His wound was bleeding more freely than he'd expected. If he lost too much, he would lose strength.

Determinedly, the trapper sought to force the right. Flint Heart was behaving as though he might be chary of closing, seeming to back off as Slingerland pushed in. The trapper decided, too, the Indian was slowing down; maybe he was weary from the long, hard search for Flower.

So Slingerland made his play. His concealed thrust was a deadly one and as he drove in, for a breath he felt triumphant, feeling he had won.

Too late, he realized that Flint Heart had decoyed him. The lithe Hunkpapa fell off, with a cougar's agility, and his knife cut deep into Slingerland's right side, the blood spurting from the terrible wound, several ribs showing white as the flesh was violently torn from over them.

Slingerland fell; with a howl of victory, Flint Heart leaped to his feet, lunging in on the white man for the kill, the gory blade driving straight for the trapper's heart.

Slingerland's right side was paralyzed; his hand, gripping the knife, would not answer his bidding. He knew he was dead, his head spun, and he was blacking out.

His confused thoughts flashed through his brain with kaleidoscopic speed. And the picture of Flower in Flint Heart's arms so horrified him that he made one final, incredibly desperate move. He didn't know how he'd managed it but he'd switched his knife to his left hand and he found the strength to hold it straight up.

Flint Heart saw it but he couldn't stop; all his great

weight and power had concentrated in ths final lunge. The dark eyes widened and the warwhoop of victory, issuing from his open mouth, died in his throat. Impelled by his own muscles, he tried to turn in midair but it was too late.

There was a sickening crunch as Slingerland's point ripped in the Hunkpapa's belly just at the soft, vital spot below the sternum, the Indian's final attempt to save himself causing the blade to turn and tear a frightful, wide gash which opened him up from one side to the other.

And the same frantic twist made his knife, plunging down, veer from its course and miss the kill, though the weapon sliced a chunk of flesh from Slingerland's thigh.

The heavy Indian lay, quivering, atop the long, lean body of his opponent.

But Al Slingerland was unaware of this. Flint Heart's weight had knocked out what little breath he had had left, and the world went black for the trapper.

X

Slingerland awoke to a strange world. He head was spinning and he was unable to move either his arms or his legs.

When he breathed, it hurt.

For a time, colored lights played incessantly before his burning eyes. He tried to speak but no sound came from his throat.

After while, he grew aware of a strange odor. It was even an effort to think, and it was some time before he remembered what the aroma was; he'd smelled it when he'd lived with the Indians years ago. The old healing women, the medicine men, mixed revolting, stinking

187

poultices with which wounds were bound, an that was it.

It was too much trouble to do anything so he closed his eyes again and slept, deeply, without dreaming at all, lying on his back.

When he came to again, his head felt clearer and the pounding in his brain had diminished somewhat.

Too, he could see better. A pang went through him as he turned his head a bit.

He was lying on a bearskin, a blanket over him. At his side, he suddenly saw Mountain Flower, squatting by him. She dipped a cloth in a pail, wrung it out, and gently applied the cool rag to his hot face.

"Flower!" He thought he'd spoken aloud but it was only a whisper.

Her small hand touched his cheek.

"Al-al!" she murmured, as he had taught her, "Ye-ess, Al-al!"

His smile cracked his dry, parched lips. She held a tin cup of water to his lips so he could drink a bit.

The she rose.

"Don't—don't go," he whispered.

But she only called, in Sioux, from the tepee entry, for now he was in a lodge, the pine poles holding the hides, the opening in the top center where smoke could issue from the fire in the middle.

Flower came back to him and sat down. A medicine man appeared, entering the wigwam. His face was streaked with special paint, and he wore two buffalo horns sticking straight out from his forehead. In one hand he held a stick with large rattlesnake tails attached to it; when he shook this, it sounded like several of the deadly reptiles giving warning.

In the other, he gripped a three-pronged wand with a

stuffed baby beaver on one tine, a dried animal heart on the second, an antelope's ears on the last. Long black hair hung down the shaman's back, the hair from a grizzly, and attached to it were bear teeth.

He knelt beside Slingerland and using the rattle and waving the special wand, began his incantations, glancing up at the home of the Great Spirit, then at the patient, then at the earth and in turn to the four great directions, north, south, east and west.

When the treatment was finished, the medicine man took his leave, and an ancient crone entered, carrying a steaming pot. The stink grew almost unbearable; she had heated the mixture of healing herbs and roots. Assisted by Flower, the Sioux squaw, her face deeply etched with innumerable wrinkles, began changing the trapper's dressings. This hurt; he evidently had four wounds, but it was the one in his right side that was by far the most serious, and he lost consciousness when the pads were removed from it . . . .

Next, Slingerland found Flower was holding his head in her soft lap. She had a cup of warm animal broth and was speaking to him in Sioux, telling him he must drink. He managed to swallow the liquid; it felt good in his stomach, which didn't reject it.

"Flint Heart?" he murmured.

"He is dead. Flint Heart died on your knife, Al-al."

Slingerland shook his head; he couldn't recall the end of the duel, or how he'd somehow managed to kill his deadly enemy.

He heard sounds not far away, the sounds of an Indian village. "Where are we?"

"Crazy Horse had a lodge set up on the far side of the creek. This was for you to lie in so I could take care of you and you would not be disturbed."

He thought this over, and drank more broth as she offered it. "How long?"

She held up one hand, fingers and thumb extended. "Five days!" he gasped.

Yes, Slingerland knew he was badly hurt. He had no desire to get up, even if he'd been able. And he had fever, he could tell that.

"Crazy Horse—is he here?"

Flower shook her head. "He rode with Touch the Clouds but said he would return. He left Oglala braves to watch so none may harm you, and warned Red Antelope he himself would deal with any who did so. And I am always at your side."

She patted her skinning knife. Nearby were Slingerland's guns and ammunition belts, while his pack and saddle lay at the rear of the lodge.

"Your horses are with the herd," she added.

His Indian friends had done everything possible for him, and he felt the deepest gratitude. And while he had lain like dead with the fever, probably raving at times, Flower must have attended to his bodily functions, cleaning him and nursing him as a mother would a sick child.

Then he remembered. "Will you bring my pack?"

She brought the roll and opened it as he asked. "The presents are for you, Flower."

She trilled with pleasure, holding up the bright cloth, trying on the necklace, examining the sewing kit, looking at the scissors, the silver thimble, the packet of needles and colored threads.

"You are the most beautiful woman I have ever seen, Flower."

At this, the color mounted in her rounded cheeks, and she dropped her long lashes modestly.

"I love you," he said gently. "If I grow well again, will you be my wife?"

Taking his big hand in hers, she looked straight into his eyes as she nodded.

He inquired what had happened after he'd left her at his camp. She had rested through the day, she said, and next morning had found her arm so much better, she'd used the awl and rawhide for mending leather to sew back the sleeve on her blouse. She made no fire, for the smoke might have been seen from far, and she dreaded Flint Heart. Even among the Indians, who could follow sign with magical skill, Flint Heart was acknowledged as a master tracker.

As the sun rose higher, so did her uneasiness increase. She'd slipped out and lassoed the chestnut gelding. She put a rope hackamore on the horse, a thick blanket on his back; taking a canteen of water and hardtack, she rode up to the north rim of the valley and hid in a dense spruce forest. Staking her mount, she slept on the soft bed of needles, wrapped in the blanket.

Awake at dawn, and watching, she saw, far below, the stealthy approach of Flint Heart and his band. Not finding her, they set fire to the buildings, and Flint Heart himself picked up the chestnut's rail. The gelding's hoofs were shod and this would make it more difficult for her to elude her pursuers.

She rode over the divide and into the next dip, seeking rock or shale areas where no marks might be left. Finally she lost herself in the wilderness mountains.

But Flint Heart was not to be shaken off, and eventually had located her hiding place, beaten her and tied her hands, brought her back.

That night Flower nestled by her man, the blanket covering them and her warm, soft body against his to

191

keep him from chilling in his sleep. Weak as he was, Slingerland felt intense joy; once he kissed her cheek, and she put her arms about him. She had given herself to him, without question, and he knew she would be his forever.

For two more days, the fever held. The healing woman left dressings off his wounds save for the bad one in his side, which was very grave. Flint Heart had come close to killing him. The Hunkpapa's blade had caused internal damage and must have cut nerves and muscles, for Slingerland had little control over his right side.

When he would ask the ancient healing woman how long he must lie there, she would only shake her head impatiently, and the medicine man came daily, making incantations.

When the fever subsided, his appetite returned. Flower fed him thick soups, venison and beat meat, Indian bread. She seldom left his side, but her squaw friends would bring her berries and roots, Nature's fruits, and give them to her.

She described the end of his hand-to-hand combat with Flint Heart, acting out parts of it, so he could visualize what had happened. At his lasp gasp, he'd somehow managed a final great effort and so had slain his opponent.

And Crazy Horse, with Touch the Clouds, had prevented Flint Heart's warriors from taking revenge by killing the white man.

"Now Red Antelope is their chief," Flower told him. "He is cruel, imitating Flint Heart, bad to his squaws, though he isn't the war leader Flint Heart was. Crazy Horse told Red Antelope not to come near you and not to say to anyone you are here. And Red Antelope fears Tasunke Witko."

When the sun was warm, she would raise the tepee sides so Slingerland could see out. Ponies whinnied and stamped, small boys shouted as they played.

There was a sound at the lodge entry and Slingerland saw a young squaw, face painted with vermilion, and her braids tied with red ribbons. She was attractive, about Flower's age. She wore a copper bracelet and a necklace of vari-hued beads, while her deerskin blouse had the wide sleeves of Sioux women. Flower went out and joined her, and for a time, the man heard their voices, though he couldn't distinguish what they were saying.

Squaws knew everything that went on around a village, and they loved to gossip just as much as their white sisters.

Soon Flower returned, kneeling by him; her friend had brought some roots and ripe berries.

"She is Pretty Swan, Red Antelope's second squaw," she exclaimed. "We are the same age and played together when younger. She doesn't love her husband very much, for sometimes he is like Flint Heart."

Slingerland felt better, in a way, but still couldn't move freely. Flower would prop him up sometimes, but his side stayed numb, and when he tried to rise and walk, he would fall back with a groan. For an active, outdoor man, lying idle was sheer torture. Only the fact that Flower was always with him, waiting on his every need, made it bearable. And he knew he really loved her from the close intimacy they shared. It was far stronger than simple physical attraction.

Pretty Swan came daily to bring small gifts and chat

with Flower, and one afternoon, when her friend had left, Flower told the trapper there was excitement in the village. "The man who pays for killing has sent word he is coming to see Flint Heart. He doesn't know Flint Heart is dead, and Red Antelope says he will deal with him instead."

"The man who pays for killing?" repeated Slingerland.

After some questioning, he realized it was George Pate, Doc Cordell's gun boss. He had been to the village before, to see Flint Heart, and Flower had seen him from a distance. With him had been a second *wasichu*, a younger one, not so powerful, and Slingerland decided this had been Joe Cordell.

Pursuing this line, he learned that Flint Heart had led out some fifty hotheads one day—this was the day he had first caught Flower when she'd run off, and had said he was going on a raid but would return.

The time coincided with the destruction of Wesleyville, and Slingerland pressed for details. Flower did not know the name of the village but Flint Heart's braves and Red Angelope, had boasted of their great victory over the whites, laughing at how the men had rushed forth in their night clothes only to be shot down by the carbines furnished the Sioux by the one who had paid them, and describing in detail how the women had screamed and tried to protect their children, before they were scalped.

The man who paid for killing said none, not even the small ones, should be left alive. The great fire had been most satisfying, too, and the triumphant raiders, who had lost not even one man and with but two slightly wounded by stray bullets, had ridden into the village with the bloody scalps flying from their war lances.

There had been a great dance and feast that night, Pretty Swan had informed Flower, who had not been present, since she'd escaped and then been rescued when Slingerland had found her.

Lying almost helpless, the trapper thought this all over. It was plain that Pate had bribed Flint Heart to level Wesleyville and kill all its inhabitants. And now Pate was again coming to the Sioux encampment.

He knew George Pate was not only a ruthless killer but a shrewd one, not easily tricked, and he wondered if Pate might have guessed who it was who'd held him off when he'd tried to overtake Lee Davis and Penny Barrington. He figured he himself would have surely decided it could only have been such an expert as himself. He would have been seen, hanging around town, and he'd talked with Vince Farley; without meaning to harm a friend. Farley would have told Pate Slingerland had been asking questions, and the gun-slinger would draw the right conclusions.

Crazy Horse had had the lodge set up on the other side of the creek, away from the main village, but if Pate found the trapper was here, he might come for his revenge. He told Flower this, and she seemed worried, but then said, "Crazy Horse ordered Red Antelope and all not to tell you are here."

But he had her move his bed to a point from which he could look out and watch the approach; then he asked her to fetch his rifles and Colt. She helped him clean them and he checked them carefully, putting in fresh loads, making sure they were ready for action.

If Pate came for him, it would be at a high cost to the gunslinger, Slingerland promised himself grimly. He could work his rifles and the revolver, in spite of his wound and the weakness, use his left hand if he had to, to shoot at close range.

Maybe Pate was riding here just to hunt him down. He asked Flower if she would see Pretty Swan, and tell her friend, who was Red Antelope's squaw, to listen as much as she could and then quickly as possible let Flower know what the white man wanted.

Next morning, word flashed through the village that the man who paid for killing was riding in.

Slingerland had Flower lower the tepee sides, just leaving a gap in the entrance so he could see across the brook to the village.

She squatted beside him and they watched.

Three whites rode slowly in from the trail, escorted by several young warriors, who had taken part in the Wesleyville raid. Red Antelope stepped forth to greet them, and the visitors got down. From a distance, Slingerland recognized Pate, in his black hat, dark shirt and gun rig. Joe Cordell wasn't along this time, but there were two other toughs that he knew were gunnies in Pate's gang.

Slingerland held his carbine in his left hand, observing the scene across the creek. After a time, Pate and Red Antelope entered the latter's lodge; and soon, bluish smoke issuing from the open flap gold they were smoking pipes as they parleyed together. Pretty Swan and Red Antelope's first squaw were serving the men.

Pate's gunnies squatted in the shade, sharing tobacco with some of the braves, talking in sign with them.

The trapper made ready as George Pate finally emerged from Red Antelope's tepee. But Pate didn't even glance across the stream. He nodded and shook hands with Red Antelope, and mounting, rode back the way he'd come in, followed by his comrades.

An hour later, Pretty Swan slipped to the lodge and

spoke for some minutes with Flower.

Flower seemed relieved when she returned to Slingerland.

"Red Antelope didn't dare speak of you, but Pretty Swan says the man who pays for killing said he'd stopped and seen your camp had been destroyed. He believes you are dead, probably slain when Flint Heart struck your home. And Red Antelope let him think this, for it seemed to make no difference, to the Sioux, anyway. The *wasichu* hadn't known Flint Heart was dead, but Red Antelope said he'd died during another raid. So the man who pays for killing hired Red Antelope to bring fifty warriors to Bubbling Spring three days from today."

"Do you know why?"

"Pretty Swan says it is to kill more whites and to burn a ranch, near the place they called Cheyenne, after our blood brothers."

Bubbling Spring, Slingerland was well aware, was about five miles south of Cheyenne. It was not far from the valley road, some distance above the site of Wesleyville.

"Did Pretty Swan say who these whites are who must be slain?"

"No. The braves will kill the males but may take the women for their pleasure, and any horses at the ranch. The man who pays for killing will direct the raid and has over a score of Gray Men, whites disguised as Indians, who will take part to make sure all is done as he wishes. There are enough Gray Men to crush this ranch without Sioux to help, but he wishes warriors to be present, too."

Slingerland digested this uneasily. Pate wanted savages along, so blame would be placed on them.

Otherwise clever lawmen might realize outlaw whites had struck. Finally he said, "When you can, find Pretty Swan and ask if she knows who is to die in this raid on the ranch."

After a time, Flower left him. And without realizing at first what he was doing, Slingerland found he was moving his right arm and leg a bit. He tried again, carefully, and hope sprang in his heart. Volition had returned to his muscles. The terrible injury was healing!

Flower came back. She shook her head; Indians seldom used whites' names, strange to their tongue. They usually referred to individuals by descriptive phases. General George Crook, was "Three Stars," while the bitter foe of the Cheyennes, George Custer, was "Yellow Hair." But as the girl told what Pretty Swan had said, he caught something which gave him a violent shock: "The raid will be at the home of the *wasichu* who builds the iron roads which split the Indians' land," Mountain Flower told the trapper.

Warren Neale! The engineer's ranch lay a short ride north of Bubbling Spring. Lee Davis and Penny Barrington had gone there.

And so Pate, with Red Antelope's killer pack and the gunnies decked out as savages, would slaughter Neale and other males, capture Allie and Penny, the Neale children. Knowing Pate's ruthless nature, Slingerland decided Cordell's gun boss had enough killers of his own and would do the job whether the Sioux took part or not.

XI

Late that afternoon the medicine man again made incantations over his patient. Slingerland was sitting patient. Singerland was sitting up. He nodded to Mountain Flower, who hovered anxiously by as he rose to his feet. He'd have fallen had she not caught his arm. The change in circulation made his head spin, and he was weak, but he was determined. With the Indian girl at his elbow, he walked slowly from the lodge into the sunshine.

The medicine man was elated. He began howling, for all to see how he had healed the one who had been dying but was now cured, thanks to his powers. He demanded more payment. Slingerland had given away all he could spare from his packs but he found a few coins in a pocket.

The medicine man knew exactly what he would do with them; he would drill holes in the metal discs and add them to his necklace.

The ancient healing woman squatted nearby, shaking her head. She still kept a dressing on that side wound and Slingerland had grown accustomed to the foul odor of the herbs.

Shrill whinnies and a bray rang out. Slingerland's stud, the mule and the chestnut gelding came trotting along, and he greeted them with pats and reassuring words.

There was a stir across the creek. Crazy Horse, Touch the Clouds and a dozen warriors appeared. Squaws hurried to take the ponies as the lithe men jumped down.

More Indians came in driving a bunch of horses stolen from whites; some had fresh scalps waving from their lances, though Crazy Horse's sacred medicine forbade that he keep trophies. The Oglala would give away whatever he captured.

"Pizi," said Flower, awe in her voice.

Slingerland knew Pizi was Chief Gall, the war chief of the Hunkpapa Sioux, noted as brave among the brave. He recognized the tall, powerful figure as Gall slipped off his paint pony, rifle in hand, arrows and bow strapped to his bronzed, strong back, hair braided with ribbon, an eagle feather drooped to one side.

While Crazy Horse and Sitting Bull were spiritual as well as military leaders, Gall was entirely practical and was a great field general.

Red Antelope and the young Hunkpapas greeted Gall with tribal acclaim. After they had washed themselves at the stream, the raiders gathered around a central fire to eat, talk, and many of the braves danced around, describing their great feats during the foray.

Al Slingerland was glad to return to his soft bed of furs in the tepee. The walking had exhaused him. Flower fixed food and hot drink for him; then, when both had eaten, he asked her to cross the creek and learn the news brought by Crazy Horse, Gall and the rest.

Darkness fell over the village; through the open flaps of the lodge, Slingerland watched the dancing red flames of the great fire, and he heard the whooping, the loud voices of the painted Indians dancing about the center of the clearing.

After some time, Flower returned. Crazy Horse and Gall had been raiding the whites' Holy Road many miles to the north. They had killed some walking soldiers, burned wagons and houses, stolen horses and other things. And Gall had brought word that Sitting Bull said because the whites had stolen *Pa Sapa*, the sacred Black Hills of the Sioux, the Dakotas would congregate at a new rendezvous to conduct their annual religious and tribal ceremonies. They would all join together on the eastern slopes of the Big Horn mountains, farther west.

So, this village must soon start moving to another site. The hunters had brought in plenty of game but it was growing scarce in the vicinity, and it was the habit of the Teton's to wander about, for better forage, easier food supplies, and sanitary reasons.

"We will fashion a travois so you can ride easily," said Flower brightly, touching her husband's hand.

"Maybe I'll be able to fork a horse soon," said Slingerland.

This worried Flower. The healing woman had said jolting might reopen the terrible wound in his side.

Dancing and feasting went on far into the night. Flower fell asleep by the tall trapper, soft and warm against him. According to Indian law, they were married; she had moved into his lodge.

Slingerland lay awake for hours, hearing the shouts and music across the creek. He must decide what to do, for it was plain to him that Doc Cordell intended to kill all who opposed him.

As long as Cordell and Pate were on the warpath, Warren Neale, Lee Davis, and their loved ones would be in imminent danger of death. And the trapper figured Pate would kill him at the first opportunity, when he found Slingerland was alive!

He must warn Neale. But how? He couldn't ride yet; a few steps had been almost too much for him. And Pate, with Red Antelope's reckless band, would soon attack Neale's home.

At last, a nebulous idea formed in his mind. He wasn't sure whether or not it would be feasible, but he must try. Then he slept, but uneasily, starting alert now and again.

Flower rose quietly at sunrise, moving about silently, preparing his breakfast. When he roused, he spoke to her, and she came to him, smiling at him. He held out his hand and she knelt by him, kissing his lips as he drew her closer, the way he liked in the white man's way.

The sunshine penetrated the mountain camp, warming the chill air, drying the frosted dew. The squaws grew busy at their many tasks, and groups of men talked together, smoking their pipes.

Later, when Flower helped him up, he found he was stronger, able to walk about for a while, his woman by his elbow. And he asked Flower to cross the brook and speak to Crazy Horse for him.

"Bring Tasunke Witko and Pizi here to me," he said.

Before noon, Crazy Horse, Touch the Clouds and Gall came into the lodge. It was a great honor to have such guests and Flower bustled about, serving them.

Crazy Horse looked at his white brother, and essayed a jest:

"Yes, you are really a paleface," he said, grim lips relaxing for a moment, and Touch the Clouds agreed, "Hoye!" Gall, too, seemed amused. For the confinement, the suffering, showed their effects in Slingerland's drawn features, chalking under his tan.

The three chiefs listened to Slingerland's plan.

Finally, Crazy Horse said, "*Hou!*" Yes, it was good.

"But Red Antelope," said Slingerland. "He has promised to meet the Gray Men at Bubbling Spring with fifty or more Hunkpapas."

Gall spoke then. "We will see whether the Hunkpapas would rather ride with Red Antelope than with Pizi!"

Touch the Clouds grinned, nodded. "The coyote flees when the lion approaches!"

Details were discussed. There was little time, for the Gray Men and Red Antelope would strike soon. The warriors would make ready the following day and start off, for they must travel on hidden trails through the rugged mountains so they wouldn't be seen, and sleep, rest at the rendezvous in order to be fresh for the raid on Warren Neale's.

That afternoon, Slingerland asked Flower to rope his bay stallion and bring the stud to the lodge. She looked alarmed at this; it wasn't a squaw's place to argue with her husband, but she feared he would be hurt if he rode.

But Slingerland was adamant, and finally Flower went off to find the bay.

She rode the big animal back and tied him outside the tepee; then she saddled him and helped Slingerland to his side. It was an effort, but the tall trapper mounted. It felt good to be in the saddle again. Slingerland drew in a deep breath of the cool, aromatic air, as he spoke soothingly to the bay. Reddy had grown accustomed to the Indian odors and the pony herd in his stay near the encampment. He whisked his long tail, showing he was glad to see his human friend.

Flower stood outside the lodge, anxiously watching as Al Slingerland moved off at a walk, and rode slowly up the creek until he came to a shallows. He set the bay across, and worked back into the village proper. The jogging hurt his side but it wasn't severe.

Up the way he saw a congregation of warriors. They were declaiming, some of them, while the rest listened. Gall was there, Red Antelope, Grazy Horse, Touch the Clouds, and others Slingerland knew.

He drew near enough so he could hear what they were saying, sitting his saddle.

Red Antelope's face was sullen. He was pointing at one young brave after another, those who had followed Flint Heart in the Wesleyville massacre, saying they must make ready to ride with him.

But Gall raised his hand.

"Who would follow Pizi?" he said in a loud voice. "I will see there are scalps and guns and horses, plenty of glory for the Hunkpapas. This I promise. Those who would go with Pizi rather than with Red Antelope will step to my side."

Now Crazy Horse pushed in. "I will be beside Pizi on this raid," he announced. And Touch the Clouds, too, agreed.

Two tall warriors moved over to Gall; then several more, and finally, Red Antelope stood alone.

Fury burned in Red Antelope's dark eyes; he dropped a hand to his knife, glaring at Gall, who coldly outstared him..

Then, Red Antelope turned and went inside his tepee. A chief was no longer a chief when he had no followers.

Gall and Crazy Horse, the towering Touch the Clouds, seemed vastly amused. "Make ready," ordered Gall. "Bring weapons and your fastest ponies. Tell your squaws to fill parfleches with food for the trip." He swung, going off toward the lodge where he slept.

Slingerland walked Reddy nearer to Crazy Horse.

"I, too, will follow you," he said in Sioux.

The Oglala looked up at him; then he nodded. It was his white friend's decision, and Crazy Horse considered it was the best way for a man to die, if he must, in battle. What else was there?

XII

It was a hard run for Al Slingerland. Every jolt hurt his side, and he felt weak. Yet the wound hadn't broken open, for he felt no blood seeping from the tight bandage the healing woman had put on before he left the village.

He left his heavy Creedmore with Mountain Flower but had his carbine and plenty of ammunitioin, as well as his Colt revolver and long knife. Crazy Horse, Touch the Clouds, Gall and the braves following them were also heavily armed.

Crazy Horse had several seasoned, veteran Oglala warriors sifting ahead as scouts for the main party.

"I do not trust the hotheads who ride with Flint Heart." he told the trapper. "They will spoil the ambush if they're not held back."

Pizi, Chief Gall, was in command of the young ones. And Gall was a master of decoy, just as Crazy Horse was. If anyone could control the youthful Hunkpapas, Gall could do it. He was a revered war leader.

They had ridden at good speed through the night, under the moon, winding on animal trails over the wooden mountains.

Two of Crazy Horse's scouts hooted as they reached a wagon road and they pulled up. The scouts reported all clear, and they formed a long, snakelike single file as they shoved north on the shadowed side of the route. Slingerland knew exactly where they were; several familiar needle spires on the right marked the range along the route to Cheyenne. Wesleyville lay miles south, and Bubbling Spring was close at hand.

The going was easier on the beaten track. They swung off it, along a path, and soon saw the glint of the pools, catching the low, soothing sound of water gurgling from the great boulders. The scouts were already in the clearing and had watered their ponies, then led them back, leaving them hidden in the trees nearby.

Slingerland grunted and cursed as he dismounted. He

was stiff, and he fought against the weakness. He let the bay stallion drink, and the Indians saw to their mounts, they lay flat on their lean bellies and refeshed themselves.

Bubbling Spring was a favorite resting spot for wayfarers. A high precipice loomed, black in the night. At its base was a jumble of huge rocks fallen from above. Melt from mountain snows and ice formations fed the spring, never failing in droughts. There was a large pool, where otters, muskrats and water birds loved to play. A brook was formed here and not far below was a beaver dam. The willow-branch domes of the busy animals' homes showing on the surface of the pond. The stream meandered off through the forest, finally finding its way into Crow Creek.

Now the masterful Crazy Horse prepared the ambush. Gall concealed the Hunkpapas in a semicircle around the ponds; strict orders were issued that no warrior must open fire until he gave the word. Slingerland donned a Sioux buffalo-horn headdress, streaking daubs of war paint on his upper cheeks and fastened a dark bandana around his neck, so he could quickly pull it up and hide his beard. He was glad to rest, and ate from the parfleches with the others as they waited.

Frogs, night birds, splashings of animals could be heard, and a wolf howled in the distance. There was a sound of brush crackling and a small herd of antelope came to the west edge of the pool to drink; the hidden, silent savaged did not startle them.

And at last, Crazy Horse's watching sentinels stole in, whispering the *wasichus* were coming.

Crazy Horse and Gall rose; Touch the Clouds, several warriors behind him, stood to the rear of the two leaders, while Slingerland adjusted his mask and waited behind the towering Minneconjou.

They could hear the white men coming long before they reached the rendezvous on the east side of Bubbling Spring.

Slingerland, peeking past Touch the Clouds, saw the dark shapes of horsemen. They wore Indian headdresses and their faces gleamed in the faint light with paint they had donned as a disguise. These were Gray Men, killers who robbed and slew, their crimes laid to the savages.

The riders pulled up in a bunch; Slingerland figured there were a score of them. Their rifle barrels glinted in the faint light.

"Red Antelope!" a man in front called softly. "*Hou, cola!*"

Pizi stepped forward.

"Here," he said. Gall could speak some English.

A match flared, and in its yellow light Slingerland recognized George Pate, sitting a big black. Pate wore an Indian disguise, but the trapper knew him at once, the shape of his torso, and his eyes. Cordell's gun boss touched the match to a bull's-eye wick, adjusted it and opened the slide a bit.

The beam fixed on the powerful Hunkpapa chief. "Say, you ain't Red Antelope! I savvy you, Gall. Seen you before!"

Gall spoke smoothly, using some English, filling out with sign: "Red Antelope—pony fall—must lie in tepee —squaw and medicine man—Red Antelope tell Pizi— meet *wasichu*—"

Pate hesitated; then he growled, "Where're your braves? All men at the ranch must die—you can have the women and horses, savvy?"

"Warriors near, we kill," promised Gall.

"If you don't, we'll do the job. I got plenty for it. It's

207

gettin' late. We better hustle."

"Guns!" Gall demanded.

Pate turned to a disguised man on a gray by his side. "Joe, get back and tell Dan Wain to bring up the rifles and ammo."

Slingerland decided the assistant was Joe Cordell, fixed up as an Indian. Joe Cordell pulled rein and started to the rear. Evidently Pate had a small pack train near the road, with the weapons for the Sioux.

And now, before Chief Gall gave the signal, for he wished to draw all into the carefully planned trap, shrill warwhoops rang out, and carbines began flaming. Hotblooded young warriors leaped up from their hiding places, yelling and shooting as they rushed upon the massed horsemen.

"It's a trap—a trap!" bawled George Pate, whipping up his repeating carbine. "Back—get back!"

He swung his rifle, aiming at Gall. It belched fire and smoke but Pizi had accurately and coolly beaten Pate to it, and the gunny's bullet shrieked past the chief's ear as he put two slugs into George Pate. The black stallion reared, snorting, trumpeting in fright; several supple braves rushed in, bodies gleaming with grease and paint. Strong hands pulled the white man from his saddle, knives flashed. Pate was slashed to pieces and a Sioux lifted his scalp, another seized the black's bridle so the fine animal couldn't run off.

The glade rang with war whoops and exploding guns. "*Hoka hey, hoka hey*!" howled the warriors as they hurled themselves on the Gray Men. Colts flamed and several Sioux were wounded, but the struggle lasted only a brief minute.

Slingerland had started in, with Touch the Clouds, and Crazy Horse, disgusted because, again, the young braves had jumped ahead of his signal.

"Hurry, or the packs will be lost!" cried Crazy Horse, rushing past the savage melee. The hotheads, eager for personal glory, were lifting scalps, snatching up weapons, stripping and mutilating the whites. Wounded horses gave unearthly screams, kicking as they lay, blood seeping into Bubbling Spring.

Several of Pate's men had been to the rear, guarding the pack horses; and when they realized what was happening, had turned and ridden back to the road. Some dropped the lines but others had tied them to their saddles and the laden animals followed behind.

Slingerland couldn't keep up with his swift Indian friends; his breath came in gasps and he was weak. Crazy Horse shot two fleeing Gray Men out of their saddles, for above all, he wanted to secure the rifles and ammunition, roped on the pack animals.

Slingerland stopped; he could run no farther. He went slowly back, avoiding the horrible melee as savages shrieked in triumph, hacking the wounded and dead, waving bloody scalps, dancing and counting their coups, boasting of their bravery.

A quick fire had been started with oil from Pate's lantern and dry brush, flames licking high, lighting the awful scene. The sickening, acrid smell of blood came to the tall trapper's flared nostrils as he found his bay stud, mounted, and started for the highway.

By nature, Al Slingerland was kind, and enjoyed helping others. He respected decent men, no matter what their color. The savagery of the Indians was frightful, but he had seen whites who excelled them in cruelty. He knew the redmen were making a desperate, hopeless last stand. Their lands, their way of life, were nearly lost to them, and they were cheated and starved by the Indian agents, looked upon as animals by most white settlers.

At the road, he found that Crazy Horse and his trusted Oglalas had caught most of the pack animals, cases of rifles, ammunition and other goods on them with which Pate had expected to bribe the Sioux to wipe out Neale.

"How many got away?" Slingerland asked the chief.

"Seven or eight," replied Crazy Horse. "We would have had all if the fool young men had obeyed me. Now we must hurry, for the alarm will be given and horse soldiers come after us."

Yes, thought Slingerland, and some who had escaped would ride hard to Cordell City, report the fiasco to Doc Cordell. And Cordell, wealthy and powerful, would swiftly and easily gather together a new band of killers. Knowing Cordell, he realized Neale, Davis, and he himself would never be safe while Cordell was free to strike.

But he was exhausted. The wound had sapped him, the hard ride here taken what little strength he'd recovered while Flower nursed him. He spoke with Crazy Horse.

"I must go to Cheyenne, to my friend," he said. "I can ride no longer, and the iron-road builder's isn't far from here. Will you tell Flower I'll come for her very soon?"

"Yes, I will tell her," promised the chief.

"If the village moves, I'll follow. But Flower and I will soon begin to live in white-man ways, Crazy Horse. She is my wife."

"It is good." The great Sioux's eyes gleamed in the faint light. "For the Indians cannot fight much longer, my brother. Already many have given up and gone to the reservations. In a few years, the Sioux will be like children, at the *wasichu's* mercy, whipped and cheated like dogs. This I know, and so does Sitting Bull and Gall, but we would die like men, killed in battle, rather than live like old women.''

Slingerland shook his friend's hand. "I'll never take up arms against my red brothers. Perhaps one day we'll meet again."

"Perhaps."

Crazy Horse ordered no pursuit of the handful who had eluded his trap, for he wished to escape with the precious arms and ammunition.

Slingerland rode off north, toward Cheyenne, with dawn at hand. His head spun and blood seeped from his bandaged side.

The night soon gave way to grayness, then fuller light. As a matter of habit, Slingerland's piercing, shrewd eyes scanned the ground ahead as he moved, and bay stallion easy under him on the road. And soon, able to make out details, he saw marks of shod hoofs, knew the sign was fresh. A rider was not far ahead of him. Noting some dark spots in the lighter dirt of the track, he dismounted to examine one, stooping and feeling the earth with sensitive fingers. The stains were wet.

"One of 'em came this way, Reddy," he told the stud. "He's bleedin!"

So he grew very cautious, glancing this way and that. He hadn't made more than a mile from Bubbling Spring when he ripped rein, turning the bay off. A heavy bullet shrieked over his head.

He pulled his horse into the thick growth along the highway, tied to a branch, and with his carbine cocked and ready, stole through the brush. Pausing to listen, he heard a horse snort, a few yards ahead. Inching on,

211

soundlessly, he crouched and studied the gray stallion, a magnificent mount, standing in a small open space. A man lay there, on his side, a Colt in his left hand, his horse's rein looped to his arm. He was staring with wide, pain-wracked and frightened eyes toward the road, his revolver cocked and ready to fire.

Slingerland recognized him; it was Joe Cordell. Carbine raised and aimed, the trapper jumped in close behind him.

"Drop it!" he snapped.

Joe Cordell let go of the pistol. He looked around and began to bawl. "Don't—don't shoot me. Please don't scalp me. My father 'll pay you a big ransom—oh, have mercy!" He began blubbering in an ecstasy of fear.

Slingerland realized he still wore the Indian headdress; to Joe Cordell he looked like a savage. "It's me, Al Slingerland, Joe. I won't kill you." He kept a bead on Cordell as he removed his disguise.

Joe Cordell sobbed like a baby. I'm dyin', Al, dyin'! Get me to a doctor, for God's sake!"

Slingerland stepped in and kicked the Colt out of reach, then knelt by young Cordell. He'd caught a bullet in the back as he had fled from Bubbling Spring. Pate had sent him to bring up the packs, and when the attack had begun, Joe Cordell had run for it, heading for Cheyenne.

The trapper carefully cut away Cordell's shirt, soaked with blood. The slug had entered under his right shoulderblade, ranging up, but hadn't emerged; it was still in there. The trapper fashioned a rough bandage from the shirttails, and lifted Cordell, who cried out in agony as he was hoisted to his saddle.

"Hold on," said Slingerland. "I'll take you in and get you a sawbone."

He led the gray to the road, picked up Reddy, and mounted, rode toward Cheyenne in the cool dawn. He used a bandanna to wipe the war paint from his face, and took his coonskin hat from a saddlebag, setting in on his head.

The sun was up and it was breakfast time as he rode into Neale's.

XIII

Warren Neale, Lee Davis, Allie and Penny had greeted their old friend with open arms, fed him and given him warm drinks.

Joe Cordell had sipped a little water but was coughing blood, and kept insisting he was dying. Slingerland and Neale had stood by him as he lay on a cot in a side bedroom. Slingerland bent over slightly.

"You were were Pate when the Sioux wiped out Wesleyville, Joe," said the trapper sternly. "I can swear to it, for I traced your horse back to Cordell City. There was a cracked shoe on your animal, and the blacksmith can identify it."

"I—I didn't do anything that night," Joe wailed. He was very weak, almost delirious with pain and fear. "Pate hired Flint Heart and his braves. My father told him to—"

"It's a Federal offense to encourage Indians to attack whites," broke in Neale angrily. "Your father will go back to prison."

"It wasn't my idea," moaned the youth. "My—my side's killin' me. Ain't that doctor ever comin'?"

"I sent a man in right away; he should be here any minute," Neale said. "Al, you need attention, too. Your wound's bleeding."

The trapper and engineer returned to the kitchen. Allie, Lee Davis and Penny, who had been married shortly after reaching the ranch, were there, and sitting down with them, Slingerland gave a quick account of all that had happened, and how he had married Mountain Flower.

"I'll have the Federal marshal in Cheyenne make out a warrant for Doc Cordell's arrest," declared Neale. "He deserves to swing."

"Sure he does. But you better hurry," Slingerland advised. "Some of Pate's gunnies escaped Crazy Horse's trap and they'll warn Jake. He can easy collect another gang and he won't quit easy. Long as Doc's loose, we're all in danger, includin' me. Joe Cordell will do anything to save his own hide, even turn in his father."

The doctor came riding in with Neale's courier. The physician had been a Civil War surgeon and was expert on gunshot wounds. The trapper insisted he take care of Joe Cordell first, and the sawbones worked on the youth for over an hour.

He came into the kitchen, and Allie poured himself a mug of hot coffee.

"Will he pull out of it?" asked Slingerland.

The stocky, bearded doctor shrugged. "I think he'll live. But he'll never be the same again, gentlemen. I got the bullet out. It looks like a carbine slug though it hit bones and is badly mashed. Did a lot of damage in there, and his arm will be almost useless."

He drank gratefully of the warm coffee. "I gave him plenty of opium, so he'll rest and sleep a while, anyhow. But he'll suffer a good deal for days. I'll leave something here for him."

Later, the doctor carefully examined Slingerland's wound. "By George, sir, I don't know how you came

214

out of this so well! The fresh bleeding is superficial. In time, you'll recover entirely. The knife slashed your liver, maybe, and other vital organs, but that Indian medicine man did a fine job, good or better'n most white surgeons.''

"I guess it was the old squaw, the healing woman, as they call her," said Slingerland. "Her poultices must've worked."

The doctor picked up the old bandage which had been on Al's wound and sniffed at it. Then he nodded. "Yes. I wish I could get some of their secret prescriptions. They've learned a great deal from nature, some of 'em.''

Later on his great bay stud, Al Slingerland led the way into Cordell City. Behind him rode Warren Neale, Lee Davis, Federal Marshal Ed Thomkins of Cheyenne with a large posse he had sworn in.

A satisfying sleep, hearty meals, fresh dressings on his wound, had braced Slingerland, though he hadn't entirely recovered from the severe hurt dealt him by Flint Heart. Neale had begged him to stay and rest at the ranch, but the trapper was determined to help capture Doc Cordell. He'd scouted ahead, approaching the settlement so they wouldn't be noticed until they were near the Colorado Queen, Cordell's headquarters.

The morning sun bathed the plaza and buildings in warm yellow light. Wagons and saddle animals waited in front of the busy stores, women in bustled dresses and sunbonnets, small children tagging along, were doing their shopping, oldsters whittled on benches near the square, and men in range clothing moved to and fro.

Slingerland eased past the rear of the structures at the north end, and rode through Tin Can Alley. He heard the clang of Vince Farley's hammer as he neared the blacksmith's forge. Near the back entry to the Colorado Queen, he dismounted, and leading Reddy between two stables, tied the stallion to a post ring. Neale, David and Thomkins, with the hard-bitter possemen, drew up nearby and secured their mounts.

Colt and knife in his belt, the tall, bearded trapper, coonskin cap cocked on his head, walked with swift, long strides toward Cordell's lair, his friends hurrying after him.

As he stepped through the doorway, eyes adjusting to the dimmer light of the long passageway to the front of the saloon, a harsh voice suddenly challenged: "Hold on there! Where you think you're goin'—" The man broke off with a voilent curse.

Slingerland dropped fast, hunkering to the wall as he whipped out his Colt. He could see the figure down the hall, a tough in cowboy garb, a sawed-off shotgun in his h ands. And the fellow was raising the weapon, evidently recognizing Slingerland.

The shotgun boomed, the explosion echoing in the aisle. But its load slashed splinters from the pine floor, for Slingerland had thrown one a breath ahead, and the shotgunner was doubling up as his finger squeezed trigger.

Warren Neale, pistol in hand, Marshal Thomkins, young Lee Davis, and the posse members crowded through. "Al—are you hit?" cried Neale.

"No. C'mon. Cordell must've been expectin' us!"

He loped to the closed door which he knew led into Cordell's private quarters, and raising the latch, kicked it open, but then drew back. He could see in now, and quickly checked the room.

"Who's that? What's the shootin'?" called a commanding voice.

Now Slingerland saw Jake Cordell. The boss sat behind a long table, facing the entrance. He was in his shirtsleeves, blue garters holding up his cuffs, which had diamond-studded gold links in them. The thick watch chain, elk's-tooth fob hanging from it, gleamed over his fancy vest, and his think hair was pomaded across his large head, bit ears reddened. The stubborn jaw was thrust out.

Slingerland couldn't tell whether Doc Cordell was armed or not; the fat, hairy hands rested easily on the table top, but he might have a gun in his lap, hidden by the table.

Warren Neale and Marshal Thomkins entered, and Lee Davis, the posse members, bunching behind the leaders.

"I have a warrent, Cordell," announced Thomkins gravely. "You're under arrest."

Cordell blinked mildly. "What are the charges, sir?"

"Yoiu instigated and armed a band of Sioux Indians to destroy the village of Wesleyville. Men, women, children, all were massacred."

Cordell gave an incredulous laugh. "Why, that's loco! I can produce dozens of witness who'll swear I never left here that night!"

"I don't doubt it. But that doesn't relieve you of the blame. It's a Federal offense to furnish the savages with guns and egg them on to attack our citizens."

"That may be, but what's it got to do with me?" Doc Cordell almost beamed, and didn't seem at all alarmed. "I'd like to see you prove such a ridiculous accusation in a court of law, Thomkins!"

"Your agent, George Pate, carried rifles and ammunition to the Indians and in your name ordered them to strike and wipe out all people in Wesleyville," said Thomkins coolly. "We have a written and sworn deposition clinchin' it."

"What goes on here?" demanded a gruff voice.

Stu Barrington, the fat town marshal, pushed through, entering the room.

"Mr. Barrington!" cried Lee Davis. "Penny is fine. We were married in Cheyenne. We are—"

Barrington scowled at Davis.

"You abducted my daughter," he growled.

"She's of age, and she went willingly. She and I want you to come live with u. Penny's worried about you."

Lee Davis held out his hand. Barrington seemed shaken; he looked down, but then he shook hands with his new son-in-law. "Well, I guess it's all right, Lee. You're a good boy."

Barrington waddled over to his master, the boss of Cordell City. "What's up, Mr. Cordell? Anything I can do to help?"

The diversion had stopped Thomkins as he accused Cordell. Now he said, for Barrington's benefit. "Cordell had George Pate arm the Sioux and sick 'em on Wesleyville, Stu. He's my prisoner."

"Tell 'em I was here that night, Barrington," ordered Doc.

"Sure he was," said Barrington earnestly. "Never left town."

"He's still guilty. He ordered Pate to do the dirty work."

Barrington shook his head, bewildered. "But, why would he do such a thing?"

Warren Neale stepped forward, said severely, "I'll tell you why. Cordell was determined to have the new branch railroad come through his town. It would have meant a great fortune for him. But the route's impossible; he tried to bribe Davis to recommend it, but no honest engineer could do so. Slingerland'll tell you Cordell sent Pate to pay the Sioux to kill me, hopin' he could make a deal with the new engineers who took over the job!"

"This is a lot of twaddle, Stu," said Doc Cordell.

Barrington stood close to his boss. He shook his head.

Slingerland noticed that Cordell had taken his hands off the table top and sat pushed back in his chair. He glared furiously at Warren Neale.

"You have no proof," Cordell declared.

Thomkins spoke again: "I told you we have a sworn deposition against you, Cordell."

"Sworn by whom?" demanded Cordell.

"By your own son, Joe. He's badly wounded, but he'll live, and will testify against you, just as he's signed the statement puttin' the blame on you!"

Cordell stared violently, for the first time, a spasm of alarm crossed his set face. "You—" He paused, then began cursing Warren Neale with intense bitterness. "You're responsible, Neale! You'd ruin my town, take away everything I built up! Your cussed branch line would draw settlers away from here, damn your heart and soul—"

"Don't—" gasped Stu Barrington.

And Slingerland suddenly realized the depth of Cordell's hate for Warren Neale.

Doc Cordell had a heavy revolver in his lap, had had it there all the time, and when he'd dropped his hands, had gripped it, ready for action. Cordell hadn't known his son was a prisoner, hadn't guessed Joe would turn against him. But now he knew, knew he was doomed.

Slingerland acted with blinding speed, Colt jumping to his steady hand, hammer spur back under a long thumb.

But Cordell had a clear bead on Neale as he threw up his revolver, taking aim at the engineer.

Warren Neale would have died then and there had no Barrington, with surprising agility for such a stout man, thrown himself at Cordell, snatching at Doc's gun.

Slingerland fired, but his shot was a second-fraction later than Cordell's.

But Stu Barrington was between Neale and Doc's weapon, and Cordell's slug drove into his breast.

Pistol raised, Slingerland jumped over.

But his first bullet had struck home. Doc Cordell slumped in his chair. His eyes were already glazing and his arm dropped, the revolver clattering on the floor. A bluish-red hole had appeared in his forehead over the left eye. Slingerland's lead had pierced his brain.

With a sharp cry, Lee Davis started toward Barrington, who had collapsed close by his former master. A door in the back of the big room was flung open and a man with a Colt in hand jumped in; behind him were several more toughs. Evidently Cordell had had them waiting there.

"What the—" growled the leader, but stopped as he took in the scene.

Thomkins raised his pistol. "Back, you," he ordered.

The armed posse surged in, and the gunnies saw the law badges, Doc Cordell dead in his chair. Silently, they backed off.

Slingerland pouched his Colt, stepping beside Lee Davis, who knelt by his father-in-law.

"Dad, how bad is it?" he gasped.

Stu Barrington turned tortured eyes to Lee's face, lip

220

twisting in a fleeting smile. He whispered, "Penny—tell her I love her—" He shuddered as he died.

Slingerland touched Lee's shoulder. "Tell Penny her dad was a real man! Warren, he saved your life."

Neale nodded. "And thanks to you, Al, we're all safe now!"

An hour later, Al Slingerland set Reddy, his powerful bay, across the river bridge, hitting the trail over the mountain.

A joyful song welled in his stout heart. He was hurrying back to his true love, pretty Mountain Flower.

THE CALL
OF THE WAR DRUMS

I

As her train jolted to a stop at El Cajon, Helen Hammond peered eagerly from the grimy window.

Yes, there were the low, flat adobes, the scrofulous plaza, the beautiful little chapel, its cross the highest point in the New Mexican settlement. Ragged brown children gaped at the train, for its arrival was a feature of the day. Goats and pigs wandered about, and yellow hounds slept in what shade they could find, for the sun was hot as it neared its zenith in the clear sky.

A few loafers, serapes drawn about them, immense straw sombreros all but hiding them, leaned against the shady sides of the mud walls, enjoying the midday siesta.

Then she saw her brother, Alfred, and beside him the diminutive Link Stevens, watching expectantly for her.

A sense of happiness, a peace came over her. She felt as though she had finally come home after a miserable journey, though she had only been in the lovely land a few years before, during a visit to her sister Madeline, for a comparatively short time.

When she'd gone back to the glittering society of New York, she'd believed *that* was her home. To her astonishment she'd found she was bored, and a trip to London and Paris had not helped. She kept dreaming of the vast wastes of lonely, rugged space, the arched vault of the azure heavens, the mountain peaks looming in the distance.

And above all, she remembered the strong, bronzed men who had tamed the wilderness, comparing the Westerners to the effete playboys of high society. At last she'd admitted to herself that what she really wanted was to go back to New Mexico.

Alfred and Link Stevens jumped on the train steps and hurried down the aisle, her tall brother shouting a hearty welcome, Link grinning and waddling on his bowlegs behind Hammond.

She raised her dust veil and stood up. Alfred seized her in a bear hug and kissed her. "Sis! Mighty glad! Just couldn't wait to see you again."

Helen returned his embrace, and as Link reached up to take her suitcases from the rack, Helen smiled and kissed his whiskered cheek. The cowboy gulped, reddening with pleasured embarrassment.

It was a royal welcome, and Helen thought how different her arrival was to Madeline's, who had come late at night to a deserted station. A drunken cowboy had staggered in, seized Madeline and forced a priest to conduct what Madeline had believed to be a mock wedding ceremony. Later, when she'd come to love Gene Stewart, the cowboy, Madeline had learned she had really been married at that time .

"We'll go to Florence's sister's in town here, clean up, have lunch and rest till the worst of the heat has passed," said Alfred, as he lifted her to the platform. "Give me your baggage checks and the boys'll take your trunks out in the ranch wagon."

A low-sided vehicle, two brown geldings hitched to it, waited nearby. Alfred signaled a tall cowboy, who hurried over. "This is Matt Hall, Helen, yard boss at Madeline and Gene's."

Hall swept off his curved-brim Stetson. He had a nice smile, thought Helen, who liked men. He kept smiling as he greeted her very politely, his blue eyes on her pretty, rosy-cheeked face. As a man will, in a glance he took in her slender, feminine figure, her large, long-lashed brown eyes, and self-consciously, Helen pushed back wisps of brown hair which had escaped from under her hat.

Helen Hammond was worth a second look, and more. She was in the prime of young womanhood, and as she put her small hand in Hall's big one, a bit of the coquette showed in her animated features.

Alfred passed the baggage checks to Hall, who turned and sang out, "You, Chris! Over here. Hop to it."

Link tossed her suitcases into the back of the wagon, except for a light bag Helen kept with her.

The man who'd been on the seat got down and came over, and Hall said gruffly, "Pick out the right trunks. I'll fetch the team around."

As Helen glanced at Chris, she couldn't restrain a gasp. He was six-feet-four, a powerful chest tapering to a slim waist. He seemed too large for the Levi's he wore, and muscles bulged in his arms, hardly contained by his short-sleeved gray shirt.

But it was chiefly his face which attracted her, as a magnet draws steel. It seemed chiseled from red bronze; his jaw was firm, and health glowed in his smooth cheeks. His hair was black, his eyes even darker.

"This is Chris Oliver," said Alfred.

Oliver touched his hat brim, and for a moment, the girl met his clear eyes. They were devoid of expression,

227

but Helen felt an electric thrill that was almost a delicious dread.

Chris Oliver moved toward the baggage car, and she couldn't help watching him. He glided with pantherish grace.

"He's a breed," she heard Matt Hall saying. "Strong as a range bull."

Alfred and Link led her to the car and helped her in. She looked around and saw Hall backing the wagon to the high platform where baggage had been unloaded. Chris Oliver lifted one of her large trunks as though it contained feathers rather than two hundred pounds of clothing, gear and gifts Helen had brought for her sister and friends. The big man set the trunk gently down in the wagon bed.

Link was muttering to himself as he cranked the car, which was balky at the moment. Alfred sat in the rear seat with his sister, who asked, "Chris Oliver, who is he?"

"He's one of Gene's hands. Great with horses."

"Matt Hall said he was a breed."

"Yes, he's part Apache. The missionaries sent him to college, though, so he's not ignorant. He's very quiet, hasn't much to say for himself. Madeline wanted to come meet you, too, but the new baby's only a month old and the doctor ordered her to take it easy. Gene's delivering a herd in Arizona, but he'll be home in a couple of days. Florence sends her love; she had to stay home and mind the kids."

The car finally sputtered and began firing. As it rattled along the dusty road, brother and sister chatted of many things.

Helen saw the ranch wagon leaving, Matt Hall at the

reins, Chris Oliver on the wide seat. She thought Oliver was looking her way, and had a strange sensation his farseeing eyes were fixed on her.

Florence's sister's home was not far away. Helen was happy to wash the travel dust away and slip on a fresh light gown. By the time she was ready, wine was being poured in the living room, and lunch was being prepared by a Mexican woman.

After a leisurely meal, Helen Hammond went to lie down, as did the others. In two or three hours, they would start for the ranch.

That afternoon they took their leave. Link Stevens was at the wheel, Helen and Alfred in the back seat. There was so much to talk about, news to exchange, but that miles rolled off swiftly, dust swirls marking the automobile's passage.

The rutted dirt track curved between two frowning rock walls. Suddenly Link applied the brake and Helen was thrown forward but Alfred caught her arm.

When she looked ahead, she saw several large boulders blocked the road. Link said in surprise, "Huh, I never knew rock falls to roll this far out!" He got down, took a steel tool, and went to lever the stones off to clear a passage for the car.

"I better give him a hand," Alfred said, as he saw Link straining at a heavy boulder.

As he rose to get down, explosions crackled in the warm air. It was a moment before Helen realized they were gunshots, and she had a brief impression of bluish smoke puffs from the low brush lining the road.

Link Stevens flexed back, dropping the tool, turned, and fell hard on the baked ground. Helen's scream froze in her throat as Alfred gave an agonized cry that suddenly broke off; his hat had flipped from his head, and he slumped by the rear wheel of the car.

"Alfred—Link—"

Gasping with horror, Helen jumped from the car and knelt by her brother. Alfred's eyes stared vacantly ahead and a trickle of blood dribbled down his left cheek.

"Alfred!" she quavered, picking up his hand.

Several lithe figures materialized, as though from nowhere; they had come around the car. She knew they were Indians, probably Apaches. They wore knee-high leather moccasins, their lean brown torsos naked to the flapping breechclout. Each carried a carbine, and snakeskins banded their straight black hair.

Still kneeling by her brother, whose head lolled on one shoulder, Helen was seized from behind. A hand was clapped over her lips, stifling her cry. She fought, kicked, tried to bite, but she was helpless. The sinewy arms wrapping her held her as though in a vise.

Another man slapped a dirty cloth over her face, covering her eyes. It was tied tightly behind her neck, and she could hardly breathe, let alone see anything. Then she was swept up, and her wrists and ankles roughly thonged.

Her cries were muffled by the blindfold. She heard horses coming up, and then she was slung like a sack of meal over the blanketed back of a quivering mustang. Grunts in an unknown tongue came to her, and then the horse lunged forward, Helen jouncing up and down as the riders picked up speed.

She could feel the Indian riding with her, and could smell him, the scent of bear grease and sweat mingling unpleasantly. Her breath was jolted from her and she was bruised from the rough handling.

Now and again her captors would exchange a word or two in their unintelligible jargon.

On and on, and Helen Hammond suffered in a confused horror.

There seemed no end to the nightmare; the horses slowed as they kept climbing steep slopes, stones clacking under the hoofs.

She had heard fearful accounts of what such Indians did to captive white women.

She couldn't guess how far they'd come before the horse under her stopped, and the Apache holding her jumped off. She was dumped down unceremoniously. Her hands were fastened behind her and she felt what seemed a stable blanket; it smelled like that.

The blindfold was snatched away, and now she could see. Two of the savaged squatted by her, cruel knives in hand. She was in a small hut made of rough adobe, the roof of thorned brush; there was a low doorway but no windows.

The Apaches scowled at her and raised their glittering blades. She expected they meant to kill her, but they only slashed off the rawhide bonds, freeing her wrists and ankles. She was sore and bruised and her limbs prickled as circulation was fully restored. The men rose, their black-haired pates brushing the ceiling; both wore snakeskin headbands. She managed to push herself up and lean back against the crumbling mud wall.

Tension mounted in Helen as she stared up at the cruel faces.

Then the Indians turned and ducked through the low doorway. They remained nearby outside, as though on guard, and before long, she caught the odor of tobacco burning. The Apaches had lighted pipes and were jabbering together.

Tears came to her smarting eyes as she thought of Alfred; she was sure her brother had been killed, and poor Link Stevens, too. She'd never see Madeline again, she was convinced of that. Not long ago, Helen Hammond had been a spoiled darling of high society, whose every whim was gratified; now—Sobs shook her as she realized what a horrible fate might be in store for her.

II

Chris Oliver brought the wagon to a stop in front of the Stewart's big hacienda and set the hand brake.

Madeline Hammond Steward, holding her new infant in her arms, stood on the long veranda, smiling expectantly as Matt Hall jumped down and saluted her. Chris Oliver had always thought the mistress of the ranch was the most beautiful woman he had ever seen. But now in his mind he corrected this, for he had looked upon her younger sister in El Cajon. He'd been unable to dismiss Helen Hammond from his young mind. He knew he was loco, as the white lords of the land put it, to dream of such a girl, as far beyond his reach as the brilliant stars in the Western skies.

"All's well, ma'am," reported Matt Hall. "Your sister and brother went to eat and rest. Then Link'll fetch 'em out."

"I'm so glad. It must have been a tiring trip for Helen."

If possible, Madeline was even lovelier than when she had arrived in New Mexico. Her love for Gene Stewart and their pretty children had brought her such happiness, she could scarcely believe her good fortune.

232

Billy Stillwell sat in a rocking chair nearby. His huge face was a maze of wrinkles, and it seemed his great bulk had shrunk somewhat with age. He sat more in the chair than he did in the saddle these days, but he still enjoyed life.

He loved to amuse and play with the little ones. He was holding young Madeline, who was three, on his lap, while Gene, Junior, who had celebrated his fourth birthday not long ago, was riding up and down the long porch on a wooden hobbyhorse Stillwell had painstakingly carved for him.

Chris Oliver saw the old man was watching him with a veiled, dormant hostility, as he always did, for Stillwell had come to the wild region before the Apaches had been subdued. He'd fought them and he would never change, Chris Oliver realized, and more than the elderly Indians, once masters of the desert all the way to the Sierra Madre in Mexico, could quence their hatred for the *Pinda Lick-o-yi*, the "white eyes," who had taken it from them in a running war, not quarter given or asked. A war that had lasted for over twenty years. Stillwell hated Apaches and that was all there was to it.

Chris Oliver was heavier and taller than the average Apache. He knew his father's mother had been a white girl kidnapped by his grandfather chief in a raid on a ranch. Oliver had been raised in a mountain rancheria, and until the missionaries had picked him out as a promising lad, he'd known only the Indian way of life. The missionaries had been good to him; a kindly Quaker had adopted the boy, and finding him of more than average intelligence, schooled him and sent him to an Indian college.

But the high hopes he'd entertained of entering the white world as a peer had been dashed. Even with his education, he'd found only the lowliest work open to any Indian. He might have worked at one of the agencies, but he'd been driven by a sincere desire to lift his people to a higher civilization.

"You, Chris! Don't just and there. Unload that stuff and put the things where Mrs. Stewart shows you!"

Matt Hall spoke to him with a contempt he never tried to veil, and somehow, Oliver resented this more than he did the ancient Stillwell's attitude. Stillwell had some reason for it, but Matt Hall was only a year or two older than Chris. But Oliver had found it best to keep quiet and hide his emotions, easy enough for an Indian.

Many whites looked down on his people. The Boss, Mr. Gene Stewart, was kind to him and paid him better than average. Chris Oliver loved horses, and the ranch animals were above average.

He carried Helen Hammond's trunks and other luggage into a large bedroom as Mrs. Stewart directed. The windows gave out on a patio, which had flower gardens and a fountain playing on a marble statue in it.

This done, he drove the team around to the rear, unhitched and rubbed down the horses, watered them and turned them into one of the pens and put up the wagon. There were a number of outbuildings, barns and stables, a long bunkhouse, a chicken run, a series of corrals. The Stewarts kept several milch cows, too.

Down the line, Oliver's beautiful paint stallion nickered to him, and his grim lips softened; he loved the animal, and had paid six months wages for him. The pinto returned the man's affection.

He washed at a trough. As he started over to the bunkhouse, his keen ears caught the distant drum of hoofs, and he turned, glancing westward. A rider was coming in, fast. Chris Oliver made a cigarette and lit it,

234

lounging in the shade outside, waiting for the horseman.

Matt Hall came around the end of the great hacienda, saw Chris Oliver and frowned. "What're you loafing for? Get over there and give Kenny a hand with them new broncos!"

"Mr. Stewart's coming."

"You're loco! He won't be back for a couple more days."

But Hall swung to watch. Oliver sayed, too, and after a while, Gene Stewart rode up on a great black horse, leathered, dusty. "Huh! It *is* the Boss. Go take his horse."

Chris Oliver hurried out and caught the reins as Gene Stewart swung a long leg off his sweated saddle. Tall, with a sharp, rawboned face, his dark hair was matted under his Stetson, and grit stuck to his flesh.

Madeline laughed with joy as she returned his embrace. "I didn't expect you till tomorrow at the earliest, Gene."

"The deal went quicker than I expected. I left the boys to come back with Frankie. Is Helen here?"

"No, but she's due any minute now."

"Howdy, sir," sang out Matt Hall. "Have a good trip?"

Stewart waved. Hall was ever trying to impress the Boss.

"I'll take good care of your horse," Hall said. He frowned at Oliver, who held the jaded black's rein, and was staring southward at the azure vault of the sky. "Move, you stupid breed," he said under his breath, so nobody but Chris Oliver could hear.

But Oliver called, "Señor Stewart! I see smoke."

Gene Stewart came down, looking at Oliver inquiringly.

"Where?" he asked, and Oliver pointed. Stewart shook his head, then took the powerful binoculars from the saddle case and focused them. "You're right. Not much but—maybe the car broke down and they're signaling. Matt, get three of the boys and a buckboard. Chris, turn my black in, fetch me another mount and pick up our own."

"What's wrong?" Madeline called anxiously from the porch.

"Nothing, sweetheart. I'm going to meet Helen. Link may have had some trouble with that old wreck of a car."

Within a few minutes Gene Stewart and Chris Oliver rode out. Oliver admired Stewart for the way he handled a horse; he was as good as an Apache. Oliver had saddled his pinto, and the two men picked up speed, the ground rolling away under the beating hoofs, wind whistling in their ears as they rode low over the withers.

"Can you still see it?" asked Stewart after a time.

"No. It has burned out."

Not far ahead was a narrows where the road curved, and suddenly Gene Stewart swore, dug in his spurs, spurting ahead. As he jumped down, dropping rein, Oliver joined him, and they hurried to the man who lay unmoving in the sandy dirt, face down, hat gone, and they could see the crusted blood in his hair.

"Alfred!" cried Stewart, kneeling by his brother-in-law.

Within arm's length was a small blackened patch where a dry sotol bush had burned.

"He must have lit it to signal before he—" Stewart broke off; he couldn't bear to say Alfred had died.

With Oliver's help, he rolled Hammond over on his back and felt inside his stained shirt for a heartbeat. He swore with some relief. "He's not gone yet! But where's the car with Helen and Link?"

Chir Oliver loped toward the gap. The sign told him that Alfred Hammond had staggered and crawled to the point where he'd managed to fire the brush. Then Oliver sighted the car, blocked by large rocks in the road.

Another man lay by a big boulder, and Oliver saw it was Link Stevens. He checked Stevens, shook his head sadly, and began looking for Helen Hammond.

She wasn't in the car, and as he read the sign, his heart jumped with dread. He ran back to Stewart, who was pouring sips of water from a canteen between Alfred's parted lips, wiping his face.

"The car's there, Mr. Stewart. And Link, he's dying. But Señorita Hammond has been carried off by Apaches."

Gene Stewart scowled up at him; he pointed back toward the ranch, and the approaching dust showed the buckboard and cowboys coming up.

Now Oliver hurried off again, ranging around, studying the sign, figuring what had happened, as Stewart headed toward the car.

After a time, he heard Matt Hall bawling at him. "You, Chris! Come back here!" Matt Hall had his hands up, using them as a megaphone.

Oliver moved back to the automobile. Four riders had accomplished the buckboard, and they had lifted Alfred into it.

As Oliver passed Hall, the straw boss said in a low but virulent voice, "Who told you to go flitting around like a coyote?"

Chris Oliver said nothing but joined Stewart, who squatted beside Stevens. Link whispered hoarsely, "Apaches!"

"Take it easy, Link," said Gene Stewart. "We'll run you home and patch you up good as new."

He knew he was talking through his hat and so did Oliver, for a glance told them Link Stevens was past saving. A rifle bullet had ripped through him from side to side, and high up, close to the heart; another had shattered several ribs, and Link's life blood was being sucked up by the thirsty soil.

Chris Oliver hung his head, sadly; he'd liked Stevens, a hearty soul and a top fighting man. He also knew why Link had managed to stay alive until he could give Stewart a final report. An Apache would have done that. Most men would have expired before, and now Stevens gave a last shudder, relaxing in death.

To occupy himself, Oliver began singlehandedly rolling aside the huge boulders blocking the automobile. The buckboard river sang out, "Hammond's coming to, Mr. Stewart."

Seeing there was nothing more to be done for Stevens, Gene Stewart said shortly, "See to Link's body, Matt," and trotted back to the wagon, climbing in by Alfred. He drew a silver flask from his pocket and held it to Hammond's lips. After a swig of the whiskey, Hammond shivered, and Stewart gave him another drink.

As Chris Oliver reached the buckboard, he heard Stewart say, "You got a little head crease, Al," in a comforting voice. "The blood's clotted. We'll run you back and send for Doc. Don't try to talk much, save you strength. But it was Apaches, wasn't it?"

Hammond nodded. "Yes, Apaches. I managed—"

It wasn't necessary to tell Stewart and Oliver more than that. Sunned for a while, Alfred Hammond had found enough strength to crawl a short distance toward the ranch. Realizing he was going to pass out again, he'd struck a match and touched off the dead bush as a signal.

Matt Hall could run the car; he cranked it, and it started easily enough. He drove it to the buckboard, and Hammond was lifted into it. The cowboys took the wagon to load in Link's body.

The valley floor was a vast red waste, broken here and there by great outcrops of rock. In the hot sky loomed mountains, the Peloncillos, the Chiricahuas, the Guadeloupes, ranges named by the Spaniards, the first white invaders. Greasewood, and cactus of all shapes, patches of grama grass, dotted the desert world.

Stewart could handle the automobile, and he took the wheel from Hall, with Hammond propped on the front seat by him. Stewart started back to the ranch, so as to get Hammond there as quickly as possible.

Chris Oliver picked up his pinto, and swung into the saddle; he started to ride west, intending to follow the sign as far as he could before night set in. But Matt Hall sang out angrily to him and he turned back.

"Where you think *you're* going?" demanded Hall, face red. "Your folks killed poor old Link and kidnaped Mrs. Stewart's sister! What you aim to do, join up with 'em?" He spoke with savage hatred, and his hands dropped to his holstered Colt as he scowled up at Oliver. "G'wan, get on back or I'll let you have it."

Chris Oliver shrugged; he turned the paint horse and galloped after the car.

A million stars twinkled in the sky as they reached the

Stewart ranch. Lights were on, and Madeline anxiously awaited them. Bill Stillwell was doing his best to calm her. Mexican servants had fed the children and put them to bed.

Alfred Hammond wasn't seriously wounded. He could walk, though Gene Stewart insisted two men hold his arms and see him to a bedroom. Madeline looked up pitifully at her husband as he took her in his arms.

"Sweetheart, be brave. Helen's been kidnaped but that doesn't mean she's been harmed. Whoever took her will demand ransom. We'll pay it and get her back safe and sound."

Chris Oliver had put up his horse, then come silently back, waiting in shadow, keeping away from Matt Hall and the other men, who stood in the shaft of light from the front door, smoking and talking in low voices.

After while, Stewart came out. He stood on the stoop as he spoke. "We can't track 'em tonight, boys. But we'll be there at crack of dawn, pick up the sign. Eat, get some sleep, and be ready to take off. I'll want Chris Oliver; he's the best tracker we got."

Matt Hall spoke up. "I'll bet the cusses are from the Eagle's rancheria; it ain't but a few miles off in the mountains. How'd they savvy Mrs. Stewart's sister was coming, Boss? Somebody here must've tipped 'em off. We're the only ones knew what time Miss Helen would come. The Apaches were told exactly. I never did trust that breed!"

"Wait," snapped Stewart. "It sounds to me like you're accusing Chris Oliver!"

Hall crawfished. "Well not exactly. I only say it's mighty queer. He's the Eagle's son, ain't he?"

Chris Oliver glided in; he didn't look at Hall, but spoke to Stewart.

"It wasn't my people," he said firmly. "They'll never war again with the Americans."

"Still, Link and Señor Hammond say they were Apaches."

"Bronco Apaches, outlaws who have sworn to fight to the death. They hide in the Sierra Madre in Mexico, raid, steal women and kill. There are a few old ones left and sometimes a fool young brave will run off to join them."

The Apache tribes had learned a bitter lesson. They had fought hard under Cochise, Nana, Mangus Colorado, Geronimo and other chiefs. For decades a mere handful had kept the United States Army busy, before final surrender. Many had been shipped like cattle to die in Florida, others restricted to arid reservations, where they were bilked by thieving agents.

The Broncos were diehards; they lurked in untracked wilderness south of the Border, waging the endless war against the Mexicans. Once the Mexican government had to pay $100 for an Apache brave's scalp and $50 for a squaw's hair, but all this was history.

Gene Stewart gave orders. They'd move out before dawn, with arms and trail rations. The boss was exhausted; he'd ridden hard all day to reach home and then to hurry to the spot where Helen had been kidnaped. He went into the house, to eat and sleep.

Soon the men turned in. Oliver's bunk was near the entrance. He removed his boots, hat and gunbelt, and stretched on his back. He lay thinking for a while, picturing the pretty, animated face of Helen Hammond. He could imagine her terror when she'd been snatched up and carried off. If those bronco devil had hurt her—his big fists clenched. Finally he drifted off . . .

He jumped awake. Some inborn instinct inherited

from savage ancestors warned him but scarcely in time. But somehow he managed to deflect the glinting long knife driving down at his heart.

The point ripped his shirt, slashing down his ribs. He snatched the thick wrist and with a mighty wrench, twisted so the man grunted in pain, letting the knife fly off.

Oliver could make out few details in the gloom, the squat shape, the black blob of the face, for the killer was masked with a bandanna. He brought up a foot and planted it in the man's belly, straightening his legs, shoving so hard the man lost his balance and fell to the floor.

He came up in a crouch and Chris Oliver heard the *cluck-cluck* of a cocking revolver, but he was already scrabbling off as the gun flamed and roared. Then he burst from the door, swerving aside in the nick of time as a second slug shrieked through the opening.

Barefooted, he ran like an antelope past the corrals. He felt blood wetting his side, and the wound stung, but he did not pause. He sang out softly to his pinto, who came trotting to him.

The moon was breaking over the horizon and the myriad stars gave him enough light to open the gate and seize the rope halter; he could ride bareback as well as in a saddle, and he sprang on the tall stallion and took off, the paint horse quickly at full gallop.

Low over the withers, clinging with his strong knees, he flashed around the lower end of the great hacienda. A lantern had been lighted in the bunkhouse and he heard vague shouts.

He wasn't sure who had tried to kill him. But he knew it hadn't been Matt Hall. The masked knifer had been shorter, heavier than Hall; it might have been Vern Olds, a dull-witted stableman who followed the straw boss around like a jackal after a lion. But there were several in the crew who might have been angry enough to do it, infuriated by the Apache murder of Link Stevens and the kidnaping of Helen Hammond. White men were like that; they blamed all Indians for what a few might do.

Oliver set his course by the stars, southwest toward the mountains. The night air was cool, a breeze in his face coming from the looming black heights. He knew the country almost rock by rock; it was his homeland. He crossed sandy wastes, skirting patches of cactus and brush, rock upthrusts.

As he hit a narrow trail up the first slopes, he pulled up and dismounted. A small rill, runoff from a spring, meandered down the rocky rise. He squatted by this and splashed cold water on his wounded side and on his face. Tearing a piece of shirt from his tail, he cleansed the long scratch and held it to the wound till more of the bleeding stopped. The stallion lowered his head and drank, and then Chris Oliver remounted and rode on, climbing into the mountain fastnesses.

III

Helen Hammond roused from a feverish light sleep.

It was inky-black in the tiny hut, though she could see a patch of sky, with twinkling stars, through the low doorway.

Tense, she listened. They were moving around outside and she heard low voices. Now the rays of a lantern showed faintly, then she saw the flickering light at the entry and someone ducked inside, setting the lantern on the dirt floor.

Helen sat up straight, looking fearfully at the newcomer. He was short and stout, and wore tight-fitting trousers tucked into high boots, a silk shirt matted to his torso by sweat. A sombrero hung by its chinstrap down his broad back. His kerchief was drawn up to his nose, but he had sober, brown eyes and there was no cruelty in them. From gray streaks in his black hair she decided he was about forty.

"Señorita Hammond," he said politely, as though they were being introduced at some social function, "I greet you. I am Garcia." His voice was muffled by the bandanna but his English was good, flavored as it was by a Spanish accent. Now he handed her a canteen, as though divining how thirsty she was. After a moment's hesitation, she uncorked it and satisfied her burning, dry throat. The water was lukewarm but sweet, with a faint alcoholic taste.

"You are hungry?" asked Garcia, in his velvety voice.

"No, I couldn't eat anything now." Hiding her fear, she demanded with dignity, "How dare you do this? Señor Stewart and the police—"

He cut her short. "Señorita, we know all this. Now, I will warn you. If you obey, you won't be harmed; I swear this by all the Saints. If you try to escape, you will be punished. Comprehend?" He was still polite but firm.

As she started to object, he warned, "Be careful. These Apaches are savage beasts. I alone can protect you."

He slung the canteen over a shoulder, took her arm and lifted her to her feet. "Stay close to me." He kept a grip on her wrist as he led her outside, the lanternlight dancing as they moved.

Silent shadows watched, like wolves ready to spring. Garcia led Helen down a rocky path. A saddled horse waited below, and the Mexican ordered, "You will ride with me."

He helped her climb to the high-pronged saddle, blew out the lantern and hung it on a hook at the cantle. Then he mounted behind her, and taking the rein, touched the horse with a spur.

The moon was up. An Indian rode ahead, and there were others behind; she heard sounds hard to identify but finally decided they were brushing out what few prints might be left in the hard ground. She'd heard of that, how skillful men could wipe out sign to confuse trackers.

The steep, rough way was like a goat path, so they were forced to move slowly. Garcia kept one arm around her so she woudn't fall off as the horse lurched from side to side.

She could not tell how far they had come when at last the ground levelled off a bit. Unused to orienting herself at night, she wasn't sure what direction they were traveling, though the moon seemed to be usually to her left.

She wasn't inured to riding astride and her legs hurt. A grove of cedars showed at the side of the track, and suddenly she saw the buggy standing there, a horse in its shafts. Garcia got down and grunted as he lifted her off. He led her to the buggy.

"Get in," he ordered, handing her up as she found the small iron step.

She sank into the leather seat. Garcia attached his mount's rein to the rear of the vehicle, and for a moment, Helen was free, but she knew the Indians were near and she had no idea which way to run if she could escape.

Garcia untied the bridle rope from the pinon limb, brought the reins up, unfastening them from the set brake. He got up beside her and released the brake. He'd lowered his mask but she couldn't make out much in the dimness.

An Apache stayed ahead, scouting the road, while the others came behind, dragging spruce branches to hide tracks. The wheels creaked as the buggy lurched over rough spots. But soon the motion grew smoother and Helen realized they were on a road of sorts.

"Where are you taking me?" she demanded.

"Be quiet, Senorita, I have told you, you'll not be harmed."

She sensed Garcia was nervous, too; he had a pistol tucked in his sash, and a knife. The moon was well up, and as the way levelled off, the buggy picked up speed. Shadows of trees sprang up and disappeared as they glided by.

Her muscles ached and strain tensed her, but Helen found she couldn't keep her eyes open, and fell into a light sleep. She roused as the buggy stopped, and ahead she saw the moonglow of a river. The horses were drinking in the shallows, she saw their riders lying on their bellies, satisfying their thirst.

Garcia got out. "Stay were you are, Señorita."

She shrank back against the seat as she saw the animal glow of the Indian eyes as they rose and looked her way. Soon Garcia came back; he'd refreshed himself, and was smoking a cheroot. He handed her the canteen.

"Drink," he said. "I have refilled it."

The water was cooler and she was grateful for it.

They resumed the journey, crossing the river at a shallow ford. Soon they came out on a sandy road. There were few trees, but she saw the shapes of ocatillos, organ and barrel cactus.

The motion of the vehicle was so smooth it was hypnotic and the girl feel asleep again.

Garcia shook her awake; he was standing on her side of the buggy.

"Come," he said, pulling her hand, as she stepped from the buggy, she saw she was in a walled courtyard, with flowers and shrubs around. A hacienda stood there and Garcia steered her to the door. The entry to the patio had been closed; lamps flickered at the heavy bronze-studded door, which Garcia opened, pushing Helen inside.

The sala was lighted and she looked about her curiously. A peon in a shapeless white cotton suit, dull eyes watching Garcia and the young woman, stood nearby. The servant shut and bolted the great door, as Garcia nodded.

Garcia gave a short command in Spanish and the servant padded off in his slippers, over thick mats with Indian designs. The room was furnished in Spanish style, with heavy, ornate tables and chairs, statues of holy figures, paintings. Helen noted the high, narrow windows were barred.

Soon a portly female came down the stairs. She wore a silk robe, and a jeweled comb was stuck in her dark hair, piled high on her head. Her white teeth flashed a welcome and Garcia bowed to her, and said, "Señora Maria, this is Senorita Helen."

Maria took Helen's hand in hers and smiled again at the bedraggled girl. She spoke softly in Spanish and drawing Helen to her, kissed her cheeks.

"Please tell me why I'm here," begged Helen, but Maria shook her head, still smiling, and said, *"No hablo ingles,* Señorita."

She led the girl up the stairs, flashing a smile back to Garcia. The steps and hallway were carpeted, and Maria steered Helen to a spacious chamber, with a dresser, water ewer and basin, a closet hung with robes, several straight-back chairs, and a comfortable one of leather.

Helen was relieved to clean up, and fix her hair before the great mirror. Maria bustled about, serving her like a mother hen. She brought forth a lovely silken robe and helped Helen remove her stained outer garments and slip into it. It had a faint, musky odor.

Someone knocked and Maria hurried over to take a tray from a Mexican woman. There was a hot meal of spiced meat, tortillas, a pot of steaming coffee, and fine silverware and china. Helen sat down to eat, while heavily flavored, the food was satisfying and though she'd thought she wasn't hungry, she ate well and drank two cups of the strong coffee.

She sat on the bed and Maria smiled, patting her, turning down the coverlet. There were three of the high, narrow windows in one wall, and Helen saw they, too, were barred, heavy draperies hanging by them. Maria drew these, and with her broad smile, said, *"Buenas noches,* Senorita." She blew out the table lamp and went off, closing the door behind her.

Helen heard a bolt slide shut outside and she knew she was a prisoner.

IV

The sun was tinting the horizon behind him with

purples, crimson and other glorious hues as Chris Oliver rode into the rancheria.

Here he had been born and raised. It was a permanent village now, though as crude as it had ever been. There were tipi shelters, long poles tied with rawhide thongs and draped with hides or old canvas, wickiups with mats for walls, a few one-room shacks of adobe with brush roofs.

The rancheria sprawled across a mountain meadow, with rock spires around the rim where sentries might stand guard. Despite the earnest effort of missionaries to change the fierce Apaches from warriors and hunters into farmers, only pitiful little patches had been scratched here and there, mostly by squaws who tended them, for that was women's work. Pumpkins, melons, a few vegetables made up the crop. The women still gathered berries, roots and other natural bounties as they had always done.

The men hunted and fetched in game. As for the seeds and grains furnished by the whites, they had dried up where they had been scattered or eaten by mustangs and birds. The soil was poor and rocky, and the braves did not fancy agriculture.

Young men with any ambition left the village to seek excitement in the white man's world. They worked on ranches or at town stables and liveries, taking any job they could find.

The rancheria was stirring and squaws were lighting breakfast fires as Chris Oliver got down and slipped the rope halter from the pinto. The horse nuzzled his arm and walked off to drink from the brook on the far side. He would graze with the shaggy ponies. A few mounts were staked nearby so others could be easily caught. There were goats to furnish milk and curds.

A pack of nondescript dogs came to fawn on him; they hadn't barked because they had caught his scent. If a stranger approached they would raise a din, but an over-noisy canine went into the stewpot, since in olden days this might betray a village.

Oliver's father, the Eagle, lean and tall, his graying hair bound by a snakeskin band, wearing a cotton shirt and long leather leggings, came to greet him. The Eagle had a hawklike visage, and his eyes were still clear and bright; in his youth, he had been a great warrior.

Now his mother came, smiling proudly at her strong son. He embraced her in white-man fashion. Seeing the blood on his ribs, she led him into the hut to cleanse and poultice the wound. The Eagle followed and sat by him, and soon the woman brought them warm food, and coffee flavored with chicory and molasses. There were hides and blankets, a few utensils, his father's old long rifle, bow and arrows, other belongings.

As they ate, Chris Oliver told his father what had happened. The Eagle was troubled; he knew the whites would blame everything on the nearest rancheria, and that meant blind repisals.

To Chris Oliver, the camp was a sad place. He'd returned from his schooling full of zeal, determined to raise his people from savagery to civilization. He'd given what money he could earn to his parents and the tribe.

But now he knew it was hopeless. The people had to stomach for the ways of the *Pinda Lick-o-yi*.

The Indians called Chris by his Apache name, which in Spanish was Cuchillo Colorado, Red Knife. The peace-loving Quakers had disapproved of this, for they concluded, and rightly that "Red" meant Bloody. They had christened him Christopher Oliver, his benefactor giving him his surname.

When he had eaten, Oliver stretched on a mat and fell into a sound sleep.

The sun was hot when he roused; his father had returned. The Eagle was a skilled tracker and had taught his son the secrets. Accompanied by two other Apaches, he'd made a swift scout down the mountain.

Chris's mother pressed another bowl of food and more coffee on him, while the Eagle unwrapped a repeating carbine Oliver had given him, a belt of ammunition for it. Any Apache would have traded his best wary poney for such a weapon, but the Eagle saved it, and now he laid it by his son, along with a staghorn hunting knife honed to razor edge. Both were first-class killing equipment.

The Eagle squatted by him, telling what the scouts had found. As he ate, Oliver listened gravely. His mother had mended, washed and dried his shirt; she again examined the hurt in his side and nodded it would soon heal.

In Apache, Oliver asked, "You'll help Señor Stewart?"

The Eagle shrugged. "We will help *you*. But the *Pin-da Lick-o-yi* will blame *all* Apaches, you know how they think. They'll shoot us on sight, it's their habit. To them we are dangerous animals to be exterminated like rabid coyotes."

"Not all are the same. Señor Stewart is a good man."

But the chief had suffered too much and seen too many awful sights. He repeated, "We will help you."

Chris Oliver didn't try to reason with his father. It was useless, just as it was to change old Bill Stillwells's

251

conviction that the only good Indian was a dead one.

Oliver donned his shirt, strapped on the ammunition belt and thrust the knife into it. He tied on deerskin moccasions, and left the shelter. The slash in his side was something not even to be noticed, and he drew in a deep breath of fragrant air. Wild flowers grew in the meadows, butterflies hovering over the blooms, birds of varied hues flitted about. Squaws were pounding and hanging up venison strips, oir baking tortillas at outside ovens. Children played games, and a group of elders squatted in the shade, smoking pipes and talking of once-great times. A brave on a high tor watched the grazing ponies.

Oliver gave a shrill whistle and the paint horse came nickering to him. He needed no saddle. He strapped a blanket bad on the powerful stud's back and fitted a plaited hair halter over the animal's nose and neck. He could guide with slight knee pressure; the pinto was a cutting horse, among other accomplishments.

The pinto insistently touched his soft muzzle to Oliver's hand, and the man's grim lips relaxed. He felt in a pocket and found a lump of sugar, which was what the horse had asked for.

The Eagle and other Apaches watched; they would never understand such mutual affection, for to them a pony was only a tool, to be used for war and hunting; if necessasry, an Indian would kill and eat his horse without hesitation.

Oliver mounted in a bound; there was little to compare with the thrill he felt with such a horse under him. He waved at his father, who watched his son ride off down the steep, winding path.

Some miles below the rancheria Chris Oliver reached the point where his father had said the sign split off to the south. The baked, rocky earth left few impressions and only the most expert eye could have detected anything, and the trail had been skillfully wiped over. He didn't dismount since his father had told him all he needed to know. He hadn't noticed the divergence when he'd passed by in the night, and he'd been hurt, intent on reaching the rancheria.

Going down was faster than climbing the steep trails. By midmorning he was nearing the plateau. Northeast lay the Stewart ranch. Nothing escaped his trained eye; several swallows swooped up, and he caught a flash, sunlight on metal, probably a rifle barrel.

He moved more cautiously; too many whites were inclined to shoot first at an Indian and check up afterwards. Soon he got down and led the stud behind some huge black boulders, tied him to a shrub pinon. Carbine in one hand, he slanted down, and waited by a flat-topped rock close to the goat track up the mountain.

Finally he sighted the van of Gene Stewart's crew working their way up. Rabbitears Walsh, an older cowboy and experienced tracker, was out front, studying the ground. A few paces behind Walsh came Matt Hall, and next Gene Stewart. A dozen heavily armed men were spaced out, ready for trouble. They were on foot; well to the rear, the horses were being led by three more waddies.

With an expert's eye, Chris Oliver watched Rabbitears pause, drop to his knees and examine a pebble, its unweathered side exposed as a horse's hoof had dislodged it. Farther on, Walsh pointed at a bit of mica glinting in the sunlight. Oliver didn't see Vern Olds, the stocky stableman he guessed might have attacked him;

253

maybe Vern was nursing injuries sustained in the bunkhouse scuffle.

When Rabbitears was fifty feet away, Matt Hall almost by him, Chris Oliver stood up, showing his head and shoulders over the flat rock. He sang out, "Señor Stewart!"

The reaction would have been comical if it hadn't been so deadly for Oliver. Rabbitears instantly threw himself down, hastily bringing his carbine to firing position. When he saw Chris Oliver, Matt Hall dropped and opened up at once with his 15-shot Henry. Bullets whanged and ricocheted off the boulder, raining bits of lead and gravel on Oliver, who was safe behind his shelter.

The rest of the posse sought cover, except for Gene Stewart, who dashed forward. Peeking from one side of the boulder, Oliver saw the Boss knock Hall's gun barrel aside and speak angrily to him.

The Boss was one of the most courageous men Oliver had ever met, and he was fair and square.

"Chris!" Stewart called.

"Here, Señor Stewart. I must talk to you—alone."

Stewart started up; Hall and Walsh tried to dissuade him but Stewart waved them back impatiently and came on, carbine muzzle pointed at the ground. When he came abreast of Oliver, Chris saw the Boss was much upset. His face was dark under his tan, and his drawl was pronounced as he spoke:

"Well, Chris. Maybe you can explain all this. I found it hard to believe wh en they told me you'd attacked Vern and run off. Where's my wife's sister? Do the Apaches want ransom for her return?"

"The Indians who captured her aren't from our rancheria. They're outlaws, even among Apaches, broncos, as I suspected."

"Do you know where they've taken her?"

"Probably across the Border. If you'll come with me, I'll show you what we've found."

Stewart's stern eyes studied Oliver, seemed to drill through the powerful young fellow.

"What do you advise?" he asked.

"Tell your men they must ot shoot unless you order it. My father and some of his braves will help. They would have run away if I hadn't talked with them for they knew they'd be blamed."

"Where are they now?"

Chris Oliver swept a powerful arm up, and Stewart stared at the crags and scrub brush above.

"They're watching," Oliver replied.

Gene Stewart nodded; he knew how Apaches could conceal themselves.

"First, Senor Stewart, about last night. I was asleep in my bunk when someone tried to stab me. When I defended myself, I was shot at. I ran to my horse and rode away."

Stewart scowled. "Who was it?"

"No time for that now, Señor Stewart. Let me show you how Senorita Helen was spirited off."

Stewart was convinced; he stepped out, signaling his men to follow but to keep back. He went down and mounted his big black horse, while Oliver brought out the pinto and led the way. The Boss stayed just behind him, the cowboys stringing out behind the leaders.

Chris Oliver climbed the steep path for a time; then he pointed to the ground. Stewart swung low on one side, studying the sign, finally shook his head.

"This is where they turned south," Oliver explained. "They wiped out sign but early this morning my father and his friends found the trail."

255

Now they began traveling along the rocky mountain side, almost due south, the horses sliding here and there. A shout caused Stewart and Oliver to swing in their leather. Rabbitears and Matt Hall were pointing at something, and when they looked, they saw a turbaned head watching over a bush.

"My father, the Eagle," explained Chris Oliver. "He's showing us the way."

The sun beat down with savage fury as they reached a tiny, broken-down shack. Stewart and Oliver dismounted and ducked inside. "They held the Señorita here for a while. See where she lay on a blanket in that corner for a time? They cut her bonds here. Several Apaches were in the party, and white man who wore boots with sharp heels met them. They carried her on a horse down the steep trail, where she was put into a buggy drawn by a horse with a crack in its rear right shoe. The buggy headed for Mexico. My father told me this. And they had not time to go farther along."

Stewart nodded; the insight of such men as the Eagle and Chris Oliver was almost miraculous.

"You wish us to help you?" asked Oliver.

"I sure do! We're in your hands, Chris. Tell your father."

They went outside, and Oliver signaled. Soon the Eagle, carrying his old long rifle, a knife in his sash, materialized from a stand of bush. Three or four other Apaches showed themselves but waited as the chief approached and Stewart held out his hand.

The posse had bunched nearby, holding their horses. Matt Hall was scowling and others seemed uneasy.

"Look, Mr. Stewart," Hall complained, "that cuss Chris near busted Vern's arm. I wouldn't trust him as far as I could throw a range bull!"

"Keep shut, Matt," snapped Stewart. "You obey my orders. Now, Chris, we better pick up that trail."

Oliver hesitated. "It will be dangerous. They'll expect it. Your men can't stay out of sight as the Apaches can, and your enemies will be watching for pursuit."

"What then?"

"Let the Apaches find Señorita Helen. I think white men hired the broncos to kidnap her, and they'll demand ransom. But if they can't contact you, what then?"

Stewart thought it over. "You're right. Here's what I'll do, lead my men to El Cajon where the telegraph is, and stay ready for action till I hear from you, Chris. I'm putting my trust in you."

Proud that the Boss should say this, Chris Oliver promised himself only death could prevent him from succeeding in his mission.

From the heights they could see for miles. The Stewarts had kept adding to their properties, and below sprawled an unusual formation of low domed hills, *Las Cabezas Negras,* which at a distance did resemble dark human heads. They belonged to the Stewarts, marking their southwest boundary.

Gene Stewart shook hands with Oliver, looked him straight in the eye, and repeated, "I trust you!"

The boss saluted the Eagle, and led his fighters back as they'd come.

Chris Oliver and his handful of red wolves sped toward the Border.

V

Helen Hammond was bored. She'd rested, and Maria had served ample meals, seen to it she was taken care of if every way.

So she was in need of nothing. But she was locked in and could only pace restlessly up and down her room, or sit and stare out at the inner patio. Her first shock of fear had abated; she concluded she was being held for ransom, that soon Madeline and Gene would pay it and she would be released.

She worried about Alfred; perhaps her brother had been killed, and poor Link Stevens, too. She kept thinking of the big young man—Chris Oliver, they said was his name. He surely didn't look like the grim savages who'd attacked the car and carried her off. She recalled that Matt Hall had called Chris a "breed."

Occasionally she heard low voices or people moving in the hacienda; she watched a peon working in the patio flower beds. Somehow Helen didn't believe that Maria couldn't understand English, but the woman would not talk with her.

She hadn't seen Garcia since he'd turned her over to Maria. But she was fairly sure she was being held in some small Mexican town.

Late that afaternoon, Maria knocked. Helen called, "Come in," and the señora unbolted the door and entered, smiling widely as usual. She announced, "Señores Garcia y Tijerina!" in a grand manner.

Garcia appeared. "I would talk with you, Señorita Hammond."

"Yes, and I would talk to you!" said the girl angrily.

He came in, and Maria stepped back. Garcia wore

clean clothing, and bowed elegantly. Right behind him was a second man, fingering a black hat and a briefcase. He was elderly, hair larded with gray. His severe dark suit hung limply on his bony body, and his wrinkled olive face was wreathed in a fixed smile, thin lips parted and showing large yellowed teeth. He reminded Helen of a vulture; during her previous visit to New Mexico, she'd seen many of the ungainly scavengers.

"Señorita Hammond," said Garcia smoothly, "I would present to you Señor Chico Tijerina!"

Tijerina bowed low, and he murmured his pleasure at meeting the beautiful señorita. He had no mustache but sported curving sideburns under his prominent ears; his skin shone, and a word which seemed to fit Tijerina occured to Helen: *oily*.

Garcia closed the door, shutting out Maria. The two men waited until the girl sat down, and then perched on high-backed chairs before her. Garcia spoke first: "Now, Señorita Hammond, I'm sure you are prepared to listen to reason. You have been brought here for a reason which will be made clear."

Garcia glanced at the other man. "Señor Tijerina is an *abogado,* an attorney, as you would say. He will tell you what you must do to gain your release."

Tijerina clicked his teeth as he opened his briefcase and drew out a sheet of paper, a pen, and a small flask of ink which he carefully uncorked. Garcia rose and brought over a ligh table, setting it before the girl, and Tijerina laid the paper on this, handing the pen and ink to her.

"You will write to your sister and her husband. Address them intimately as you would do. Say you are well and unharmed, and that if they follow instructions, you'll be returned safe and sound. Señor Stewart must be at the El Cajon railroad depot tomorrow afternoon at three o'clock, and alone. If he plans a trap and fails to obey the orders which will be given him they, your family will never again see you alive, is this clear?''

Helen Hammond shrugged.

"Just how much money do you want Mr. Stewart to bring with him?'' she asked, contempt in her voice.

"Señorita, I said nothing about money. Write as I have said.'' For an instant the fixed smile wiped off Tijerina's face.

Helen hesitated; then she dipped the quill pen in the ink and began. "Dearest Madeline and Gene: I am well and haven't been harmed . . .''

As she was composing the note, Garcia and Tijerina spoke in rapid, low Spanish. She didn't understand what they said, though she heard the words, *"El Jefe,"* which she knew meant "Chief,'' and twice a name, "Folsom—Folsom,'' which meant nothing to her.

She signed her name and handed the note to the lawyer, who put on a pair of pince-nez and carefully read it, nodded, and had her address an envelope, in which he enclosed the folded message.

He passed this to Garcia, corked the ink bottle, wiped the pen nib, and put them back in his briefcase. Rising, Tijerina bowed low before Helen, and left the room.

Garcia said, "You'll soon hear, Señorita,'' and trailed out, shutting the door. Helen heard the bolt slide.

She turned and stared down at the little patio below; the sun had dropped so it no longer came into the inner square, the evening shadows grew long. Helen wondered why no sum of money had been mentioned; but then she decided they'd tell Gene this when they met him in El Cajon.

Maria brought her supper, removed the tray after she'd finished, locked her in again.

Helen walked up and down the room, lit her lamp for a time, and finally lay down in the big canopied bed. The feather mattress was soft and she closed her eyes. . .

A faint light came through the barred windows, and she could see the yellow line under her hall door, as a lamp was kept burning all night in the corridor. She had half roused; some light sound had disturbed her.

She wasn't sure what time it might be, but thought it must be late, as she was refreshed by a good sleep.

As she was about to close her eyes again, she caught another faint noise and looked at the door. It was opening, very slowly, a few inches at a time, the perpendicular shaft from the hall light growing larger.

She sat up, suddenly afraid; someone was stealing into her room, and now she saw the man's shadow as he slipped inside and pushed the door to behind him.

"Who—who is it?" she gasped, hardly able to find her voice.

She wanted to scream but before she could, an urgent whisper came, "Señorita Hammond! Be quiet. It's Chris Oliver, your brother's man. I've come to help you."

She clutched the silk coverlet about her, and the man moved to her side. The light was faint but she could see the powerful figure. His hair was banded and he wore dark clothing. She seized his strong hand.

"Oh, Chris, I'm glad! I've been terrified."

"Keep your voice low," Oliver warned, sitting by her, holding her hand. His touch, his presence, comforted her immensely. "We found where they had brought you, but the hacienda is large and closely guarded. I had to find which room you were in. Are you all right?"

"Yes. They haven't hurt me. The Indians turned me over to Señor Garcia and he drove me here. My brother, Alfred—" She almost feared to ask this.

"He's fine, he had only a head crease. But Link was killed by the bronco Apaches, who are outlaws, not of our people."

Helen Hammond could feel the strength of the young man as she clung tightly to him. He was her friend, she felt she could trust him fully and affection welled in her. He listened carefully as she told him about the letter to Gene Stewart, which the lawyer, Tijerina, had ordered her to write, that Stewart must be at El Cajon railroad station at three o'clock the following afternoon, and alone.

"Strange they demanded no money. I have heard of this Porfirio Garcia; he's a mining engineer, and he has a bad reputation on both sides of the Border. He must have hired the broncos to kidnap you. Is he behind all this, do you believe?"

"I'm not sure. They spoke of someone, a chief named Folsom."

"Folsom?" The name seemed to puzzle Chris.

A shout came, followed by two sharp gunshots. Helen clutched Chris Oliver, and he warned, "Get down on the other side of the bed and stay low. Quickly!"

Oliver pressed her hand, and jumped to his feet. Helen rolled to the far side of the wide bedstead, and crouched on the mat.

Her door burst in and three armed vaqueros, one waving a lantern, rushed into her room. "Chris!" she called, to warn him.

Then in the shaft of light she glimpsed him, pressed to the wall by the entry. A breath later the big man launched himself at the bunched trio; the lantern clattered to the floor and went out.

Helen screamed as pistols roared in the room, and a knife glinted in the shaft from the hall lamp.

A man gave an agonized cry which stopped in a horrible gurgle, and the girl had a confused impression of clashing bodies and cursing fighters in an insane melee. She saw Chris's great figure as he rose up, a squirming vaquero held overhead, and hurled him at another who was taking aim with a revolver.

The pistol exploded but the man Chris Oliver had thrown hit the gunny a moment ahead of the shot, and the two sprawled in a tangle near the open door.

Oliver vaulted the third one, who lay ummovin across the entrance. He turned down the hall, out of Helen's sight. She heard groans, muffled profanity. Somebody in the corridor bawled, "*Alto!*" and a gun roared twice. Then glass tinkled and the lamp in the passage suddenly went out.

More shouts, running feet throughout the big hacienda. Bursts of gunfire came from the lower level. The shocked girl listened intently, praying the Chris Oliver would somehow manage to escape from the death trap.

As quickly as they had begun, the noises of the battle stopped. She still caught voices, and soon a dancing light, from a lantern, came along the hall. "Señorita Hammond!" It was Porfirio Garcia, and the squat man entered her room, holding the lantern up.

He had to step high to clear the body across the sill. He looked at this and prodded it with a boot toe, then shrugged and turned to glare at the other two, who had risen.

He spouted angry, rapid Spanish; she didn't know

263

just what he said, but he was evidently scolding and reproaching them. They replied defensively. Finally, obeying Garcia's orders, they picked up their comrade and carried him off down the corridor.

Garcia was in a bad temper. He wore a holstered revolver and a sheaf knife, and his Latin politeness had entirely disappeared.

"Put on a cloak," he snapped. "Come with me, at once."

"Where?" she demanded.

"Do as I order."

Sensing his contained fury, Helen found a mantilla with a silk hood, which she wrapped around her night robe, and thrust her feet into slippers.

"Hurry," Garcia cried. "Walk ahead of me."

"Señor Garcia, was anyone killed in the fight?"

He said icily, "You saw one of my men with your own eyes just now, stabbed to the heart in your doorway. Besides that, others were wounded; while two Apaches were shot dead in the wanton attack on my home."

"Apaches? Who were they?" Her voice quavered in spite of herself.

"Who can say who an Apache really is?"

He was sullen, and would answer no more questions. She left the bedroom and walked through the inner passage; the lamp had been swept from its bracket and lay on the floor, fragments of glass stewing the rug, and she avoided the larger pieces which might pierce her thin slippers.

"Your friend did that," said Garcia. "I was at the far end of the corridor and would have killed him with my next bullet had he not knocked the lamp from the wall so I could no longer take aim."

Hope sprang into her heart. "Then he escaped?"

Garcia's eyes narrowed as he realized the big fellow he'd glimpsed was of special interest to her.

"I did not say he escaped, I only said *I'd* missed him. Many of our vaqueros were downstairs, and they saw to him."

"He was shot?"

A cruel smile touched Garcia's lips. "Who was he? He seems to be an Apache. Tell me his name so we many notify his family."

Helen shook her head. Chris, then, might have been killed.

Garcia steered her down a narrow rear staircase, through a kitchen. She didn't see Maria, but was aware of armed Mexicans in the shadows as she was led outside into the walled stableyard. A peon waited, holding a horse hitched to a buggy, and Garcia roughly lifted the girl in and climbed in by her. The groom opened a gate, and Garcia drove through into an alley, soon emerging on an unlighted street. Silvery moonbeams streaked the road.

"You'll regret your amigos attempted to rescue you, Señorita Hammond. The place we're going to isn't as comfortable as the hacienda!"

He turned another corner, stopping before a dark adobe hut. Getting out, he unlocked a padlock on the first door and shoved the young woman inside. One barred window showed in the back wall and the place smelled of moldy straw. The lantern dances as Garcia pointed at a bench with a horse blanket on it.

"Si, thank your friends for this," he snarled, unable to hide his resentment. "No one can hear your cries."

She felt she really knew Garcia now. He was tough and evil with the thin veneer rubbed off. "How long do you intend to hold me?"

"*Quien sabe*? If your people do not quickly do as Señor Folsom and I order, it will be necessary to dispose of you. And soon, for you are too dangerous a witness against us."

He seemed to relish frightening her.

He took the lantern with him, slamming the door when he was outside, and Helen heard the padlock snap shut.

Little light filtered through the tiny window. She groped her way to the bench and sank down, fighting her panic. Somehow, Chris Oliver had found her. But they had moved her here, and her friends wouldn't know where to look for her, even if Oliver hadn't been killed at the hacienda.

It hurt her cruelly to think he'd died for her. She could never forget him, though she had only seen him at the El Cajon railroad depot, and then when he'd come to her in her bedroom at the hacienda. It seemed to her, in her emotional state, that all her life she'd been waiting for the big man. She recalled his soothing voice as he'd whispered to her, and above all, the intense comfort she'd felt as he held her in his strong arms.

She leaned back against the dank mud wall and shut her eyes. She dozed a bit but would start awake at every little sound. She was sure big rats scurried in the dirty little place, as she heard the straw rustle now and again.

She wasn't sure how long it was before the padlock clicked open; she tensed, nails digging into her palms as the door opened and saw men's figures outside. The concentrated beam of a bull's eye lantern blinded her, and she jumped to her feet.

"Who's that?" she called.

She was seized from either side. A silk kerchief was tied over her lips and she was carried out. Saddled horses waited nearby, and she was lifted on one. A man mounted behind her.

Commands were snapped in rapid Spanish, and she believed it was Garcia speaking. She heard the word *Agua*, which she was sure meant water. It was coupled with another word she didn't recognize, twice they said *Agua Honda*, and then they started off, the saddle leather creaking, the horses picking up speed as they left the silent town behind and moved along a sandy road.

The moon was up and the myriad twinkling stars; the shapes of giant armed cactus, bunches of thorned brush threw shadows as they flashed past, on and on.

Jouncing in the seat, Helen heard the mustangs blowing now and then. The man behind her held her slim waist with a firm, muscled arm, following in the rising dust of the leader, the others stringing behind.

Her breath was jolted from her several times; she slopes were few and far between, and the land seemed to be desert.

It seemed endless, her discomfort, but finally she saw lights twinkling ahead, and the pace slowed. They came to the gate of a large enclosure made of crooked poles covered with high brush.

Some challenged and Garcia answered.

The gate swung in and they passed on through, dismounting before a low, rambling house. There were stables, corrals and smaller outbuildings, spread about the spacious yard, which seemed to be entirely circled by the crude fence. Then, as she was lifted off the saddle, she saw a patch of trees and the moon shining on a round pool of water.

Garcia came to her. Her legs were sore and stiff from the uncomfortable ride.

"You will come with me, Señorita Hammond," he said coldly. "Señor Folsom awaits you."

He led her to the low veranda of the adobe house. The front door was open, and she entered as Garcia urged her through.

She stood, glancing curiously about her. The room wasn't furnished with the elegance of Garcia's hacienda, but looked homey and comfortable enough, with woven straw mats on the rough plank floor, wicker stands and chairs, and a lamp burned on the center table.

"Sit there," ordered Garcia, indicating an armchair. Then he called, "Folsom, she is here."

A tall man in a cool silk shirt of crimson hue, wearing Mexican trousers banded with a sash, his head bare, came from an adjoining chamber.

He had a glass of liquor in one hand, and he smiled down at Helen, and said, easily, "We meet again!"

Helen gasped; her eyes widened and she would have cried out, but the gag chocked her words, and she could only stare in amazement at the man called Folsom.

VI

The bell in El Cajon's church steeple slowly and majestically tolled three times as a friar pulled the rope below.

It was extremely hot and the tiny settlement seemed asleep. Even the goats were quiet in the siesta hours, the brilliant sun burning mercilessly down.

Gene Stewart rode to the little railroad station,

holding his powerful black horse to a walk. He got down and tied his rein to a post on the shaded side, then went inside. His shirt stuck to his hide, and runnels of sweat streaked his dark, strong face.

The waiting room was deserted—no, behind the rusty potbellied stove, in the corner, which was lighted only on wintry days, lay a peon under an old serape. A huge sombrero of plaited straw covered what must be his head, and an empty bottle which had held tequila lay nearby. The man was obviously dead drunk.

Stewart could never forget this place, for here he had first set eyes one night on "Majesty" Stewart, now his beloved wife Madeline. He'd been drinking himself the evening he'd accosted the veiled lady, who was alone after getting off the train. Unaware of who she was, he'd forced a priest to marry her to him, although at the time, Madeline had believed the ceremony, in Spanish, had been a mock union.

He glanced again at the drunken peon, who hadn't budged, then shrugged and went to a grimy window. He stood, watching; he was right on time, three o'clock, the note had said. Some of his crew had gone back to the ranch, among them Matt Hall and Rabbitears Walsh.

Several awaited orders at the hotel up the plaza; they'd begged to accompany him, or at least let them trail him, in case of trouble. But the letter delivered to him had ordered him come alone, if ever the Stewarts wished to see Helen Hammond again.

Stewart was a brave and daring man; he had ridden into many tight spots by himself. Only death could stop him.

He took off his Stetson and mopped his face with his bandanna.

269

Then he sighted the buggy, drawn by a bay gelding, clopping in from the south, from the direction of old Mexico. It slowed as it crossed the boards laid to ease passage over the iron rails. The driver seemed in no hurry; he pulled up on the shady side of the building, and got down carefully, a bony man in a black suit draped on his skeleton form. A sober black hat sat straight on his head. He put on the brake and tied to a post. Carrying a briefcase, he entered the station.

"Señor Stewart," he said with a bow, thin lips parting to show large yellow teeth. "I am Chico Tijerina, *abogado*. I am an attorney representing those who would deal with you."

Suddenly Tijerina noticed the heap by the stove. "You were to come alone! Who is that?"

"A drunken loafer, sleeping it off, I don't know him. Now, get down to it. How much ransom do you demand? We will pay what you ask, so long as she is returned unharmed. I have a good deal of money in my belt, and I have made arrangements with our banker so I can get even more within a short time."

Tijerina kept smiling, his skin sheening like olive oil. "Señor, have we asked for money? No, we have a business proposition. If you will accompany me to *Agua Honda*, it will be disclosed to you. If you agree, your sister-in-law, who is being held there, will be released. I assure you she has not been hurt in any way."

"*Agua Honda*? Si, I know that place. Deep Water, an oasis not too many miles over the Border from here. Once it was a secret hideout for Sheriff Pat Hawe, who was no friend of mine!"

"Señor, all this is nothing to me, it is long past. I am only an agent, and I am carrying out my client's instructions. This is the duty and obligation of an attorney."

"All right. I'll go wherever you say, Tijerina. I've been all through that country. Maybe you know I once fought with the Mexican rebels."

"Si, who will ever forget the brave deeds of El Capitan Stewart?"

Tijerina's smile never left his lips, but Stewart thought he detected a faint sarcasm in his voice.

"Let's get down to the business," said Gene Stewart shortly. "You have papers in your briefcase you wish me to sign?"

Tijerina shook his head. "Nothing can be accomplished here. You must come with me to *Agua Honda*, alone, and at once. I will drive you there."

"My horse?"

"Tie him behind the buggy. Are you coming, Señor? I can delay no longer, for I must be at *Agua Honda* by dark. I have been instructed to inform you this is the only chance you will be offered to save the life of your wife's sister."

The smile had wiped off Tijerina's bony face and he looked more than ever like a buzzard.

"Of course I'll go with you, Tijerina."

"Make no attempt to signal," warned the attorney. "I'm sure you have followers near at hand. Once across the Border, we'll be under constant surveillance, and if we are trailed, the spies will be shot from ambush on the road. It may have occurred to you that you might have me arrested before leaving the United States. This will do you no good, for it's my word against yours, and if I fail to arrive on time at *Agua Honda*, Señorita Hammond will never be seen again."

Tijerina gave a short nod, and walked out. He stood,

watching to make sure that Stewart gave no signals to anyone spying from the center of town. Sweat beaded Stewart's bronzed face. He curbed his frustrated rage, aware he must obey instructions or Helen Hammond might be killed, or worse, handed over to the bronco Apaches, who would spirit her off to their hidden encampments in the Sierra Madre, to be a slave and plaything for the braves until she died.

He didn't doubt the viciousness of his foes. They had killed Link Stevens, and come close to killing Madeline's brother, when they had kidnaped Helen. They had done this cleverly enough, for the first impulse had been to throw the blame on the Eagle's rancheria.

Right up to this moment Stewart had been convinced the motive for snatching the girl had been to hold her for a large ransom, since it was common knowledge that the Stewarts were extremely wealthy people, not only in land and cattle, but the Hammond family fortune.

So Gene Stewart was confused, and racked his mind, seeking some other explanation, but he was unable to decide what it might be. He slowly left the little station and under Tijerina's sharp eye, fastened his black horse's rein behind the attorney's buggy.

Tijerina nodded and waved his briefcase, telling Stewart to climb in first. When Stewart settled on the leather seat, the *abogado* untied, took the reins from the brake and joined the rancher. He slapped the leather on the tall bay gelding's back, and they started off, crossing the tracks and heading south for the road to the Border and *Agua Honda* . . .

The serape by the potbellied stove in the station stirred and was thrown off, with the large straw sombrero.

Chris Oliver rose, stretching his long limbs, taking in

a deep breath of the warm air. It had been difficult, lying in a heap, hardly daring to stir while Chico Tijerina was nearby. He was bathed in sweat; but he'd heard everything which had been said, and an Indian, especially an Apache, would withstand discomfort and hardship, even pain, with a stoicism most white men couldn't muster.

He looked from the south window, seeing the big bay trotting as the buggy headed southward, Tijerina flicking the whip over the horse's ears, dust rolling under the rubber-tiled wheels. Then he checked the other direction, and saw three of Stewart's men in the road outside the saloon, staring after the buggy, with the Boss's black following behind.

They were older fellows, trust employes of Gene and Madeline Stewart. They had been watching for some sort of signal from Stewart. He had left strict orders they must stay put until the Boss called them. There were several more on the saloon veranda.

They began consulting with one another, evidently trying to decide what they should do. Some wanted to pick up their mounts and follow the buggy, others weren't sure it would be the right move. After all, Gene Stewart had his guns and his black horse, and would be more than a match for such a person as the Mexican they'd seen driving the buggy.

Chris Oliver crouched there, waiting. He hoped they wouldn't attempt to trail, even at a distance, for he had overheard Tijerina's warning, that they would be shot from ambush. He had no doubt this would happen. His father, the Eagle, and the braves with him, had killed two of the broncos during the fight at Garcia's hacienda; without his father's help, Oliver would not have been able to escape from the place. But the enemy still had several of the outlaw Apaches, dangerous foes, probably even now concealed along the route to *Agua Honda*, on the watch for anybody following Tijerina and Stewart.

Chris Oliver was by inheritance and breeding, by years of hard physical work, a man of steel. He could go for days with only snatches of sleep, as could even the older Apaches. He had some bruises, and a bullet sear along one thigh, where a slug fired from Garcia's revolver had burned his skin as he zigzagged through the hall leaving Helen Hammond's room. Then he'd swept the bracket lamp off the wall as he passed, and Garcia had no longer been able to see him as he rushed off, and, covered by the Eagle and his friends, gone over the wall and melted into the night.

He hadn't known that Helen had been moved, almost immediately, by Garcia, to another point. Chris Oliver and his aides had regrouped, made ready for another strike; one of the Eagle's braves, wounded in the fight, had ridden home for the rancheria.

At the first touch of dawn, circling the hacienda like so many prowling wolves, the Apaches had found the fresh buggy tracks leaving the rear of Señora Maria's and Garcia's spacious establishment. They'd caught the peon groom as he slept in his small room off the stables. At knife's point, the frightened Mexican had told them that Garcia had spirited Helen off. Trailing, they'd discovered the hut where she'd been held a short while, and the sign left by Garcia's vaqueros. The sign led them from the tiny town, heading northeastward.

Oliver had detached himself from the Eagle's band. They would make rendezvous later, in ways known to the Apaches. Chris Oliver had ridden hard for El Cajon; Helen had told him that Gene Stewart had been ordered in the enemy note to be in the station at 3 P.M.

There were few trains that stopped at the little place, and the agent was on hand only at certain hours. Oliver had left his paint horse down the line, and moved afoot, watching his chances. A half-drunken Mexican had been glad to sell him the worn serape and straw hat, his almost empty bottle, for double their value.

By noon, Chris Oliver had settled; in the corner behind the stove, covered by the cape and sombrero; he'd catnapped ignoring the discomfort of the mounting heat.

He was armed with his sixgun and long knife; he'd left his cartridge belts and rifle, his Stetson, with the stud.

He was in no hurry to leave the station building, since he'd overheard Tijerina say they were going to *Agua Honda*, an the buggy could not travel with the speed of a fast horse. And he had not the slightest doubt that the Eagle and his braves had by this time determined that Helen Hammond had been carried to the fenced oasis.

He sat down and chewed methodically on a strip of dried meat. He had a hide pouch of ground corn, and he'd hidden his canteen and small supply of food in the cold stove. With lukewarm water, he had a substantial if tasteless meal.

It was well after four o'clock before El Cajon came back to life; people appeared on the dusty plaza, the stores took down sun shutters. So far, Stewart's crew had stayed put, though now and again one of them would step out and stare toward the railroad station.

Chris Oliver went through the door on the track side.

Not far away stood the freight station. He flitted toward this, not wishing to be seen by any of Stewart's men. Keeping the bulky building between himself and the plaza, he reached the deserted barn where he'd left his paint horse. The stallion whickered at him; Gene Stewart had fed him, and given him water before he'd left the animal.

Oliver rode eastward, along the north side of the track for a mile, then turned south. The sun was lowering over the mountains as he swung on a slanting course for the river. This was desert country, sagebrush, cactus growths, rock formations, except along the watercourse which were running almost dry in the arid months.

Aware of the warning Tijerina had given Stewart as to possible trackers being ambushed, he watched most carefully for any sign of danger, riding a quarter mile away from the sandy road leading eventually to *Agua Honda*.

He rode slowly, glancing right and left. The land grew more parched, and the paint stud's hoofs dug into the sand. He crossed the winding river, and paused at a shallow pool to let the horse drink, and to refill his canteen. He squatted for a time, holding his rein, and washed his face and hands, took off his sweat-soaked shirt and dipped it in water, wrung it out, and after washing his torso, put the shirt back on. The evaporation would cool his skin.

He led his stallion to the steep south bank; when there was an occasional cloudburst, the river, like an arroyo, would overflow its bed. Remounting, he shoved on southeast for *Agua Honda*, and the sun was now dropping behind the great mountains to the west.

Some instinctive warning came to him, and he slowed. A thicket of cresote bushes, cactus, long wands of the ocotillo, giant saguaros and barrels, low clumps of prickly pears breaking through here and there, blocked the way.

Then he heard the insistent rattles. He stared ahead but could see no snake, though it sounded like a large one. However, his grim lips softened. "One—two—three. One—two—three." No snake ever signaled with such regular cadence!

He started on and the Eagle, crouched by a thick bush, grinned at him, shaking the snake rattles at him. As though by magic, one of his father's old warriors materialized, an they led him through a narrow aisle to a deep, completely dry arroyo, screened by low bush. Here, the rest of the Eagle's war party waited, with their horses. They had snared two rabbits, had plenty of ground meal and dried meat in their pouches. Chris Oliver got down and led the stallion into the ditch.

As he turned to fasten his halter rope to a root, he saw the two dead, half-naked bronzed figures stretched in the sand.

"Broncos," nodded the Eagle, with a satisfied smile.

Chris counted four extra mustangs, and his father explained. "Two more enemies lie dead on our back trail from *Agua Honda*. We took their food and the money paid them by the *Pinda Lick-o-yi*. There are no more bronco Apaches to be dealt with nearby, only a dozen vaqueros."

The young giant, worthy son of the Eagle, nodded. He knew that only the most expert Apaches such as his father and his comrades were could have overcome the murderous, stealthy broncos.

VII

Pale, drawn and exhaused by strain, Helen Hammond still held up her head proudly as Garcia ushered her into the main room at the *Agua Honda* rancho. The young woman started as she saw Gene Stewart seated at the table, on which a lamp with a round white globe shed a yellow light.

"Gene!"

"Helen, are you all right?" he asked anxiously rising.

"Yes, I'm—I'm fine." She sat in a chair, and Stewart resumed his seat.

"We wouldn't expect you to pay us, Señor Stewart, without seeing the goods are undamaged," said Garcia smoothly.

An armed Mexican stood by the front entry, a carbine slanted under one arm. Another was at the doorway to the rear of the house, but the room was unlighted. Chico Tijerina came in, a fixed smile on his face. He held several documents in his thin hands, and there was a pen and an ink bottle by the lamp on the table.

Tijerina nodded politely as he drew out a chair and sat down.

Stewart's pistol had been taken from him shortly before, as he was kept covered by the vaquero guns.

Stewart stared coldly at Garcia. "I know who you are, Señor," he said. "I've heard of you."

Garcia smiled but it wasn't friendly; he disliked Stewart as much as the rancher did the stocky man. "Si, I am well-known as a mining promoter. My fame has spread north of the Border." A touch of irony was in his voice.

Helen knew nothing of Garcia's reputation as a shady

278

mining engineer, but Gene Stewart knew all about him.

"I would like to put my money on the table," said Stewart.

Garcia shrugged and Gene Stewart carefully extracted a wad of large bills from his inside pocket and put them on the board.

"There is plenty more where this came from, once I am sure you will release Miss Hammond and me," he said quietly.

"Señor, there is more to this than what money you might wish to give us," said Garcia. "Tijerina, please show Señor Stewart the documents he is to sign."

The lawyer spread several legal papers out and handed them to Stewart, who began to read them.

"Gene," began Helen. "Matt—"

"Be quiet, Señorita," ordered Garcia sternly, scowling at her.

Stewart read over the documents; a puzzled look spread over his bronzed face. "These turn over part of our property to Patrick Folsom and to you, Garcia. The sections enumerated take in all the territory, including *Las Cabezas Negras,* to the Border. *Las Cabezas* are practically worthless, for grazing purposes, the rest is chiefly desert stretches."

"Please, sign the quit-claims and the conveyances, Señor Stewart," order Tijerina. "You will also sign Señora Stewart's name, since we're aware you have power of attorney to act for her."

"True, I do. What else do you want?"

"Only this, Señor Stewart," said Garcia quickly.

Gene Stewart glanced at Helen, then began signing the documents as Tijerina directed, the bony attorney sitting close to Stewart, making sure everything was in

279

order. Two vaqueros came and signed at witnesses.

Tijerina glowed with satisfaction. "Everything is now in order, Señor Garcia. *Las Cabezas* will be your property as soon as I have registered these documents with the proper authorities."

Steward said nothing; he wasn't an attorney, but he well knew that documents signed under duress would never be upheld, in the United States or in Mexico, either. Once Helen was safe, and they were back across the Border, the quit-claims and other conveyances could easily be declared void. As an *abogado,* surely Tijerina must be aware of all this, but Stewart held his tongue. Maybe they were fools.

He saw Helen start, and look past him, and hearing a soft footstep behind, he swung and saw a tall man, smiling at him, a cheroot dangling from his lips. The man wore soft Mexican garments, but Stewart immediately recognized his straw boss, Matt Hall.

"Matt!" he exclaimed. "What are you doing here?" For a moment, he believed his own crew had somehow located the place and had come to help him.

"Hello, Gene," Hall drawled easily. There was none of the usual deference accorded one's employer in the tall fellow's voice.

He pulled out a chair and sat facing Stewart, still almost laughing, convulsed by inner amusement.

"I believe you knew my father," he went on.

"Your father? Hall? I may have, but don't recall the name, and you never mentioned this before, Matt."

"Not Matt, Pat. Pat Hawe, Junior. My father was sheriff of the county, and was brutally shot down, murdered by your man, Monte Price, with his friend Don Carlos Martinez!"

"But-but you—?"

"I was a lad at the time and lived here with my mother, Pat Hawe's wife. She died soon after my father, cursing your name with her last breath. And so I determined to avenge my father and my mother. This is why I went to work for you, Gene. At first, I simply intended to kill you at the first opportunity I could do so without being suspected.

"But Garcia, a frequent visitor here, told me about *Las Cabezas Negras*. He secretly prospected through these strange hills. Under the almost bare surface, the great domes are solid silver, metal and extremely rich ores. And so we decided to take, not only revenge, but the mines, which will make us wealthy men."

"And Folsom—?" asked Stewart.

Hawe stopped smiling; the fury in his heart darkened his face. "A name I assumed, because you, Stewart, blackened mine with your lies about my father, Sheriff Pat Hawe!"

With difficulty Gene Stewart kept silent, staring at his arch enemy, son of the thieving sheriff who, with Don Carlos Martinez, had come close to shutting off forever, for Stewart and Madeline, the Light of Western Stars.

It was plain that the man was the leader and instigator of all this, that Garcia had been his partner in the project, so carefully planned. Flashes of thought ran through his mind, how Howe, as his straw boss, Matt Hall, had insisted Helen's kidnapers had come from the Eagle's rancheria. How someone in the bunkhouse, undboutedly egged on by Hawe, had nearly killed young Chris Oliver, and other things that now dovetailed as the puzzle grew clear.

Hawe was speaking again, "You must realize now,

Stewart, we're not such fools as to think you'd let us have *Las Cabezas* if we let you go. And anyhow, I have other plans for you and for your pretty sister-in-law. I really am most fond of her and intend to keep her for myself. You'll simply disappear into thin air; no trace of you will ever be found.

Stewart already understood. He was as good as dead, and Helen would serve young Pat Hawe.

Gene Stewart was a fighting man; he'd held himself in with a tremendous effort. Now he gave a hoarse cry and shoved the table at Hawe, who was reaching inside his silk blouse, pulling a revolver. Stewart hoped to knock over the lamp, it rocked crazily, flickered, but righted itself as Stewart dropped to his knees.

"Run, Helen—" Stewart gasped.

The room suddenly rang with blasting guns; the vaqueros on guard had turned, carbines firing as they aimed at shadowy figures thrusting through the windows. They went down, riddles; lean Apaches sprang into the room, and Chris Oliver ran in as Pat Hawe cried out with sudden pain, his revolver falling from his hand.

Hawe clutched at his punctured shoulder: Oliver had put a slug through it. The Eagle drove a long knife into Garcia's back just as the Mexican took aim at Stewart, and Garcia fell on his face.

Tijerina, bleating in terror, screamed for mercy as he groveled on the mat near the rocking table. Blue gunsmoke clouded in the room, curling around the lamp chimney.

Stewart started at Hawe, meaning to seize him with his bare hands, for he had no gun.

Chris Oliver had swung toward the girl, but suddenly whirled, throwing himself bodily at Hawe. Spewing his hatred for Gene Stewart, Hawe drew a small, large-calibered derringer from his pocket with his uninjured hand, raising it. At such close range he couldn't miss, and the heavy ball would rip a hole the size of a saucer in Stewart's breast.

Oliver hit Hawe a breath before the derringer belched death.

The .44 caliber bullet whizzed past Oliver's ear and lodged high in the wall across the room. As Hawe went down, bowled over by Chris Oliver's lunging weight, the Eagle sprang in, driving his bloody knife again and again into Pat Hawe's vitals . . .

"No, no—" began Chris Oliver, getting to his feet, but it was too late to check his father's flashing blade.

Pat Hawe quivered on the mat, gaping wounds showing through long rips in his silken shirt.

It was over. The Apaches had stolen up, silenced the guards without a sound, as only they could do. Hawe and Garcia were dead, while Chico Tijerina, on his knees, pled for his life.

Sickened by the awful sights, Helen Hammond turned away, her kneed almost giving way.

She stared at Chris Oliver, towering in his youthful power. He's shoved his gun back into his sash.

She went to him and threw her arms around him, crying, sobbing like a child. Oliver held her, seeking to comfort her. She felt the beat of his strong heart as she pressed her body close to his.

"Chris, Chris! You must never leave me. Promise me this."

She felt him tremble and she knew he loved her as she loved him. And she would be his as long as the Western stars lighted the heavens.

GUN TROUBLE
IN TONTO BASIN

ROMER ZANE GREY

Gun Trouble In Tonto Basin signals the reappearance of Arizona Ames, the title character of one of Zane Grey's most memorable novels. Young Rich Ames came to lead the life of a range drifter after he participated in a gunfight that left two men dead. Ames' skill earned him a reputation as one of the fastest guns in the West.

In these splendid stories, Arizona Ames comes home to find his range and his family haunted by the shadow of a terror they dare not name!

WESTERN
0-8439-2098-X
$2.75

THE RIDER OF DISTANT TRAILS

ROMER ZANE GREY

The Rider Of Distant Trails marks the return to print of one of Zane Grey's most memorable characters, Buck Duane, first introduced in Grey's novel *Lone Star Ranger*. Forced to turn outlaw as a young man, Buck later teamed up with Captain Jim MacNelly of the Texas Rangers and proved himself to be the Ranger's deadliest gun.

In these stories, Romer Zane Grey, son of the master storyteller, continues Buck's adventures in Texas and as he takes on outlaws who are terrorizing ranches and towns in this tough cattle country!

WESTERN
0-8439-2082-3
$2.75